JOSHUA V. SCHER

AFTER THE END

THE VIRUS WAS THE EASY PART

aethonbooks.com

AFTER THE END
©2021 JOSHUA V. SCHER

Aethon Books
www.aethonbooks.com

Print and eBook formatting by Steve Beaulieu.

Published by Aethon Books LLC.

AUTHOR'S NOTE

I wrote this story while my wife was pregnant. Nothing makes you consider the end of life-as-you-know-it like looming parenthood. Watching my wife and family grow also gave me a sense of stakes that I'd never had before, as well as an understanding that perseverance isn't a choice but a necessity. Both processes (writing and gestation) led to two surprising, inevitable discoveries. First, control is an illusion, but losing that illusion is terrifying. Second, optimism is a crucial delusion for anyone trying to nudge the world in the right direction. I also had one other revelation: whoever said writing a book is like giving birth has never been in a delivery room.

ACKNOWLEDGMENTS

This has truly been my most enjoyable brush with the post-apocalypse thanks to a handful of dedicated people in my life. First, Ron Hanks for setting this whole thing in motion and excitedly accelerating towards the cliff edge with me; Jeff Ourvan, who is more than just an agent, but an ideal reader and a sherpa; the show Doomsday Preppers that initially introduced me to this ~~worldview~~ end-of-the-worldview; my wife and children for filling me up and draining me dry of every ounce of life every day.

God broke his promise.

—graffiti in a cave
outside Sicily, Oklahoma

PART I

1

THUMPER

God broke his promise.

thumpTHUMP.

To the world. To me. Even to this little bastard.

thumpTHUMP.

That's right, take the bait.

thumpTHUMP.

What? You shy now? No one's watching. Far as you know.

thumpTHUMP.

Take it, you son of a bitch.

I shouldn't curse. I know. But it's not like I'm taking the lord's name in vain or nothing.

Truth is, it's not really even cursing. It's thinking. I'm not actually saying it out loud. Can't get mad at me for that. I mean thoughts move so quick. It's not like you even got a chance to rein them in. They just shoot out at, well, at the speed of thought.

Not to mention the fact that the little bastard eating my broccoli is a goddamn thief. Neither shalt thou steal.

thumpTHUMP.

That's it. Get in there. Just like you been doing. Get that last little bit left from yesterday's raid.

thumpTHUMP.

Won't touch my tomatoes though. Will you? You never do. Too smart to meddle with my nightshades. Too much to hope for, I guess. I wonder, is that 'cause of generations of instinct or just a personal preference? Or is it just the draw of my broccoli…

thumpTHUMP.

Go on. Dig in. Relax. Champ that little motor mouth of yours to your heart's content.

thumpTHUMP.

You can rotate those furry, goddamn radar ears as much as you want. I ain't making no sound. No, sir. I greased up the idler wheels slicker than buttered cat shit on a linoleum floor.

Don't matter none.

The air is alive with crickets. Everywhere and nowhere. But loud enough to give me the cover I need.

thumpTHUMP.

Not a groan from my bowstring as I draw it back. Quiet as dark.

thumpTHUMP.

Come on, Addie, you got him. Breathe in, breathe out.

Shoot between the heartbeats—

thumpTHUMP.

It's a dog-eat-dog world now. And, you know what they say, life gives you lemons… make rabbit stew.

thumpTHUMP.

Breathe in—

Look past the arrow.

Look right through Thumper the Thief.

Breathe out.

thumpTHUMP.

The arrowhead disappears into a blur.

Breathe in.

See only the target. Shoot between the heartbeats.

thump.

Loose the arrow—

THUMP.

The arrow stabs into the dirt a good meter to the right of the rabbit.

"Sheee't."

The little bastard doesn't even have the common decency to flinch. Just takes another nibble and waits just long enough for me to consider nocking another arrow in place before bouncing off with a bellyful of my bounty.

Maybe a snare'd be better. There's no aiming with a snare. Find me some good fishing line. I think there's a whole chapter on traps in the Good Book.

Maybe I just need more target practice.

I should get a pet.

The vegetable garden looks worse up close. The beans've been pillaged. The broccoli's decimated. And the peppers never even took. The only ones that are doing ok are the tomatoes and zucchini. But they're all just so goddamn small.

They need more water. Get in line.

The arrow's still got some dirt on it when I draw it out of the earth. A mark of shame. I wipe it on my shorts. Just below my pistol holster. The soil blends right in on my camo cutoffs. Not sure whether to be proud or repulsed.

I check the fletchings. Straight as an… arrow.

I got to clean the dirt off. Or it won't fly right.

Shee't, maybe that'd help me.

. . .

It takes twenty-three pumps of the handle to get a thin stream of water to pour out the spout. It took fifteen last week. I just need the pump to last two more weeks. Two more and I'll be good to go.

I rinse and rub the arrow clean. Dry it on the other leg of my camo cutoffs. I fill up both hydration packs. Going to be covering some good miles today and can't trust the water out there. Least I'd rather not have to.

A rusted coffee can lies on its side in the dirt nearby. Looks like a piece of detritus. Its own version of camouflage. I pick it up, fill it with water, then egg-on-a-spoon-race walk it over. Not a drop spilled.

I only water the zucchini and tomatoes. Let the broccoli wilt. I'm done working for Thumper. Let the little bastard eat it wilted.

2

THE HOUSE

It ain't a shit-shack exactly. More shit-shack-esque. In nature. *Good bones*, Momma would call it.

Like the front door's a nice old thick piece of cedar, but the red paint's peeling off like it's got a wicked case of eczema, and the rubber on the doggie door's all pockmarked and ragged.

The porch swing would be *positively charming* except for the snapped chain on the back-right corner. As it is, the weird tilt makes it super creepy swaying in the breeze like that.

The creaking don't help nothing neither;

groaning as the wind shoves it up into motion: *eeh...*

sighing when it can swing back down: *aww…*

eeh... aww...

eeh... aww...

Doing its best impression of an arthritic donkey. Or a horror-flick soundtrack. Either way, it's creepy as shit.

Don't think about that. Think about the donkey sounds. Anything else.

If a porch swing is on a veranda, is it still a porch swing? Or—

A flicker between the trees and the left side of the house catches my eye. I swing the binoculars towards whatever it is.

Nothing there.

I roll the thumbscrew back and forth.

The twin circular worlds breathe in and out of focus, finally sharpening in juxtaposed clarity. Well, at least the right side does. The left one has a pretty nasty crack through it. If I'm being honest, at this point, they're more monoculars than binoculars.

Blurs of dead cornstalks flutter in front of the lenses. I dig my elbows into the dirt and army crawl a little ways forward. Just to the edge of the cornfield.

If anybody is in the house, they'd still be hard-pressed to spot me, flat against the earth, motionless beneath a rippling sea of rotting maize.

Plus, you know, my camo shorts.

My lenses won't glint in the sun at all neither. No, sir. I got me the best polarized and antiglare lenses. And fitted them with a top-of-the-line, military-grade, antireflection filters with guaranteed kill-flash.

The movement flickers again. Somehow I see it but still don't *see* it. Takes a second for me to stare through the middle distance, until—

Shee't. It's just a wire leash dangling from its pulley on a dog run. Scared by the wind.

I shrug. *Always better to flinch than get hit*, as my uncle used to say. Dog's probably long gone by now.

The corn's desiccated; the front lawn's overgrown with cat's-ears and sow thistles. Nothing's moved for the entire twenty minutes other than Eeyore's veranda swing.

Normally, I'd take at least thirty minutes to recon. At least. A good half hour, if not longer, staked out in some hiding place, hiding at a safe distance, watching, waiting, taking my time. Assessing. God is in the details, and haste is of the Devil.

But there ain't been nothing to raise an eyebrow at for going on several months now. Not even a false alarm. And I got to cross nine square miles off the map today if I'm going to be ready and set in two weeks.

Screw it, I'm going in.

At first, I used to fret about whether it was better to leave my bike and trailer in hiding, so they were tucked away and secure. Or whether it was best to ride them right up to the door, so they were at the ready for a quick getaway just in case.

As it is now, I ride it right up, close as possible so I don't have to hump a lazy-man's-load of my haul any further than I need to.

Also, the jury-rig trailer clatters nice and loud as I ride up over the lawn. I mean, once I'm committed and out in the open, I may as well beat the bushes, just in case.

I pull up right next to the veranda steps.

I catch the sole of my right sneaker on the lip of every step as I walk up. It makes a satisfying *fwapFWAP* with every footfall.

More bush beating, I guess.

Or foot dragging. Depending on how you look at it. The two ain't "mutually exclusive" or nothing.

Can't help but smile at that one. My honors geometry teacher would be proud of me for remembering that little gem. Ain't no arguing about it now. He was right, of all the maths, geometry is the most useful out in the world. It's why they invented math in the first place, he used to tell us. To measure out farm fields so they could tell whose crops were whose and how the pharaoh could tax accordingly.

Although I guess that taxing part was more arithmetic.

I squat in front of the red, rash-ridden door, shrug my pack off my shoulders, and get ready. I always put on the safety goggles first, the surgical gloves second, and the surgical mask last. It don't save me a lot of time, but a least a few seconds extra where I don't have to breathe the hot, claustrophobic air.

. . .

Quick, quick, get under, Addie. Under here, ain't nothing that can get us.

I'd curl up against her bent legs that propped up the duvet, eyes wide in the diffuse light that leached through our cavern of covers. Reaching my hand across the bed, traversing the cotton landscape to find her outreached fingers.

The night mares can't gallop through here. They don't like the heat.

I can't breathe, Momma. It's too thick.

It's all right. Just hold my hand. We'll keep each other safe.

She'd straighten her legs, and the sheets would close in closer. Thicker. And we'd stay there as long as I could, until I had to claw my way to the surface to catch my breath—

I press the doorbell. Don't hurt to be polite. It don't work of course.

I knock.

I wait.

Nothing.

Of course, the door's locked. I can probably break it. It'll be harder than breaking a window, but at least I won't have to deal with shards of glass.

I take a few steps back, to get a running start. And that's when I see it. Dummy. I should have thought of that first.

The pockmarked rubber *fwaps* back down into place behind me. Christ, they must have had a big dog. Like a mix between a Great Dane and a grizzly bear. I almost could have walked through, except for wood shards. I guess there was no getting around shards of some sort.

There are bits of the shattered boards I had to kick in. Some nails too. I just shove them out of the way, over to the wall.

"Hello?"

Nothing, save a quiet *beep* of a plea for maintenance from some neglected electric device.

Dust covers everything: the front table, the car keys hanging from a hook, the chair one would sit in to put on shoes. It blankets the runner rug that extends down the hallway all the way to the kitchen.

I turn to unlock and open the front door, but it's been boarded up from the inside. Just like the doggie door was. I yank off a couple more wooden shards from the doggie door opening. Good enough for an escape route.

I do my thing, and I do it quick.

First up, front hall closet. Jackpot! I press a pair of practically brand-new hiking boots up against the flappy sole of my sneaker. Close enough.

I toss the boots out the doggie door onto the veranda.

beep.

Kitchen: piles of crusted-over plates. Bare cupboards. No spare food. Par for the course. Food's always the first thing to get used or stolen.

Dining room: pretty much a bust other than the 9-volt I snag out of the smoke alarm. I don't bother sifting through the flatware. It's clearly silver plated, and I've got sterling back at the CC.

Family room: the TV remote leaves a silhouette of itself in the dust on the coffee table. Like a chalk outline at a crime scene. The LED bulb doesn't light up when I press power. Batteries're dead. I drop it on the couch. Over the fireplace, there's another faded silhouette in the shape of a shotgun.

beep.

Downstairs bathroom: empty medicine cabinet and drawers. Just old soap shaped like seashells. Decorative and utter crap at cleansing.

This here's the good soap, Addie. You leave it be. Guests only. Momma can't stop her interrupting.

The stairs creak under my weight. I can't help but tiptoe up them. Like I didn't make a huge racket kicking my way through the doggie door. Dummy. I still hear the donkey on the porch swing outside, singing its horror-film soundtrack, *eeh... aww.*

Of course the door to the upstairs bathroom is closed. Shit. Closed doors always make me… nervous. I can see the sun reflect off white tile through the crack beneath the door. No shadows. Nothing moving. I turn the knob and nudge it just enough for the tongue to latch out and keep it ajar.

Again. Nothing.

eeh... aww...

Screw you, Eeyore.

beep.

I tap the door; it swings open a few inches. Tap it again. Widens its arc. I shake my head at myself and just go in.

The counter's covered with empty containers: rubbing alcohol, witch hazel, three tubes of Neosporin, Tylenol, aspirin. Every box open, every bottle empty, every tube dry.

It's hot in the upstairs hallway. I swat away a couple of flies. The master's at the end of the hall, I'm guessing. The smaller bedrooms were fruitless. Two little girls' rooms and a guest room turned sewing room. I swiped a box of needles and a few spools of thread. I'd probably be more excited about that if I knew how to sew. I mean, I get the basics of it, but—

The smell hits me before the sight. Well before the image registers and I process it. By then, I'm already halfway down the stairs. But it's the stench—like a rotting skunk raped a honeycomb—that instantly lifts me up and shoves me out of the master bedroom, kicks me down the hall. Bursts of retching toss me down the stairs. The odor of old gray meat doused in cheap perfume nips at the back of my throat. I accelerate towards the door with every heave. No comprehension, no reason, no thought other than GET AWAY!

I burst out of the doggie door into cleansing sunlight. Not quite getting the surgical mask off fast enough as I spew vomit all over the veranda.

Between the surges of sputtering ejections, the images catch up with me.

An ashen, desiccated hand gripping the bedpost. Its tense fingers calcified with rigor mortis.

I shouldn't've opened the door to the master so fast.

Another surge gags its way out of me.

A petrified foot wedged between bed rails.

This was not a peaceful death.

Seizures of disgorgement rack my torso.

A petrified body twisted, like dried rubber cement, hooked over the edge of the bed, head bent at an unnatural angle, hovering above a pail

—acid burns my throat—

and the smaller corpse. Behind her. On the bed. Spooning—

Waves of bile rise out of me as I pull myself to the edge of the veranda.

It's not until several minutes after the dry heaves subside that I feel it. The pool of sweat running down my leg. I sit up and see the hiking boots. A streak of crimson smeared across the left one. A trail of scarlet tracks past it, following me, up to my leg.

It's not sweat.

The gash splits open just below my shorts, just above my knee. A six-inch-long grin spreads down the side of my leg, drooling blood out of the corners. It leaches up my shorts, a rusted umber splotch of "drool."

Goddamn shards.

Panic takes over.

3

CC

"My" house shudders. I try to hold the monoculars still, but my hands won't calm down.

I roll onto my back and scooch into the embankment out of sight. The sun bears down from its apogee and rolls torrid waves off of the road.

It's the heat.

It's the heat and how fast I was hauling ass. I'm still breathing heavy. I should have stopped at the farm. Gotten more water out of the pump.

I'm dehydrated.

I'm tired.

I'm overheated.

I'm…

full of horse shit.

Breathe, long breaths. Innnnnn, oooouuuut. You're fine. You're fine. Just nerves. And exertion. And sweat.

Not a fever.

A gentle breeze blows up the slope, and a chill ripples across my skin. The shaking stills for a moment. Finally.

There's plenty of water in the CC. I just have to wait a half hour, that's it.

I scooch back up and take another survey. My house stands still. The pasture's quiet. The road is empty as far as the eye can see.

Still, though. I've got to wait. Protocol is protocol.

Yeah, but this is an emergency. Time is of the—

An emergency caused by you not following protocol.

It's not like I got jumped. I went in *ten* minutes early. I could have waited thirty hours and it wouldn't've been no different. The protocol's about—

Safety. Precaution. Survival.

My house has started shuddering again. Bouncing all over my field of vision. I scooch back down, breathe, and wait.

It's a solid house. Well-crafted. A fossil. Built way back when, to last through the ages. Thick stone walls that shelter the cool in the summer and hold onto the heat in the winter. Practical and suited to its environment.

I've never been inside. Don't want to leave no signs. No clues about the CC. Wouldn't really be an effective decoy if I'd already ransacked it. So I never went in.

Not even when I torched it. Just tossed the Molotov cocktail through the window. Still, the stone walls held strong. Never burned, never weakened.

The bike and trailer clatter loudly on the worn, cobblestone driveway as I ride past the house and swing around to the back.

The garage's made of the same stone as the house. I never been in there neither. I swing around the far side of it. The north side, out of sight of the house, but not the road. I should hop off. Less weight, less time it takes for the bike tracks in the grass to spring back and blend in. But my leg burns with every throb of my pulse, and the bloody smile grins wider and wider up the side of my knee. I won't let protocol be the death of me.

As soon as I round the far corner and cut off sight lines to the road, I'm off the bike. It careens a few more yards of its own accord and clatters to the ground as I already make quick work of clearing away the pieces of junk and small boulders I covered the steel doors with this morning.

The CC doors rise only a few inches out of the earth, a metallic plane, sloped at an angle just so this sort of pile of debris wouldn't cover it up in a storm and turn the sanctuary into a trap. The steel sheet warbles like thunder as the doors swing in quick opposing arcs, orbiting around their hinges, and quickly crashing into the ground.

If someone were watching from a distance, it'd be a peculiar sight. Flat land in every direction and me somehow stepping down into the earth itself. Like I'm descending Hell's staircase… 'cause Jacob's ladder don't reach this world no more. Disappearing into some barrow, then rushing up and out, clutching a polished cherry-wood case and dumping sterling flatware onto the ground. Leaping back down into the depths, groundhogging up and out, tossing about a glass jar, a roll of duct tape, a plastic tube, a pasta pot, and an empty two-liter soda bottle. Only to slide back down into Hell one last time and emerge dragging a large Igloo athletic cooler full of water. All the while, me barely reining in the chaos. Only controlling it with severe focus. Like blinders, to keep the panic out of my periphery.

Start a fire—

Get water boiling in the pot—

Dig a hole three feet away from the fire; bury the soda bottle up to its neck—

Fill the glass jar halfway with water—

Duct-tape the plastic tube into the glass jar; seal the jar with more duct tape—

Run the tube across the ground and into the buried soda bottle; cover the tube with dirt—

Place the half-filled glass jar into the boiling pot of water—

Wait.

Cyclone cellars were made so the twisters wouldn't have nothing to grab ahold of as they clawed their way along the earth. They'd tear past, glance off the lip of the underground shelter, and move on. The CCs weren't designed to be invisible hideouts. That was just a collateral convenience for me.

I've taken my temperature three times already: 99.2 degrees.

The jar floats around the pot, the water inside it is almost done boiling off up into vapor, floating along through the tube, and condensing back into liquid inside the soda bottle buried in its cool, shallow grave. What's left in the jar is cloudy. Good.

Good enough.

I unearth the soda bottle now a quarter full of distilled water.

I have a sort of makeshift workstation next to my cot in the CC. The *U.S. Air Force Survival Handbook* sits on the edge. I've pretty much memorized the process outlined in chapter 7, but I keep it there for reference. Just in case. The cover curls back, and Uncle Izzy's inscription winks out at me.

Pour the distilled water into another glass mason jar—

Connect four 9-Volt batteries in series—

Snap on a lead connector to one of the empty battery leads—

Strip the wire end; twist some copper wire onto the lead—

Tie the copper wire around the sterling silver knife—

Pinch between a pair of unsplit, disposable chopsticks—

Secure with electrical tape—

Repeat with another sterling silver knife—

Wrap copper wire around the other knife; lead it back to another battery's snap-on connector—

Scrub the knives vigorously with a Brillo pad and some distilled water—

Lower knives into the distilled water—

Rest the chopsticks across the mouth of the jar so it holds the knives suspended in the solution—

Attach the other battery snap-on connector to the empty 9-volt lead—

Wait.

I do my chores to pass the time. Unload the wood I collected from the bike trailer, do inventory on my dwindling food supplies (canned goods, dried ramen, etc.), clean the shotgun, clean the pistol, count bullets, update my calendar—it goes back to October of last year. Each sheet ripped out and tacked to the wall. My notes at the bottom of every month: people in red Sharpie, bodies in black. October has twenty-two red hash marks and four black ones. The red marks taper off through March as the black ones multiply. After May, there's only the sporadic black mark. No red ones.

I x out August 6 and, at the bottom, add the first two black hash marks to the month.

I survey my food shelf again. Screw it, it's been a day, and I need the nutrients. I grab a can off the bottom shelf.

The beans give off a sweet, pasty aroma. Normally I'd relish the aroma. But the problem is I can still smell that master bedroom. That scent of perfumed rot scraped trenches all the way up my nostrils, right into my brain. And even now, it stains every inhalation with streaks of decay.

I rotate the can a half turn on its rock sitting at the edge of the fire.

In the process, my leg accidentally bends a little, unleashing a thousand stingers along the length of the cut.

The strips of T-shirt I used to bandage it cling to the cut. Dried parts have unstuck themselves and dangle in jarring clumps. The wound's stopped bleeding. For now. It's definitely inflamed though. I just can't tell if the surrounding flesh is turning red with infection or if that's just bloodstains.

I lift my shirt to check my ribs.

No stripes.

Yet.

Dark, crystalline barnacles grow on the sides of the knives suspended in the solution. I unclip the batteries and slowly pull out the knives. The liquid in the jar has a yellow tint to it. It worked. Colloidal silver. Time to disinfect.

It feels good to be full. Even though I know I shouldn't've opened up the second can of beans. Starve a cold, feed a fever, though. Right? Thermometer still reads 99.2 degrees, but I feel hot. Especially from the waist down. The dark air sits on me, a thick layer of insulation. Even with leaving the CC doors open.

Still not too full for Oreos. It's been a day. I deserve a treat. I don't remember the last time I allowed myself to dip into my prized box of Oreo two-count packs. I've kept those on severe rationing status since I found them. Who knows when I'll find more.

If I'll find more.

Stars are brighter nowadays. Not the biggest silver lining to everything…

One glints in the sky, cruising across east to west.

So, satellites are brighter too. I flip it the bird. See if your all-seeing lens can see that.

I suck at the last remaining morsels of chocolate biscuit and sweet crème filling I got wedged up between my jaw and my cheek like it's a hunk of chaw. The Oreo lasts longest if you don't chew it.

My good leg dangles off the side of the cot. I reach over, without looking, and take a wet strip of T-shirt out of the jar of colloidal silver and replace the strip on the bad leg. Antiseptic cool. For the first few seconds. It'll kill all the bacteria, at least.

Probably not the Stripes though.

4

LIFE'S FITFUL FEVER

I dream in fiery flashes.

A hospital. A heart monitor: *bee-beep.*

My childhood bed. Damp sheets, stick like dried glue on skin.

bee-beep.

Whispers at the door.

He's burnin' up. Doc said—

I know what the goddamn doc said, Emmie. We just gotta bring it down.

It's over 104.

We just gotta break it.

Ice trays crack above the tub.

bee-beep.

Plastic bags of cubes, ripped and emptied. Hailing down into the bath.

A green Hulk fridge magnet holds up a crayon family portrait.

The high-pitched thrush of water singing its way out of the old pipes.

I can't—

Goddamnit, Emmie. Fine, go git 'im. I'll do it, I'll do it. Just git 'im.

We can just take him to the ER.

What, they givin' out employee discounts now?

I-I dunno. Yes. Maybe.

Just go git 'im. This'll work fine. It's just about lowering the boy's temperature. That's all it is, Emmie. This'll do it. Go git 'im.

Brown liquid swirls inside in an art deco bottle.

Soft lips cauterize against my forehead. Whispered kisses.

bee-beep.

A handoff.

Warm bourbon breath. White lines of grout octagons in an ocean of sea blue bathroom tiles.

We just need ta cool you down, little man. This'll cool you off.

Searing ice water. I explode in frenetic fury. Trying to get out of the singeing cold. But his weight bears down. Holding me under. Callous pressure.

beebeepbeebeepbeebeep.

Icebergs calve and shatter against the porcelain cliffs of the tub. Waves of frigid lava ricochet off them, swamping me in livid chills.

Get him out! GET HIM OUT!

Hol' still, goddammit. S'for your own good. HOL' STILL!

I'm screaming. I'm burning.

We gotta break the fever!

I'm clawing. I'm drowning. *MOMMA!!* Scorching artic water floods my throat.

GETHIMOUTGETHIMOUTGETHIMOUT!

A blur of movement, lightning quick. And a crack of thunder snaps her back.

The weight has lifted. I can breathe. I can get out. I can sit up.

She shields her left eye with her hand, a belated afterthought postattack. It'll purple up into a shiner for sure. A spiderweb halos out in the mirror behind her, where the back of her head hit.

Whispered apologies follow us down the hallway. My wet, shivering skin sticking to her blouse.

Frantic search for car keys.

A white *H* on a blue road sign.

bee-beep. bee-beep. bee—

5

EXOTHERMIC REACTION

—beep.

It sounded like it came from behind the wall. Down a linoleum hallway.

I wait. Nothing.

It's in my head. It has to be. No echoes can survive beneath the suffocating blanket of humidity. Instead of collecting a pool of cool night, the CC traps heat, an earthen incubator.

A film of dried sweat stifles my skin.

I lie still. Listening out of the corner of my ear. The heart monitor stays mum. It's made its point.

What time is it?

No crickets. Must be late.

It's a relief to surface into the open air. Not a breeze exactly, but movement.

The fire's out.

Venus winks up above the eastern horizon. The morning star.

I try not to clink the thermometer against my teeth. I hate that sound. Feeling the clink of glass on bone.

Memory interrupts—

"Beep?"

No. I'm not going back.

No.

It's not worth it.

"…"

It was just the dream.

"You heard it. Clear as day. S'why you dreamt about it."

It's not worth it! Ok!?

…

Ok.

I peel off the sliver of colloidal-silver-soaked T-shirt and replace it with a fresh one. It melts into me like a ribbon of snowflakes. Good chills.

The edges of the gash look better. Less angry. No redness, no inflammation. If only honors chem had had tests on making colloidal silver disinfectant instead of asking about electron orbitals, then maybe I would've passed. Context is king.

The only useful thing I really got out of that class was learning how to swipe rare chemicals from the supply closet.

LG!

I didn't have to look to know Elmore was sitting on the bleachers. I didn't have to check to see if his crew was with him. I just had to run until I hit a full-out sprint.

Come on, Shooter. Don't be like that.

My bookbag shuttled back and forth, shoulder to shoulder, as I picked up speed. But it didn't matter.

Whatta I say 'bout running, LG? We talked about this.

Two of his boys held my arms out. I braced for the inevitable gut punch.

Come on, man. I ain't gonna hit you.

Why? Why wouldn't he hit me? I risked a glance up from my shoes. Riley Anne hovered behind him. She looked different than she used to, back when she was in all the accelerated classes with me. Distant behind the black eye shadow.

Yeah, you interested now, LG.

His name's Addison, Riley Anne said. It wasn't quite clear if she was sticking up for or narc'ing on me. When she first started hanging out with him and his crew, she told him about me scoring her some government grow from my uncle.

He beat the shit out of me for stealing his client.

All I had been trying to do was just get to first base.

I know his fucking name, don't I? he growled at her. *LG and me go way back. Ain't that right, Shooter.*

Yeah, you used to steal my lunch money in grade school. I don't have any now. I bag lunch it.

Come on, LG. E'rrybody know you as poor as church mouse shit ever since yo' daddy disappeared.

I shrugged. Silver lining.

I need a favor.

This should be good.

Need you to get me some phosphorus from the chem lab.

Get it yourself! I thought. But didn't say. *Why?* I knew why.

Da' fuck you care?!

You're trying to make meth.

I'm upgrading my game is all.

That shit's volatile as hell.

Volla—wha'?

Dangerous. Unstable.

Me too. His crew laughed at that one. *Come on, brother. You can't tell me the Lone Gunman cares about dat shit. Ain't you an anti-Christ?*

Anarchist, Riley corrected him.

I'm a prepper, I corrected her, rolling my eyes.

We on da same team, LG. Disruption is our game.

I don't believe in teams.

You believe in money? I'll pay you... There it is, that shut you up. Even an anarchist gotta price.

That wasn't it. I just knew the only way out was appeasement... in the moment. So I agreed. And I did it.

After I got it for him though, that was a different story.

When I took the phosphorus, I nabbed some strips of magnesium too. More stable than phosphorus. You don't need to keep magnesium sealed in an airtight container at all times. And a strip of it was more than thin enough to easily slip through the vent at the top of his locker. Pinched it between my fingers, ignited the end with a Bic, and let go.

Once magnesium's lit, it turns exothermic, fires up brighter than the sun, and burns almost as hot.

The first link in a chain reaction.

As I strolled away, the burning white magnesium lit up his entire supply of pot and ignited phosphorus. And once that shit got going, it melted a hole right through the locker door. Volatile as hell.

The fire department came. Found the remains of his stash.

He got expelled and tried as an adult.

In history class we read about how some philosophers say man is originally good, but society makes him bad. While others think that at heart, man is a vicious animal and it's society that tames him. The truth is, good and bad only exist with others. Morality requires society. There are no ethics on a desert island.

If I had known then what was coming... I just would have let Elmore have the phosphorus.

The thermometer reads 98.8 degrees. First light breaks the horizon.

Screw it. I'll go back.

6

WORTH IT

eeh... aww...

No goddamn wind, yet somehow the damn porch swing is still going. Still giving me the heebie-jeebies. This was a bad idea.

Dead cornstalks itch me. Been over forty minutes. Not 'cause of protocol. 'Cause I ain't worked up the nerve yet. They're not mutually exclusive though.

The pockmarked rubber doggie door cover bends back inside, snagged on one of the broken wooden shards, like a soldier's corpse caught up on barbed wire.

Did I kick it back inside during my rushed escape, or has something else gone in since?

My elbows dig into yesterday's dirt divots as I roll the thumbscrew to sharpen the focus.

Dried-out chunks of evaporated vomit map out the topography of my panic across the veranda. Better put on the surgical mask now.

The house slides back and forth as I pan over every inch of it.

Nothing moves. Including me.

. . .

Short, hot, humid breaths bounce back off the mask. Other than the runner rug I must've accordioned against the wall yesterday, the dusty hallway looks untouched. It's all I can see through the doggie door.

I crouch on the porch. I listen. I delay. I hear it.

beep.

Son of a bitch. It was there the whole time. That plea for maintenance from some neglected device. It just hadn't really registered. And now, damn it.

The "new" boots make it easy work clearing away all the wood shards. I'll be damned if I'm going back in without a better exit route.

I move real slow like. A glacier in lead hiking boots. Like the virus has some sort of motion detector and I'll be safe enough if I just don't trigger it...

I steer clear of the stairs. Don't even risk a glance up them.

beep.

Relief sighs out of me. It's on the first floor. Somewhere. I track it by sound, like a bat hunting at dusk.

Doesn't take long to locate the beep. Through the dining room, past the kitchen and its piles of plates and empty cupboards. Stuck to a wall, in the mudroom out back. A keypad to an alarm system. Sentinel 300 with backup juice and a reminder that beeps when it's running on auxiliary power too long. And a second electrical wire that runs along the floorboard, then snakes through a hole near the boarded-up back door, and slips outside.

Once again, back through the doggie door, circle around to the far side of the house, to the kitchen and the back door, and there's the wire, popping out, and climbing up the wall…

Up.

No. Not a chance in hell. Not up those stairs, not down that hall, not up in that room. Not on your life. Or mine.

Eeyore's distant *eeh... aww* finds its way out back around the far corner. Pulling my focus. And there, nestled against the base of the house, lies a ladder half hidden in the overgrown weeds.

It's a small solar panel mounted on the roof, at the edge of an eave. I cut the cord, yank it off, and flee.

The ashy ember scent catches up with me on the road about a mile downwind. It carries with it memories of Christmas and s'mores and pyres.

I stop and look back at the cleansing conflagration. It was a precaution, not revenge. Safety. Least that's what I keep telling myself.

Flames reach out of the windows and doors, yellow and greedy lashings. Frenetic fiery flapping in search of a handhold, a way up, desperate for air. Smoke drifts at an angle, a leaning column of black cotton balls billowing up.

A beacon of Babel visible for miles. I'll be long gone by the time anyone could follow it home.

For better or for worse.

The only difference between a beacon and a warning is who's doing the looking.

7

JURY-RIG

This world is a warehouse of artifacts and castaways.

The volleyball smiles at me with its painted face. A quiet taunt from its perch atop a rotting bale of hay. Another bale decays behind "Wilson's" mocking gaze.

Quiet draw-back.

Breathe out—

thumpTHUMP—

Release—

FHWK! The arrow dives halfway into the hay six inches to the right of Wilson.

"Sheee't. Really?? Goddamnit."

A cluster of arrows juts out of the hay, flanking the vandalized, but intact, volleyball. My own little monument to precision's triumph over accuracy. So I'm consistent in my suckage. Awesome.

Dead grass crunches beneath my boots with every stomp of my angry charge. My last arrow seamlessly drawn out of the quiver and nocks into place in one smooth movement.

It'd look badass in slow-mo. Real Rambo-like. At least until the camera pans down to reveal Wilson a mere ten inches away from my drawn arrow tip.

THUNK! The pierced volleyball lets out a satisfying hiss. While it finishes its dying breath, I nab all of my misses out of the bale of hay and put them back in the quiver.

I glance up at the hayloft. Sunlight glints off the solar panel.

A watched pot never boils.

I practice knife throws to pass the time. They bite into the soft, old wood wall. Well, with knives at least, my aim is good enough to hit the side of a barn.

My jury-rigged solar-panel concoction continues to tempt me to look up at the loft to check and agonize, to prolong my wait. I turn a deaf ear to its silent prompts.

Got to get away.

I do a walkabout.

Check the snares.

Empty. Thumper's too smart. Or I'm too incompetent.

Collect firewood.

Refill my hydration packs. It takes twenty-nine pumps of the handle to get it going.

Fill the rusted coffee can and go to water the zucchini and tomatoes. The broccoli has been completely decimated during my absence. At least Thumper has the decency not to eat it in front of me anymore.

BWEENNNNNG!

It worked! Son of a bitch, the solar panel worked—

Don't get ahead of yourself, Addie. It just sounds like it worked.

I finish watering the vegetables. Taking my time. The solar panel can wait. Stroll back to the pump, and make sure to place the can just right, so it looks like it was haphazardly discarded.

If you're too eager, God'll lash out and snatch away your small victory.

Stroll over to the barn; climb the hayloft.

It looks downright poetic up there, dust motes lit up by the waning light, dancing in an invisible whirlwind.

I check on the solar panel first. Make sure it's secure. Don't even glance sideways. It's good though.

Check every inch along the length of its tail. To where I stripped the cord bare, exposing the cathode and anode leads, and spliced them to the leads from the white cord, following its twists to where I had left it, gently placed on a pile of hay.

I tap it.

Enter Passcode.

Your passcode is required when phone restarts.

My hollering startles a thrush of starlings into flight.

8

HOME, VIDEO

A younger me pushes through the bushes in front of our house.

"It's flashing red. Don't that mean it's recording?" Her voice is off-screen.

Hearing it twists the core of my Adam's apple into a knot and swells it up to the size of a grapefruit. It feels like a choke hold. It feels like when I was little. And I was trying to get a handle on a staccato of sobs before he decided to come over and *give me something to cry about.*

"Yes, Momma. The flashing red recording sign means it's recording."

I watch myself find the extension cord I was hunting for and follow it.

"Oh Lord, you sure you wanna be sassin' your momma when Santa's on his way, Addison?"

Her index finger dips down in front of the lens and covers up a good third of the screen while she adjusts her grip on the phone.

"Seven sons a sassin', six moms oh Lording, five golden zings!"

My smile stretches into a large shit-eating grin as I murder "Twelve Days of Christmas." "Got it!" I yell, holding up two ends of two different extension cords.

My voice sounds high, womanish in the video. What was I, twelve? Thirteen maybe. I could check the timestamp on the file.

But I don't.

"Ready? Hold it steady, Momma!"

The whole image tilts down as she—

"How do I zoom in, Addie? I'm pinching the sides an everything, but ain't nothing zooming."

"No, no, no. You pinch in the sides."

"I'm pinching the sides!"

The world twists and flips.

Me too.

"Not the sides of the phone. The sides of the screen."

"They ain't the same thing?!"

"Just—don't! Don't pinch. Don't zoom. Just man the switch. Ok? You need a wide shot, Momma." My voice cracks halfway through the sentence.

"Ok, I'll *man* the switch," she says in her best bass voice.

"Mom—" I was always supersensitive to her teasing. Especially the delight she took in highlighting my puberty.

"Ok, ok. I got it."

The old world straightens itself out. Younger me stands dead center. Slightly annoyed.

"Ready, Addie."

My womanish voice rings out, “Three, two, one…” Young me plugs one extension cord into the other.

The porch railings, the rain gutters, all the window frames, a plastic Santa Claus, and a plastic candy-cane candle erupt in festive light. It actually looks kind of nice. The lights seem to polish over the piece-a-crap acreage we lived in. One step above a trailer park.

“Oh, Addie… It’s just so damn Christmasy I could cry.”

Momma forgets she’s manning the camera and yanks the world downwards as she drops her arms to her sides.

“Momm—”

The video freezes.

The CC feels blue, lit up by the phone screen.

The knot in my throat rears up big as it can and coils into a fist, grabbing my windpipe from the inside.

I can’t get a full breath down.

Only one a day. That’s the deal. Rationing is the key to survival. One video a day. So the newness of her stays fresh.

Like an open wound.

I turn off the phone.

Darkness.

And sobs.

From somewhere outside, a coyote yips back in response.

This world is an artifact.

9

THE PLAN

Two of the Igloo coolers are totally full. The third's got about half left.

Ten gallons, ten gallons, five-ish gallons.

Average person needs three quarts a day, just for consumption. Add one more for a safe margin and cooking. Call it a gallon a day, seven gallons a week… three weeks and change. That's what I got.

I look around the CC, hoping I'll find an answer on one of the shelves. But all I got are my dwindling dried and canned goods. And books:

Self-Reliance

Walden

The Bible

The Decameron

Robinson Crusoe

To Build a Fire and Other Stories.

How to Survive the End of the World as We Know It

U.S. Army's Complete Guide to Edible Wild Plants

U.S. Air Force's Survival Handbook

And my favorite sci-fi book by Tate Avess. Because it can't all be business.

On the opposite wall hangs my body-count calendar and map of Oklahoma.

Out behind the garage *The Guide to Edible Wild Plants* holds down one side of the map, and *Survival Handbook* pins down the other on top of the old door repurposed with some cinder blocks into a desk. The wind pushes open the warped cover of the handbook. Below Uncle Izzy's inscription, his Bible quote admonishes me:

> Go, my people,
> enter your rooms
> and shut the doors behind you;
> hide yourselves for a little while
> until his wrath has passed by.
> —Isaiah 26:20

I shrug and circle the empty spot between Woodward and Fairview on the NW corner of the map. Home base.

Mark an X on Ouachita National Forest at the SE edge. Using *Walden* as a straight edge, I draw a line from one to the other. It passes through Oklahoma City.

"Unh-unh." I shake my head at myself. "Might still be some wrath out there."

My leg itches along the length of the healing scab. A warning of what-if.

Cross out Oklahoma City. And Tulsa. No cities. That's where the Stripes started.

I draw a new line, due south to Wichita Mountains and the Wildlife Refuge, then another straight east to Ouachita.

Tick off distances with the edge of the book. Use the map legend to calculate.

"'Bout a hundred and fifty miles to the Wildlife Refuge. Then another three hundred or so to Ouachita," I announce. "Loaded down, maybe thirty to forty miles a day. At most five days to Wichita, ten to Ouachita. Just over two weeks."

Ok. Draw a course, leave the sanctuary, and set out. I guess that's the plan. Bike my ass clear across the state. To Izzy.

Noah didn't build the ark while it was raining. So why should I wait until the farm well pump dry heaves?

Twisted Sister, Eminem, Nas, Metallica, Taylor Swift.

Music makes everything better. Especially chores.

Like tuning up the bike and battening down my Frankensteined trailer.

Loading up and securing the heavy-as-shit Igloos onto the trailer, along with shotgun, pistol, bow, arrows, ammo, pots, tent, jar of colloidal silver, Ziploc bag full of lighters, Ziploc bag full of matchbooks, scavenged fireworks, dried and canned goods, lots of ramen, my prized box of snack-pack Oreos, bag of batteries, and my books.

The campfire burns bright. Light flickers off the packed bike trailer. Empty cans glow in the umber coals. A blurry reflection of myself winks back at me between the flames.

It makes me think about cold winters, a fire in the fireplace, and me pretending the floor was lava and the couch was home base and I had to make it from the hall to the dining room. The CC ain't got nothing on a good pillow fort.

"Satellite," I announce to the emptiness as if I saw a punch-buggy VW. It shimmers past overhead. Maybe it's the same one as before. Hell if I know. I don't give it the middle finger this time. Just turn and spit.

I check my phone. No bars. Without working cell phone towers, you ain't going to get no bars, no matter how many satellites glide past. Still had to check though.

I can barely move with my belly so distended and bloated. That's what I get for eating as much Prepper Surprise as I could stomach. It was either that or leave it behind.

PREPPER SURPRISE

INGREDIENTS:

- 1 can of whatever you're not taking with you
- 1 can of whatever else you're not taking with you
- 1 mystery can (that the label got ripped off of a long time back)
- 6 small zucchini
- 15 cherry tomatoes *(Either of these last two can be substituted with whatever variety of every goddamn veggie morsels you managed to grow in spite of the rabbit ransackings.)*
- Sprinkle to taste any other stuff you don't want to drag along on your Oklahoma odyssey, but sure as shit aren't going to leave for someone or something else.

PREPARATION

Step 1

Open up the various cans. Empty into one pot. Make sure not to peek inside the mystery can; otherwise you risk ruining the surprise later.

Step 2

Chop up zucchini and cherry tomatoes. Toss into pot.

. . .

Step 3

Simmer it all together over an outdoor, post-apocalyptic fire for five to fifteen minutes depending on whether you actually have a working timer. And how much you like playing botulism roulette.

Step 4

Gorge yourself.

Step 5

Belch like a boss. Belch the alphabet, trying to get at least to *H*.

Step 6

Gorge yourself again. Because you don't want to be wasteful. And there are starving children in Africa.

YIELD: 1 massive serving

TIME: Five to twenty-five minutes (depending on how lucky you're feeling)

10

BROKEN PROMISE

"Santa Looked a Lot Like Daddy" plays on the stereo.

A somewhat older, but still younger me *mans* the camera now.

I grab Momma's present from under the tree. Inspect the other gifts and grab a book-stack-sized one for me.

"Can I open the one from Uncle Izzy?"

On the couch sits Momma—

I got myself a large personality and even larger costume jewelry, she'd always tell people. *Call it a folksy joie de vivre.*

It's the first time I've seen her since—

I prepped myself before opening the clip though. And I manage to catch that emotional choke hold before it makes it up to my throat. I grab ahold of it, push it down, and lock it up in my chest. But it don't miss a beat, just jigs quick to the right, grabs ahold of my heart, and starts to squeeze. Tighter and tighter.

. . .

"If that's the one you want to open for your Christmas Eve gift." Momma's wearing her old raggedy Christmas sweater. *It's my holey holy sweater*, she'd joke every December, sticking her fingers through nickel-sized holes.

Momma unwraps her snack pack of Oreos. We always stuff each other's Christmas stockings with them. They are Momma's favorite cookie. Were. That year I surprised her with Winter Oreos.

"I cannot believe how adorably festive these are! They're filled with red cream! Correction." She unscrews one cookie side from the other and takes a lick of the filling. "Filled with *delicious* red cream."

I plop down on the couch and hand her the present. "You first."

She smiles, takes another lick, and places the cookie cream-side-up on the table. Then delicately unwraps the present, careful to save the paper. We always had to save the wrapping paper and reuse it.

Why? It's just paper. What, are we that poor?

No, Addie. We ain't that poor. And we ain't that wasteful neither.

She opens the box and pulls out a brand-new Sooners hoodie. She'd gotten her nursing degree at OU. I bought it with the money Elmore paid me for the phosphorus (after I delivered it to him but before I burned down his life).

"Oh, I love it. How'd you know?! It's so soft. I love it." She's already taking off her ratty sweater and putting on the Sooners sweatshirt. Then… she models it.

"How do I look? Like a sorority girl?"

The repulsion in my tone is not subtle. "No. Momma. UGH! Please never say that again."

"Woo! Spring break!" She starts to lift her sweatshirt as if she were flashing.

"MOMMA!!"

"Oh hush. I'm not gonna flash nothing at Christmas." She winks. "I gotta save the girls for Lent and Mardi Gras."

. . .

Her laugh fills the CC and rattles my chest. The tendrils wrapped around my heart constrict, squeezing tighter. I can feel it warping like a balloon, bulging out to escape the constricting grip. Pushing up again towards my throat. No matter how much weight I bear down on it with.

"Your turn!!" Mom grabs the camera.

Young me tears open my present. Inside is a Leatherman multi-tool and two books: *U.S. Air Force Survival Handbook* and *How to Survive the End of the World as We Know It.*

"Awesome!"

"That's great, honey." She's underwhelmed.

I unfold all of the Leatherman blades and tools. "You think this summer I can go work with Uncle Izzy?"

"I'll talk to him about it. You might still be too young for forest ranging all the way over in Ouachita." She sighs. "I'm worried that maybe you're too worried. You know, 'bout the end of the world and all. I mean, it's ok to just be like everybody else sometimes, Addie.

"Nah, if you're just like everyone else, you're going to end up like everyone else."

I was so sure of myself. I was right. Just not the way I thought I'd be.

Momma takes another lick of her festive Oreo. She could really milk a cookie, so to speak. She used to say it was about taking the time to appreciate one of life's yummier blessings. Make it last. I knew it was really about keeping her "figure." The more time it took her to eat one, the less likely she was to eat two. Same reason she liked the snack packs even though buying them that way cost more.

"Right. Right. You gonna take your momma with you though when you bug out?"

"No." It comes out so quick. A thoughtless reflex. The look on my face, it kills me. Suddenly serious and practical. And oblivious.

Momma makes a mock aghast sound… mostly mocking. Maybe

there's a penny of hurt mixed into that pound of joke. "Why not? I'm whatchu'd call an asset. A hot asset."

"No, you gotta choose smart. You know. Numbers can be bad." I'm so serious. A devoted prepper.

"You'd leave your momma?"

My eyes drop. Her humor finally cracks through my walls. Her hand reaches out from behind the camera. A chunky turquoise bangle clacks against her faux pink pearl bracelet. She tenderly cups my chin and lifts up my head until I look up at her.

"No. No, I would not leave my momma," she prompts me.

Obstinate as a mule, at least in tone, I repeat her words back to her, "No, I would not leave my momma."

She smiles and pans down, pulling at her Sooners hoodie. "And I will never leave my soft new sweatshirt."

The video freezes.

I wipe my eyes on the Sooners sweatshirt balled up beneath my head. It used to still smell like her. Now it smells like dirt mixed with a hint of hand lotion.

The videos disorient. There's no past. Only memories. There's no future neither. Only hope. Living is just a constant balancing act in the moment between memory and hope.

I pick up the *Air Force Survival Handbook* from the bottom of the cot. The phone gives off enough light to read.

The more you know, the less you need. —Merry Xmas, Uncle Isaiah

That part of the inscription is way better than his Isaiah quote.

Uncle Izzy's dog tags clink together on the chain around my neck as I shift positions and turn to the chapter on psychology.

11

GOING, GOING…

All the packing yesterday makes for quick work this morning.

I plug the charger cord into my phone, tuck it inside the rolled sleeping bag on the trailer, and bungy strap the solar panel on top so it can charge up during the ride. Like on a trip to Walmart. You know, "normal" like.

The steel doors warble as they swing closed. They thunder in protest with every piece of junk and small boulder I throw on top. Maybe the camouflage is overkill, but just in case I ever need to come back, there's no need to advertise the whereabouts of my CC.

I give myself permission for the briefest bit of pining.

Then I piss on the fire embers, get on the bike, and head south without looking back.

Ok, that last part might've been a lie. But it would've been epic if I hadn't looked back. And if I had burned my house down again.

PART II

12

FRIEND OR FOE OR FIGMENT

Someone's following me.

Paranoia whispers in my ear. Tugs at the corner of my eye. Brushes up the hair on the back of my neck. It keeps me company.

No one's there though.

Not really. Just movement beyond my periphery. Blurs of action that I never quite see. Odd noises muted in the distance that I don't quite hear. Like when the chorus of crickets suddenly fills the air after being quiet. And I'm not quite sure if they actually had been quiet all this time or I had just stopped hearing them for a spell. It's real. It's a delusion. A ghost that's only there if I don't look.

So I ignore it. Sometimes.

Sometimes though, I talk to the misbelief, out in the unseen. After setting up camp for the night in a copse. Teach it lessons on survival, like how to use a bow drill and a stick to start a fire.

"...and press down with the rock on the stick, hard enough that its firm and got some resistance, but not so much that friction locks it in place. S'all about the right amount of resistance. And tinder. Like this dried corn hair. Nice and flammable. Press down on the rock and piston your arm back and forth with the bow. Spinning back and forth, back and forth, and blow. And back and forth…"

Until my arms get tired and I'm sick of blowing and nothing's smoking, not even a little—

"Screw it."

I get out the disposable lighter from the Ziploc bag in the trailer.

I start awake.

Something's here. I heard it. For sure. Something's outside my tent.

I think.

What is it?

Don't move. Don't make a sound. Nothing to let on I'm here. I'm awake. I'm savvy.

I try to flex whatever muscle rabbits use to rotate their ears without moving their heads.

The fire pops. Coals're still burning down. So I couldn't've been asleep that long. Couple of hours at most.

Other than *popPOP* though, camp's quiet.

There—

A huff, a patter, in the underbrush. Not a lot. Not constant or nothing. But not part of the landscape neither.

Something's out there. In the dark.

Slow like, at snail speed, I reach over and grab the shotgun.

SOMETHING DEFINITELY JUST MOVED.

Control your breathing. Panic demands oxygen. I still need too much though. Breathing way too loud. I can't flare my nostrils wide enough to muffle my hysteria. Open your mouth. Short, metered breaths. That's right. Quiet. Stay quiet.

Fingers find the tent zipper in the dark. Tug it up centimeter by centimeter. The tent's teeth sigh apart in a maddeningly slow yawn.

Until finally I can slip out.

Peer into the blackness.

Where I can't see shit.

But I keep staring. Waiting. Outwaiting. Days pass in those minutes in the dark.

Nothing.

There was definitely something though.

Quietly, I kick dirt over the remains of the fire, snuff it out.

The darkness gets a little darker.

Sunrise. The tent's empty. Fire's buried and cold.

And I'm one big cramp, wedged into my perch up a tree, with a lockjaw death grip on my shotgun. Sooner hoodie constricted around my head.

I lift up my monoculars dangling from my neck and scan.

Empty fields.

Empty roads. Except for the abandoned truck I passed yesterday about a mile back. But ain't no one used that for a while.

Looking down, nothing jumps out. No footprints (other than mine). Least not in camp.

Nothing gone or disturbed.

Paranoia's just playing tricks on me. I guess. Maybe.

Maybe not.

13

DOG DAY AFTERNOON

Different scenery, same emptiness.

And worse heat.

Fevers ripple along asphalt rivers and douse me in sweat at every rise in the road.

It's overkill, I know, but I stop atop each knoll, pull out my monoculars, and scan the upcoming horizon.

Best way to get ahead in life is ta always look forward. Uncle Izzy had a lot of these fortune cookie thoughts. Never used to make sense to me, but I get it now.

That said, up ahead's always deserted.

Nah, that's not right. For it to be deserted, there'd have to be deserters.

Hollow? Vacant? Unfilled. Yeah, that's it. Unfilled.

I also check the phone atop each knoll. Still no bars.

The miles melt past. Fallow fields. Motionless towns (that I steer clear of). And the occasional roadside ruin of a building. With its welcome shade. A brief oasis hidden from the afternoon sun. Mostly these pit stops are just an excuse to try to rub the soreness out of my thighs. Or play a game of *Angry Birds*. But only one game. 'Cause those zippy little bastards really burn through battery life.

I can't help but wonder about the various decrepit buildings. Is today's a new ruin or an old one? BS or PS. Before Stripes or Post Stripes. Hard to tell sometimes. Lot of this land was forsaken long before the Stripes scraped through. A withering world pockmarked with sink holes and pustules of dilapidated monuments: crumbling churches, disintegrating schools, degenerating factories.

Poverty hastens havoc.

The gas station shimmers in the distance.

An old F-150 and a rusted Subaru Outback splay out in front. Askew, haphazard. Like a flood washed them up and left them there in its wake. The F-150's hood leans open, like the truck can't stop yawning.

No movement. No people.

I suck a couple of swigs out of the adjustable tube clip on the shoulder of my hydration pack.

Something feels off.

So I pan my monoculars across the whole junction.

Still nothing moving. Nothing suspicious.

A shimmer patters through my neck hair, and I flip 180 degrees and scan behind me.

Hell if something didn't just dart into the tall grass. Or it could just be my cracked lens making me see things. I close my left eye and squint with my right.

Road, telephone poles, cypress tree, dog, barbed-wire fence—

Dog?!

Pan back quick.

Son of a bitch.

A black dog sits like patience on a statue in the cypress's shadow.

Staring right at me. Droopy jowls, droopier ears. Looks like a Lab, but way thinner. Maybe part pointer. Maybe just goddamn starving.

A dog.

That's who's been following me.

Son of a bitch.

I laugh so loud the hound tilts her head sideways with canine confusion. Which only makes me laugh louder.

She darts off, an ink blot dissolving into the untended field of tall grass.

And that was it.

I hook my two index fingers under my tongue, but stop short of whistling.

She knows I'm here. Been tracking me for days now. Just not sure if I'm friend or foe.

It takes a second to find it in the trailer. Buried way down, since it's only for special occasions. Double-bagged, trussed with rubber bands, and stuffed in an oatmeal tin. My stash of beef jerky.

Saliva swamps my mouth as soon as my nose gets even the slightest whiff of it. I tear off two hunks and rebag it, rebag it again, rubber band it, and seal it in the tin.

I place one piece on top of a rock nearby. The other I tuck up into the corner of my jaw, like a pinch of chaw.

It's hard as hell not to chomp into it, but like Oreos, jerky lasts way longer if you don't chew it. You can suck on the juices a good half hour before it dissolves.

High on beef broth, I mount up and head down to the station.

Both pumps are tapped. Figures. Gasoline's volatile, and people are pigs.

What, you saying people burned that shit up like you melted my locker?

No, Elmore. I'm saying it evaporates quickly, and fuel's one of the first things folks rush out to horde. Water, Wonder Bread, and fuel.

You think you're so effing smart. Just a smug, smart little Shooter. Ain't you, LG?

Smartest one in four counties. Leave me alone, Elmore. I got shit to do.

It's better when it's Momma who's interrupting.

There's a first aid kit in the back of the Subaru, but it's already been scavenged. And the F-150's just full of old fast-food wrappers.

An ice machine sits out in front of the station. Open wide and bone dry.

Inside the station's just as barren. Decimated shelves, save a stale pack of sugarless gum, some artificial sweetener, a random bunch of fireworks, and half a carton of Marlboro Reds. I grab them all.

No actual food. No water. No oil.

Damn.

A key chained to a large wooden plank hangs off a nail behind the counter. RESTROOM.

I find it outside. Around the back of the building. I prop open the door with a rock to let in light.

About what you'd expect. Small, dark, dirty. Definitely not a place worthy of a spot on my Best Places to Lunch on Dry Ramen Yelp reviews.

Any other day, this might've gotten me down. The same old, same old, can't-catch-a-break rigamarole.

Oh, I just love that word, Addie. It feels like what it means, you know. When you say it.

My momma had a bunch of favorite words.

Like it's onomatopoeia. Only not quite, 'cause that's about somethin' sounding like what it means. I wonder if there's a term for this though, words that feel like what they mean. Like shenanigans or glee. You can't say glee and not get a little happy.

You wanna know the secret ta happiness? Uncle Izzy always turned philosophical when he'd had too much Crown Royal.

Izzy—

No, now. No, no. Don't tone me. Don't Izzy me in that I know what's what, no matter what *tone you grin at me with. This here, these things're important fer Addie to know. Life lessons. Yes, sir. You wanna know the secret ta happiness?*

Another swig. Like the answer got caught in his throat and needed to be greased out with Crown Royal so it'd slip loose and he could spit it up.

Low expectations. Thass the secret. 'Specially when it comes ta pee-pal.

Maybe I meant cynical, not philosophical. Although, I think cynicism's a type of philosophy, ain't it?

Rigamarole. Yes, sir.

Ain't nothing getting me down today. I got a mouthful of jerky juice and a dog.

And apparently a supply closet tucked back in the shadow behind the bathroom door I wedged open.

Jackpot.

There are towers, towers of toilet paper in the supply closet. An actual shit ton. I can't stop smiling, loading up the trailer with armfuls of two-plied heaven. That's right, this place splurged for two-ply TP.

Hot.

Damn.

On the third trip, I notice the dog. Watching me, head tilted to the side again. This time she's sitting in my stakeout spot from before. Where I left the jerky for her. As if she'd been there the whole time.

Still like. An onyx statue that changes location every time you glance away.

I smile and nod to myself. It worked. Now she knows I'm a friend.

I try not to let it, but the pride swells up in me. Makes me light on my feet. Taller. Feels nice. Pride. Don't feel like a sin at all.

Happier than a dead pig in sunshine, my momma would say. Some of her sayings were better heard than parsed.

Today's a good day.

By the time I'm done strapping everything down, there's a mountain of Charmin teetering behind me.

Charmin. That's a good dog's name.

Dog names nee'ta be two syllables and vowely. Or t'least have a consonant you ken hold onta.

Izzy had an insight for everything.

That way, you ken really yell it. Soooo-phieeee! Sey-mour!

Charrrr-miiinnnn.

Before I head off, I leave another hunk of jerky on the curb.

Today's a good day.

14

BAIT...

"So by digging a small pit and surrounding it with rocks, you keep the fire contained. But, and this is the secret, by digging this here little trench inta an' outta the circle, you got yourself a channel for the air to flow in and feed the fire. Not e'rrybody thinks about that."

I can't see her, but I know Charmin's out there. Listening.

"It's all about the oxygen. That's why you arrange the sticks of wood into a little teepee. Like so. It guides the flames without smothering 'em. Gives 'em room to grow."

I haven't seen her since the gas station. But she's out there. Blending into the shadows.

Maybe I should've named her Pepper. Pepper the Prepper. I still can, I guess.

"Then there's your tinder. And I got just the thing."

Marlboro Reds.

I smile real big. There's that pride again. Still feels good. Warm even.

"If there's one thing a cancer stick's good for, it's catchin' fire."

I break open a couple of cigs and sprinkle them into their own little pile atop a green elm tree leaf.

Now I suppose I could've just gotten out my lighter. But pride's like fire. Once it catches hold, it spreads. Fast.

As proud as I felt, I weren't about to embarrass myself with that damn bow drill neither.

"This here's fire steel."

I pull out the ferrocerium flint rod that hangs off of my dog tag chain from under my shirt.

"Some folks call it a ferro rod, on account of it being thirty percent ferrous, which is a fancy word for iron. Others say metal match. I like fire steel because, well, it sounds coolest."

I unclip the metal striker from the necklace and fit it around the ferro rod.

"It's basically like a big piece of flint. Although there's no real chemical relationship between this and actual flint."

I squat walk up close to my kindling teepee.

"I guess there's no real steel in it neither, but, like I said, it sounds cool. Cooler than fire iron. Don't really matter whatchu call it though."

I resist the temptation to look around. I don't want to see she's not there. If I don't look, it's easier to feel her presence, her head tilted, gaze fixed on me.

"You just drag'n scratch the metal striker down the length of it and—"

Sparks fountain off the ferrocerium rod, pouring down onto the cigarette innards. It catches immediately, and flames dance out from in between the tobacco grinds.

I blow. Light soft breath.

It swells brighter. Happier. Hungrier.

Slowly, I pick up the elm leaf and place the seed flame inside the teepee of wood and watch it flare to life.

It catches ahold of the kindling, like a vine, and climbs its way up. My pride does the same.

. . .

A hundred and fifty paces out, I set down a hunk of ramen atop a rock. Then another piece at a hundred paces out. At fifty, I switch up to a piece of jerky. It's running low, so I've got to be a little more measured with it. Figure she'll like the jerky the most, so she gets the best reward for coming the closest to the campfire.

I watch the pot, waiting for the water to boil. Anything to distract me. It ain't true what they say. Eventually it will boil. But a gun-shy dog don't have to show no matter how long you wait.

Soon as the surface roils with bubbles, I toss in a packet of ramen.

I set the timer on my phone. I still can't get over it. So easy. Amazing how something as simple as a timer is a luxury these days. Maybe it's a good thing I can't get over it. Better way of being to not take for granted even the littlest of things. Especially toilet paper.

It's only after watching the phone tick off a full minute that I allow myself a glance.

No dog.

I don't recommend sprinkling artificial sweetener on ramen. Unless Hell's gone and freezed over, in which case have at it. Hard to say if it's good or not. It's different though, there's that. And sometimes any difference makes all the difference.

I'll call it dessert noodles in my Yelp review.

It don't take me no time to scarf it down. No matter how much I try to draw it out. *Make an evening of it*, as Momma would say.

I also don't seem to have any say about my gaze drifting out past the fire: fifty, one hundred, and one hundred and fifty paces. They just keep going there. Checking on my spots.

Still no dog.

Forget it. I got more important business to take care of.

. . .

It's not like I couldn't do all this before. Find a nice quiet spot in the woods, dust off part of a fallen tree. Sit a spell and read another story in *The Decameron* as the fire pop-pops in the distance and the crickets whirr to life in the fading light. Bask in the goddamn bucolicness of it all.

I could always do that.

I have done that.

Just, I don't know…

Having a roll of two-ply toilet paper sitting there next to me makes it so much more civilized. More satisfying.

Like it's a choice instead of a reality.

Screw it. I'm going whole hog.

I reach over and thumb my way to my music app. If I'm going to be civilized, I'm going to be goddamn civilized.

The fourth movement of Beethoven's 9th fills the forest.

An inspiring finale encapsulating all of mankind's struggle against the darkness. Least that's how my European history teacher used to put it.

On the walk back, I feel positively gleeful. With my trowel and book under one arm and my roll of TP under the other.

Lighter. That's what I am.

So light, the dead leaves don't even crunch beneath my feet.

The fire flutters as I approach camp. The glow of it kaleidoscopes through the underbrush. It's not until I push all the way through the bushes that I see her.

A silhouette sitting fifty yards from the camp, licking her lips.

It's the first time I've seen her move.

I freeze in my tracks a moment. Then move real slow so as not to startle her. I squat at the trailer. Put down the book and trowel. I slip the TP into a Ziploc baggy.

She clocks every one of my movements, her big, droopy hound ears perking up.

Staying low, keeping the trailer between us, I finally risk a few words. In my softest voice I say, "Hi. You been following me? Come 'ere."

I pat my thigh.

She doesn't move.

I pat it again. "Come on. Come 'ere? No? Smart. You should be cautious. You hungry?"

She tilts her head, trying to understand.

"What's your name? Charmin? You like that? Charrr-miiinnn!"

No reaction.

"Pepper?"

She straightens out her head.

"Pepper. Ok. You like Pepper more? Pepper the Prepper it is."

She stares at me like a toddler inspects a menu.

I slowly sift through my trailer. "I bet you're hungry enough to eat the balls off a low-flying duck."

Found it. The half-eaten pack of ramen. She tilts her head further at the *SNAP* of the dried noodles. I hold it out.

"Want some?"

The dog doesn't move.

Maybe she doesn't know what it is. I mime like I'm eating it.

"Mmm. It's good. You can have some. Come 'ere and get it."

She stays put.

"All right. I get you. How 'bout I come to you?"

I stand up, hold out the noodles, and take a step towards her. Then another. Then another. I get within about fifteen yards of her before she stands up.

I take another step, and she starts to back away.

"Ok, ok." I stop and squat down to her eye level. I take a nibble of the noodles and hold the rest out.

"It's ok. Want it?"

She's focused on the ramen. Ok. Good enough.

I break off a hunk of noodles and toss it at her. Pepper scoots to the side, letting the hunk fall to the ground. She takes a cautious whiff and then scarfs it up.

I break off another hunk and hold it out.

She still won't approach. So I place it right next to where I'm squatting and retreat about ten paces back towards the fire.

The dog takes a couple of steps towards it, veers off to the side, backs up, looks at me, takes another couple of steps towards it from a different angle. Stops. Finally, she gets real low, like a coiled spring, and sort of crouch-crawls the rest of the way.

"That's it. Good girl."

I repeat the procedure, backing up towards the fire. One at twenty paces from camp, fifteen, ten, five—until I make it all the way back to the fire, where I sit down. And wait.

She trots up to the twenty-yard one, eats it.

Slowly paces to the fifteen-yard one, eats it.

Then zigzags back and forth, trying to take a pass at the ten-yard one. But she's too skittish to get that close.

"It's ok. You can get it." I give her a wink. "I won't bite."

Pepper takes another pass, but refuses to get close enough, and then, just like that, she darts off into the darkness, like ink into velvet.

"That's all right. That's a start. We got time. Plenty a time ta build some trust. You gotta get to know me. See I'm ok. Yeah."

Yeah. Well, all right.

15

...AND SWITCH

Momma sings me to sleep that night.

She never knew I shot this video. It was while she was getting ready for church one morning. I'd lied and told her I wasn't feeling well 'cause I didn't want to go. I'm sure she knew. But she didn't push it. Just kissed me on my forehead, ran her fingers through my hair, and whispered in my ear to rest up.

She's in her room. The door's cracked open. She's sitting at her little makeup table that we'd snagged in front of one of the rich folk's houses on trash day.

Well, ain't that just darlin'.

It's just garbage, Momma.

Hush, just because someone doesn't want it no more don't mean it's trash.

I didn't get it then that she was talking about more than just furniture.

Momma, it's literally on its last legs—

A little TLC and sandpaper will tart that there up real sweet. Now quick, 'fore someone beats us to it. Go'en grab it and pop it in the trunk.

Momma—

That set her off but good. She was out the door, muttering to herself. As she stormed around the car to get it—

You gonna Momma me. Momma, nothing. Always going off on how big and strong and self-sufficient you are, all you can do is sass me when I need you to help—

Too slow, I hopped out right quick to help, embarrassed as all hell. Not sure if I was more ashamed about taking someone else's garbage or about making her do it. Either way, I felt so goddamn small that when we got home, I spent the whole afternoon sanding and revarnishing it real good.

Oh, Addie.

Oh, Addie. She was so dang happy. Like I'd polished up the Lord's crucifix on Good Friday.

Truth is, I spent all that time working on it so no one'd see it was secondhand shit. She was right though, a little sandpaper and TLC and it turned out nice enough.

Momma's putting on her makeup she got on sale at Big Lots. And while she's doing it, she sings softly to herself. One of her favorite hymns.

> ...I need Thee ev'ry hour,
> In joy or pain;
> Come quickly and abide,
> Or life is vain.
>
> I need thee, oh I need thee.
> Ev'ry hour I need thee...

The video plays on repeat I don't know how many times. A ghost's lullaby—

The *CRASH* launches me out of the tent into a confusion of movement and disheveled clutter. Shotgun in hand. Disoriented and still more than half asleep.

Upright, somehow, pumping a shell into the chamber, my brain's sticky and still tangled up back in the sleeping bag.

Nothing makes sense.

It's dark. It's night.

Something's here.

Something was here.

Something crashed.

I rotate the radius of the 12 gauge three hundred and sixty degrees.

The trailer's turned over.

The trailer's…

I can't.

The gun swings down. I guess I lowered it. I don't know. I don't really feel like I'm moving me. Just still trying to parse what I can make out in the murk.

Torn-up ramen wrappers. Confettied beef jerky bag.

Shredded dried-goods containers.

Shards of the shattered solar panel scattered everywhere.

The Igloo coolers are tipped over. The top of one has popped off. All the water's spilled out.

In the fresh-made mud: a paw print.

The ground rushes up and catches me as my legs give out.

Instinct turns me fetal, arms wrapped around my knees, rocking.

"I can't, I can't, I can't—I'm ok. I'll be ok. I just need to, I need to… I just wanted—"

And then I'm yelling at the blackness, "I was trying to be nice. I thought we was friends! We coulda helped each other! Goddamnit!"

The yells dissipate in the emptiness.

My voice catches, weakens. "Goddamnit. Goddamn you. Damn you right to Hell!"

The stars stare down. Unblinking. Uncaring.

God? God either ain't all-powerful, or He ain't all-loving. Take your pick. Uncle Izzy-ism.

"Why would you… Why won't you help me? I was being good. Why you gotta be such a dick all the time? Christ, what am I gonna do?" My head drops. Weighed down with worry. "What am I gonna do?! What am I gonna—"

The stars stare up at me.

Out of the water.

The water.

A wet finger has stretched its way across camp, to the tent. Reached out in the dark and pooled itself around my phone that'd somehow found its way outta the tent and landed facedown.

In the dirt.

It must have gotten thrown free.

In the bedlam.

I snatch it out of its puddle, but I already know.

It's a fucking paperweight now. Bricked to all Hell.

A dead artifact.

I feel calm. No thoughts. No feelings. Just a sense of surety.

And then I'm in motion.

Gun. Bow. Bike. Go.

16

DOG EAT DOG WORLD

It doesn't taste like you'd think.

Fattier. Not as much as pork. Gamier.

Don't look. Don't think.

Waste not, want not. Especially in this world.

The problem is the bones. So many small bones.

The bones keep reminding you. And the tanginess. Super strong tang.

Between those two things you just can't forget, can't pretend that you're not eating—

The night sounds go quiet. Like all the birds and cicadas and crickets can't believe their ears. Like I burst into their midnight gala. And they all just stop and stare at me:

On all fours.

Retching.

My abdomen trying to twist itself inside out. Trying to hurl itself out of me, break free, and get away from the monster that holds it in, this sick shell of a man.

Choking on gags and heaves.

It's all out, but that's not good enough.

Dry disgorgements.

Gasping to catch breath.

Still attempting to somehow yank my insides out. So I could better scrape the viscera clean from me.

At some point the retches change.

Devolve.

Into sobs.

The animals turn away and go back about their business. Not wanting to see this… boy. Break down.

Back at camp, I grab the rest of its carcass off the makeshift spit over the fire. The flames splash up, hungry, yearning, reaching for every drop of rendered fat that wicks off.

It takes a good chunk of time to dig the hole. Lay her down. Give her a good Christian burial.

I stay stone faced the entire time.

Well, I try to.

Exhaustion climbs into my sleeping bag and sits on top of me. A relentless, weighty hobgoblin. But sleep won't come.

It's still hard to breathe deep at all. Like when you were little and had been swimming all day. Taking in anything but the shortest of breaths sets off a fit of wheezes.

Wriggling on my side makes it a little better. Curling my knees up to my chest too.

The hobgoblin spoons me. Scratches at the back of my brain. Opening up a crack just big enough so the flashes of thoughts and images can slip out.

Eyes closed, I can't help but replay it all.
Eyes open, I stare at the dead phone.
And listen.

> …I need Thee ev'ry hour,
> In joy or pain;
> Come quickly and abide,
> Or life is vain.
>
> I need thee, oh I need thee.
> Ev'ry hour I need thee…

17

REFUGE

It's a blur after that. The mile markers, the fields, the ruination. Broken white lines flicker past along Interstate 54.

The empty Igloo cooler rattles on its side. Random detritus slip slides around inside.

In every direction just fields, trees, drooping fences.

Without even slowing down none, I lean a left on Route 49.

East.

It barely registers.

At some point a sign flashes by along the shoulder: "Wichita Mountains Wildlife Refuge."

It should've felt like a milestone.

It didn't feel like nothing.

The road starts to lean towards me as it curves around a bend of trees. I only notice as it presses down on my legs. Slowly burning apart the muscle fibers. In the distance, some wooded mountains reach up into the sky.

. . .

A dam arches sideways across a valley. The contrast of it gapes out at the world. Emptiness on one side, weight on the other. The border between void and water.

I roll across the in-between, biking its concrete ridge.

I sit in silence and stare down at the dam. Maybe I eat too. I don't know.

In the land of the blind, the one-eyed man is king.

That must make me a cyclops.

Surveying his kingdom.

In the land of no-man, any man is king. Even a boy.

In another life, it'd be spectacular.

Splendor, wonder, beauty.

They're just words. Nothing more.

There's no beauty if ain't no one there to see it. No ugliness neither, I guess. No good, no bad 'less I think it so.

This world is rotten.

This place is a refuge if I call it so. Or a prison if I name it such.

This world is Eden with no escape.

I try to take it in. Zen away the past, chanting Uncle Izzy's mantra, *The more you know, the less you need. The more you know, the less you need. The more you know*, and let the "magnificence" wash over me.

At some point, I leave the road behind and ride through a field of wildflowers, where jackrabbits jackrabbit away from me.

Glide across a rolling landscape beneath a murmuration of starlings.

Navigate undulating grasslands bordered by bison silhouetted against the setting sun.

A shimmering lake smolders orange with the last light of the gloaming.

I try to marvel at the majesty of it all.

But the blackness rushes up out of nowhere. Slams into me at full speed.

Smashes me, the bike, and the trailer down into the depths.
We disappear into the earth. And shatter.

18

THE GIRL WHO HAD THE POWER TO CALL THE BUFFALO

The Caddo tribe tells stories of a girl who could call the buffalo. Her six brothers were stars. They left her every night to cross the sky. And every morning, they'd come back and place their sister in a lariat swing hung from the heavens. She'd swing through the air, and buffalo would come to watch her. And her brothers would kill as much as they needed to fill their bellies. In this way, the family always had plenty to eat.

Coyote visited once, saw the bounty of meat, and decided to stay and live with them. He watched every morning as the brothers swung their sister. He watched the buffalo come. He watched the boys hunt. The brothers didn't like Coyote much, but allowed him to stay once he promised to never swing the girl.

One night though, when the brothers were gone, Coyote beckoned the girl and told her to get into the swing. She refused, but Coyote threatened to hurt her. She still refused. So Coyote threatened to hurt her brothers if she didn't swing.

The girl climbed into the swing, and Coyote pushed her.

But the buffalo stayed away.

Coyote pushed her again, harder. She sailed higher into the air.

Still no buffalo.

Coyote kept pushing harder and harder, trying to get the buffalo to come and see. He pushed so hard though, she swung through the air and disappeared into the sky.

Coyote grew frightened. He yelled at the sky for her to come down.

No one answered Coyote.

In the morning, when the brothers returned, they asked Coyote where their sister was.

A monster took her away, Coyote told them.

But they knew the truth, and they chased Coyote away, cursing him. He and his children would always be hungry. That was the punishment for his disobedience and lies.

Missing their sister a great deal, the brothers gathered in council and discussed it. They decided to leave this world and go up into the sky for good so they could live with their sister.

Stars wink up through the dark. The sky flutters in and out of existence as I struggle to open my eyes. The world reeks of petrichor.

Something circles down below. Behind me. Somewhere. I hear it, out of the corner of my ear. Footfalls and sniffs.

I don't move. Too much effort. Or maybe I can't move. Either way. Best to stay still. Stay quiet. Not make my presence known.

Is it a buffalo? Buffalo don't hunt.

I can't see the girl swinging in the sky. But I hear distant singing. Muffled. Might be ringing. Not singing.

A river of blood dams up deep inside my ear canal. Swells with each pulse, trying to break through. Cracking the walls. Like a vise opening up inside a pipe.

I reach up, quiet like. Slow and heavy. Like I'm moving through mud. I find my earlobe and pull, try to stretch open my earhole. Try to relieve the pressure. Pull a release valve, so the blood can empty out and not burst the Eustachian tube.

It doesn't work. Nothing comes out. No relief. Just more pressure pushing from the inside out.

More sniffs and snuffs down somewhere behind me. Circling. Like a coyote. Stalking prey. I could probably take a coyote. But not a pack.

I can't tell how many there are.

Shh. Don't make a sound. Moving my hand away from my head, gravel falls off my palm, plunging up into the night. The stars ripple, blur, and cohere again.

I squeeze my eyes shut against the disorientation.

Breathe.

Open.

The sky shimmers below. Up is still down somehow. More footfalls circle behind me. I try to get my bearings, but can't make tails or heads of it.

I reach down into the darkness, and the stars ripple away again. Disappear like the girl who could call the buffalo.

My hand dips into a pool of wet, cold night.

It takes a moment, but it finally clears up.

And I can see.

It ain't poetry. It's a puddle. I'm staring down into a puddle.

I push down into the wet sky and lift myself out of the mud. Caked in clay that weighs a ton if it weighs a pound. Mired in earth, I struggle up to sitting. The world hesitates, but finally joins me.

I'm at the bottom of a massive pit.

The unseen beast circles above. Beasts? Pacing the edge.

Just out of sight.

Orienting somehow makes it worse. Makes me tense. I try not to breathe.

Not to move. Not to make a sound.

Whatever it is pauses. Dissolving into silence.

I let my eyes wander around the bottom of the pit. A disheveled chaos surrounds me.

Dead leaves, broken branches, my mangled bike, and busted trailer. Everything that was in it scattered every which way.

Including the water coolers. That's what made the puddle that caught the stars. All but a quarter of one cooler has poured out.

Sheee't.

I should tip it upright. Save what I can. I don't move though. I listen for predators. I wait. And close my eyes. May as well rest until they—

The pit spins. My stomach slips loose and slides right up into my throat.

Ok. Open eyes it is. Breathe. Don't throw up. I must be concussed. Don't moan. Moans'll only embolden the hunters. Wounded prey and whatnot.

Keep hush.

Keep still.

Keep it together.

One minute. Three minutes. Thirty minutes. Maybe just a handful of seconds. Can't really keep anything straight.

It moves again. I think.

Something rustles off through the grass. Fades into the night. It lost interest. Or wised up and didn't want to get itself stuck in a pit.

Or it was never there, and I'm just hearing things through earfuls of blood.

Exhale. Inhale.

Tip the cooler upright.

It only takes me about ten minutes to move the foot and half over to the cooler. Least it feels that way. Like I'm moving through mud. Which I guess I sort of am. But I did succeed in saving the remaining water. There's that. So now I can stay hydrated and last a good long while. Down here. At the bottom of a hole.

Awesome.

I gaze up at the edge of the pit. As far as pits go, it's a good one. Big. Deep. Baffling.

What in hell is a pit doing here?

And how did I not see it?

Fuck.

I make my way to standing. My knee objects. Sharp lashes of pain whip out of it, unravel up my leg, and wrap around the base of my spine.

Ok, ok. I get ya. Somewhere on the way down, my knee got banged up but good. Makes sense. You can't very well Thelma and Louise your way at full speed down into a huge pit and not expect a couple of bumps and bruises. Or a knee swollen up to the size of a bruised softball.

Now those two, they know how ta live right. Thelma and Louise was Momma's favorite movie. She licks the last bit of cream off her Oreo.

They're driving themselves right off a cliff, Momma.

They're refusing their circumstances and deciding their fate. Momma pops the de-creamed cookie into her mouth.

By dying.

By living like they need to until they can't live no more. 'Cause what was before wasn't living. You of all people should understand. All your prepping, ain't that just about making it so you can do things your way on your terms?

My way's about surviving. Not dying. No matter what it takes. I'd've figured something else out. Some other option. Yes, ma'am. Broke outta jail or something.

I bet you woulda, Addie. I bet you woulda.

We watch the two women accelerate towards the edge.

Their way's just so joyful. And sorrowful.

She looks at me and smiles. Pulls me close and kisses the top of my head.

Ain't no sorrow in death. Death swallows sorrow right up.

Death feeds the darkness. Gives it life.

Somehow I manage to climb up atop what's left of the trailer, stand on my good leg, and reach up to the edge.

Not even close.

I grab the empty cooler, wedge it into the bent corner of the trailer, and try to get up on it. Neither the cooler nor my knee feels like cooperating, and I crumple back to the mud amidst a fit of caterwauls and curses.

I scream at the world in frustration.

The world doesn't respond.

I'm in a hole.

Injured. Cold. And wet.

I'm in a hole.

Eff it.

The hole'll still be here in the morning.

I clear off the trailer, unroll my sleeping bag, and go fetal. Again.

On the bright side, at least now I'm staring *up* at the stars instead of down into them. I guess that's something.

A satellite glimmers across the sky. It don't pause or pay me no mind. Just speeds along on its way. In a constant rush. Like it's late. *Oh dear! Oh dear! I shall be too late!*

19

NO EXIT

It must seem a sight, for the bison. They're just enjoying their day, sipping water from the lake, munching on some grass in the meadow, when a grunt echoes out of the earth, and with it, a makeshift grappling hook launches up into the air, seemingly out of the ground itself. Twists up, reaching into the sky, only to crash back, empty-handed, to the earth.

Maybe they take a moment and lift their massive heads while still masticating a cud of grass. Take note of the downed thing-a-ma-bob, a sort of clawlike rat-cluster of tent poles, tent hooks, and duct tape. With a tail that esses its way back down into the hole it flew out of.

Maybe instinct kicks in and they shuffle away a bit, mistaking the rope tail for a snake. Wary, watchful, but still eating, just keeping an eye on the serpentine ess as it straightens out, turns taut, tenses and makes the claw jump and back a couple of inches. Still watching as the "grappling hook" rests. Jumps again. As if it's trying to grab ahold of something, anything. Searching for a toehold and coming up empty. All the while its tail hisses along the ground, dragging the claw scampering back across the ground, to some unseen edge in the earth, and down—

A *WANG* clanks out of the pit when the grappling hook hits the trailer below.

Back to grazing, this time paying no mind to the object skyrocketing into the air once again as it tries a different direction. The bison ignore the non-threat as it repeats the same rhythmic jump, jump, skitter, skitter—the grappling hook hunting for a handle while scampering in retreat to the pit. And plummeting once more into the depths.

A third toss. A third failure.

Repeat. Repeat. Repeat.

Until the jury-rigged claw gives up or gives out.

Nothing worked. Not the grappling hook. Not piling the water coolers on top of one another. Not wedging the bike vertical against the wall and using it as a sort of ladder. Not digging footholds in the earth (especially when they seem to crumble just as I get high enough that falling effs up my knee all over). Not screaming for help. Not praying to God. Not a damn thing could get me out of that grave.

The only win of the day was taking apart the darn grappling hook and rejiggering the tent poles and duct tape into a "splint" for my bum leg.

It's cooler here at night. Maybe it's some microclimate in the refuge; maybe the weather's changing. Either way, I'm freezing.

And I ain't got no kindling.

I stare at the small teepee of leaves, twigs, and roots. None of which will light worth a damn, 'cause the pit's microclimate is chock-full of damp.

I half-sit, half-squat wrapped in my sleeping bag, Sooners hoodie pulled tight. Staring at my belongings, which I've organized and stacked. Guns, bullets, bow, arrows, books, clothes, what's left of the food, water, miscellaneous objects.

Books.

Neatly stacked.

And wouldn't you know it, right on top, Jack London's *To Build a Fire and Other Stories*.

I laugh. Almost. The chuckle never actually surfaces.

I rip out the pages only as I need to. Starting at the front. One leaf of literature at a time. Just enough to feed the small flame as it consumes the pages inside the teepee. It takes the entire introduction and the first three "Klondike" short stories before the wood teepee finally warms to the idea and ignites.

The cooked ramen feels good, its salty warmth filling my stomach and spreading. I make sure to save the water in the pot to reuse tomorrow.

Fill my tin cup with a weak stream of water from the cooler. I don't want to, but I peek inside the cooler.

The water supply's dwindling.

I put another small broken branch on the fire and pull the trailer and sleeping bag a smidge closer. Fire ain't that big and won't last long, so I may as well enjoy what I can while I can.

I crawl into the sleeping bag and lie back on the dry trailer bed.

My remaining books rest near my head. Maybe I should read them again before I have to 451 everything.

Walden sits on top. Thoreau wrote *Walden* while living on Emerson's land. During that two-year stint, his mother brought him lunch every day and did his laundry regularly. Basically, Thoreau was a momma's boy.

I pick up *Self-Reliance* from beneath it. "Man is his own star."

I put it down.

The stars are only half out. High cirrus clouds blur out parts of the sky.

The fire pops. It smells good. The coals breathe orange. Another pop. A thin column of smoke rises and melts into the dark above.

Native tribes used smoke signals to send messages of distress.

I smile. Why the eff not?

A flame shoots up out of the earth, whistling loudly into the night sky, and explodes with a bright flash and loud bang. Another one screams its way up into the sky.

The small, but significant assortment of fireworks is arranged from least to most powerful: bottle rockets, Roman candles, aerial repeaters, aerial shells, parachutes, missiles. They survived the journey, the dog pillaging, the fall, the moisture.

The tip of my Marlboro Red grows brighter as I blow on it. The lightest of touches to the next fuse sparks it to life, hissing and spitting smoke.

The Roman candles kick up a series of star shells. I light up the aerial repeaters too. The fireworks explode in bright blossoms.

I whoop and laugh and holler with delight. It's a sight to see. A right last night. Hot meal and a show. Joyful…

Rave at the close of day...

When just the right amount of bourbon went into him, poetry sometimes came out. Too much though turned verse to violence.

Grave men, near death, who see with blinding sight

Blind eyes could blaze like meteors and be gay.

In another life, he'd been a schoolteacher. Like everything else in our world that dried up and blew away.

When they take away your purpose, what've you got. A choice, that's it. Suffer and bear a life sentence of indignity, or buck the sentence. That's what killed Hemingway, you know. Not the booze or the depression or the brain traumas. No, sir. Just he woke up one day and couldn't write no more.

Never could quite figure if the bourbon was the cause or the effect with him. Momma was always tight-lipped and secretive after he was gone.

And you, my father, there on the sad height,
Curse, bless, me now with your fierce tears, I pray.

Burst of pigments painting the sky, followed by delayed *BANGS* rushing to catch up. I bet you can see the fireworks for miles across the valley.

Like all good pyrotechnical displays, I build up to a finale, launching my last half dozen missiles one right after the other. Detonating iridescence lights up the night. Flashes of color reach past the horizon.

Do not go gentle into that good night.
Rage, rage against the dying of the light.

Until the last flare flutters down and fades into darkness.

And I'm left back alone.

Sitting with my small fire.

Awash in scents of sulfur, charcoal, potassium nitrate, and ozone. Drowning in the silence.

For a moment, I was better. But I got over it.

I'm not really sure what I was expecting, but I find myself underwhelmed.

"Yay."

The blackness swallows up my sarcasm, unmoved.

Ain't nobody like a SASS-quatch, Addie.

Ok, Momma.

She never appreciated my sass. She could've just stopped though after *Ain't nobody...*

I take a puff of the Marlboro. And give myself a coughing fit. Real smooth.

PART III

20

DEER WOMAN

It was just a dream, baby.

No, Momma. I wasn't sleeping, so it couldna been a dream.

Sometimes though that's how dreams feel, Addie.

No. No. I was lying on my side, in bed, staring at the hall light spilling in under the door. I could hear you down the hall.

And what happened?

I realized someone, somethin' was at the foot of my bed. Standin' there. Starin' at me. But I couldn't turn none. I couldn' get up t'all. All I could do was keep looking down at the light on the floor.

You couldn't move none?

Uh-unh. It was like there was this pressure holding me down. Every part of me.

Awful.

And then it *started walking. Around the other side of the bed. 'Til it was standing behind me. I mean, right behind me, Momma. And I still couldn't move. Or even breathe. Just lay there, watching the light, and listening—as it started to lean over the bed, its breath hot against the back of my neck... And then finally I bolted upright screaming, and it was gone.*

She hugged me close, like when I was little. Littler.

Shh, shh, shh. It's ok now. I'm here. And it *ain't. That there was just the Deer Woman. That's all that was.*

Deer Woman?

Mm. Part shape-shifting spirit, part black-tailed deer.

What's she want?

Well, the Lakota say she's drawn to good souls, wants to see if she can tempt 'em bad. The Potawatomi see her more as a sign that change is coming. But all the tribes agree she's easy to be rid of.

She is?

Mm-hm. As you figured out, she scares easy. And you did perfect. Waited 'til just the right moment to snap into action and scare her away. Once the Deer Woman realizes she's been seen, she runs off. Just perfect, Addie. Just perfect.

Deer Woman.

The cold bears down heavier in the deep night.

I pretend to sleep. Listening to the footfalls.

It don't sound like coyote. Too heavy.

Maybe wolf. Or bear.

Maybe the Deer Woman.

Bundled up tight, cuddling my 12 gauge, I silently slip the barrel free of the sleeping bag. In spite of the cold, I've been leaving it unzippered ever since that damn hound ransacked me.

Lying on my side, I stare into the embers, as whatever *it* is stares down.

I don't move none.

As it circles, around the other side of the pit.

Behind me.

Watching me.

Leaning in.

I don't exhale as it peers over the edge.

Knocks loose a clump of dirt that tumbles down and—

Sets me off.

Spin—cock—set—fire—

The *BOOM* thunders out for miles, waits a few seconds, and then rushes back after ricocheting off the mountains. The blast shakes dirt loose all around the earthen walls.

I scan the edge of the pit, focusing down the length of my barrel like a telescope. Still startled, tasting metal, pumping out adrenalin.

Listen.

Did I get it?

What was it?

There's nothing there.

I'm dreaming.

I'm hallucinating. My solitary confinement's finally getting to me.

The crickets come back to life.

I shake my head at myself. Just wasted a perfectly good shotgun shell. Shee't.

And for what?

For nothing. For trying to bring down a nightmare mid-gallop.

Good effing job, Addie. Real smart. You burned through all your fireworks, may as well shoot off all your ammo too—

"Throw up your gun," her voice says.

That ain't real. That ain't nothing.

My throat disagrees. It's caught my breath mid-inhale and refuses to let go.

What would a wolf or a bear want my gun for anyhow? Without thumbs, guns're just heavy sticks—

"Hello?" she asks.

It's the Deer Woman!

"Hello?" I don't mean to, but I can't help but say it. Good manners demand a call and response. Even if it is the Deer Woman, it'd sure be nice to conversate with something other than me.

Nothing comes back though.

Shee't, it was nothing. I really am nuttier than a squirrel turd.

Nerves shiver through my whole body. I can't control it. I can't help nothing. "Hello?" I try again. What could it hurt? "Are you, like, real?"

I wait…

"Are you, like, stupid?" she says. "Throw. Up. Your weapons."

This woman is *not* the Deer Woman. She is a woman woman. A real woman. Who I—

"Oh my god, did I shoot you? Are you ok?"

"I'm fine. You're a shitty shot."

"Oh, thank god." I can't shut up now. The dam's done broke. "I'm really sorry about that. I thought you were the…" No. Nope. Don't say it.

"The what?"

What do I say?

"I dunno." It's all I can think of in the moment. She don't say nothing back. Shee't. "Hello?"

She's gone.

She was never there.

She's not real.

"Are you gonna throw up your gun, or you just want to rot in my punji pit?"

"What's a boon-gee pit?" Again the words come out before I can catch them. I ain't got no control.

"Punji pit. Like a tiger pit."

"There ain't no tigers in these parts."

"Apparently not. Just jackasses."

Ha effing ha. My anger don't keep the blood from rushing to my cheeks in embarrassment. It's ok though. No way she can see my blushing in the dark. From behind the edge.

"Ain't no way *you* dug a pit this big."

"Maybe it wasn't just me."

Now there's a thought. Maybe it wasn't just her. How many're up there? Just beyond the edge. Wanting my guns. I look around the pit. It's effing big. It've taken six people six days. On the one hand a pack of people is way more lethal than just the one. On the other, security in numbers should make them feel less threatened.

"So, what? Were you all trying to, like, catch people?" I need to buy time. To think.

It sounds like she sighs. "You really are… No, Shere Kahn. We was aiming for bison. Or antelope. Either one. But you've successfully scared them to the other side of the valley with your little bottle rocket show."

"Sorry. I was trying to, I dunno, call for help, I guess." Why the EFF am *I* apologizing??

"You find many folks to help you these days?"

Her question sinks down into the pit like a lead fishing weight. It's dense. Packed with portent. That there aren't many folks anywhere. Especially these days. And folks who might be around sure as hell aren't interested in helping. It's a loaded question all right. Loaded with hollow-point rounds. Alone or in a group, the voice is a survivor. Smart too.

I cast out my own line. "You came, didn't you?"

"I ain't here to help."

Her words plunge down into the hole with force. This girl's fishing with dynamite. It detonates and ripples a chill up my spine.

I make my voice real flat. Not threatening, but not cowed none neither. Just matter-of-fact. "Then I ain't throwing up my gun." Either she and her friends don't got any guns themselves, or they don't want to waste any ammo. I'll be damned though if I'm just going to toss mine up and make it easy for them to go on and leave me to die in this grave. It'll cost them at least a bullet of their own. My life's worth that, I guess. One bullet at least.

For some reason, I add, "You know, your tiger trap banged me up pretty good."

Not sure what I was expecting, but no apology came out of the dark.

No demand either though.

"Maybe we could trade. I've got water and food," I offer.

"No. You don't."

I wonder how long they were checking me out, evaluating me and my situation, before I finally got savvy to them. My gaze skips across all of my belongings. A frantic hunt for something of value. "You like books? I'll trade."

"I like guns."

"Don't you got a gun?" If she was going to be this direct, then so was I.

She doesn't say nothing. I got her. Them?

"Well?"

Still nothing.

I literally dig my heels into the earth and yell up, "Tough shit. The shotgun's mine." Beneath the cover of my shouts, quick and quiet, I tuck my pistol down my waistband against the small of my back.

She still doesn't say nothing.

"Hello?"

Is that footsteps walking off?

"Hello?! Please!" Frenzy chokes out of my throat. I hadn't planned on her leaving. "Please! Don't leave! There's gotta be sumptin' we can do… PLEASE!! PLEASE DON'T leave me…"

My unhinged pleas dissipate in the dark.

She and hers don't need to waste a bullet at all. They just need to wait.

The tears well up and out.

I ain't got no control.

These days, the night sky is so strewn with stars, there's hardly any black at all. Silver lining. I eat one of the six remaining Oreo snack packs I salvaged. The other five I stash in a secret pocket inside my hydration pack. A cream-filled communion wafer for my last supper.

Later that night, lightning flares soundlessly somewhere in the distance. Least I think it was lightning.

21

CAPITULATION

Knowing the truth of things is an act of resignation.

These days, the land abounds in bounty, yet this here is hungry country. These days, man is ignorant, and nature remains indifferent. It's the way of things. As always though, to endure one must adapt.

Come morning, alone and half mad, I watch gray daylight stab down into the pit. Exhaustion and thirst spent the night honing my thoughts to a point. I've made a decision.

More rightly put, I've resolved myself to the only option.

With a grunt, the shotgun takes flight. Up into the rectangle of sky and over the edge. It thuds onto the ground out past the border of existence.

Then nothing.

A few moments more.

More nothing.

Come on.

"The pistol too," her voice courses down into the pit.

Sheee't. She knows. She saw.

I sigh. And mutter. Put on a show of it.

The pistol flies up and arcs up past the edge. Off in the same direction as the shotgun. A close grouping most likely.

Footsteps approach, slow. Then stop, still a ways off.

Through strained ears it sounds like she might be crawling the rest of the way. Smart. Avoid my line of sight. In case they missed some third gun.

They didn't.

I can hear her retrieve the weapons and shuffle back.

It's not long until I can hear the slow click of pressing in the shotgun release. The sliding of metal as the action bar's pulled back halfway, then all the way. The quick release of metal sliding back on metal. The thunk of dropping the shotgun to the ground.

Immediately followed by the lighter click in opening up the break action hinge on the revolver.

Then a moment of quiet.

And another.

A big shit-eating grin spreads across my face as I stand by for the inevitable.

"Where are the bullets?" She sounds annoyed.

Her annoyance stretches my grin out further.

I affectionately pat the pack resting in the crook of my crossed legs. "Down here, with me. You want 'em up there, you're gonna hafta pull me up with 'em. That's the deal."

I wait for her response. It's a while coming.

"You sick?"

"What?"

"You infected?" she clarifies.

It's obvious what she's asking. Just unsure how to answer. A charged query. Her question mark hangs like a snare.

Like I said, smart.

"Don't seem like it. But wouldn't I say no even if I was? Wait, are you infected?"

I twist my question mark into a noose.

Then quiet.

A head crowns the edge of the pit. Not at all where I was looking. Either she moves real quiet, or someone else is up there, and they're the ones who went and retrieved the guns.

Backlit by dawn's blood-red clouds, her dark hair hangs down, like blinders framing her sharp, high cheekbones, hollowed cheeks, and eyes black like burnt chestnuts.

The chestnuts narrow, peering down at me.

"Lift up your shirt."

I can't stop staring though. She's there. She's real. An angelic demon looking down from above, framed from behind by a sky on fire.

Back in the CC, I'd hash a line in red Sharpie on the calendar. First red mark in months.

"Come on, Shere Kahn. I need to see if you got stripes."

The sky spins and snaps into place.

If she's asking, she's thinking about helping.

Or…

She's considering shooting me. And is concerned about sending the Stripes airborne by puncturing my body. It moved so fast, scientist on the news were theorizing it had to be airborne. Back before the airwaves went dead.

My resolve has not wavered.

I lift my shirt. Expose my chest. Lift the left arm and turn to show the left side and armpit, back, then right arm, right side, right armpit.

Beneath a layer of dirt, all remains pale, pinkish, normal.

I lower my shirt.

"How old're you, fifteen?"

Her disbelief irritates me. Might be her surety of my youth.

"Seventeen." It comes out way too angry. In a scramble to cover, I demand, "Your turn."

It's out of my mouth before it hits me what I'm asking her to do. My eyes go wide, grasping it just as the moment slips away. As blood flushes my cheeks. "I mean, I meant I don't, I'm not, uh—"

She stands suddenly and lifts her shirt and peels back her bra to expose her left armpit, side, back, right armpit, side. Her belly's slightly distended like one of them malnourished African kids on the TV with the flies all over their face.

And then she's gone. Walks off and disappears behind the edge.

I'm left alone with my mute humiliation. Unarmed, unmasked, confused.

So awkward.

I guess that's it, then. I played my only hand. The only hand that—

A rope drops down the far side of the pit.

It seems alive. Dangling to and fro. Tempting. Like the snake in the garden. It ain't real. Can't be.

I stare.

I doubt.

I capitulate.

Rush over, grab ahold. Give it a yank.

It holds. And emboldens—"So you going to help pull, or you just want me to climb up? Hello? Hello?!"

Sigh. Shee't. She did it again. Goddamn disappearing act.

Resigned. Resolute. Desperate. I test the rope again. Stable enough.

The knee and brace slow me down, but hold together well enough. The strain of it keeps me from thinking too much about what's waiting for me up top. A knife. A gun. A laugh.

I prairie dog my head up. Scan the surroundings.

Nothing. She's gone. Like a black-tailed deer bolting into the night. The Deer Woman.

I pull my way up and over the edge. And collapse on the grass. Spent.

The rope's anchored around a small boulder.

Standing, I do another 360-degree scan.

She's nowhere. Ain't nobody else neither.

No set or sets of footprints. Just a couple of different disturbances in the dirt where she'd, where someone'd shimmied over to the edge.

And a Caterpillar backhoe and abandoned Bronco truck parked a couple of hundred yards back behind a berm I didn't notice at all the other night. That'd explain the pit. Some old construction project from before the outbreak. Ranger station foundation, or septic system, or mass barrow tumulus.

Shee't.

That's when I notice something on the boulder.

I walk over.

It's a cooked rabbit leg. Left for me on the rock. Like I'm some sort of feral animal.

22

TWO'S COMPANY

It took the better part of the day to get what was needed out of the pit. Every descent was an argument that ended with a forced march over the edge. A leap of faith that the rope would hold. That it would stay put while I was down there.

It did. On both counts.

No one, no thing came by at all. To the point where I couldn't help but wonder if I'd imagined it all. That somehow, my grappling hook had worked. I'd made it out of my own accord and tied the rope to the boulder for better ballast. That I'd set myself to excavating my own would-be grave. And the exhaustion of it all had simply wiped my memories clean. In a way, short-term amnesia made a hell of a lot more sense than the Deer Woman and her possible pack.

Even so, don't hurt none to prep for both realities. Hence why I lit two campfires, down by the water I'd been so taken with the other evening that I didn't see a lake from a hole in the ground.

Two fires, twenty yards apart, each near its own tree. A healthy distance in a quarantined world. And me, sitting by one, under the assumption that all her actions (whether or not she was accompanied by a pack of others) were based on prudence, not predation.

Also operating under the assumption that she does, in fact, exist. Which I reasoned out based on my own adaptation of Pascal's logic (thank you, AP European History). Pascal argued you should believe in God according to basic game theory. Either God exists or he don't, and you can believe or not, and all you need to do is evaluate the pros and cons of it.

	God Exists	**God Don't Exist**
Believe in God	Good. God happy, so I'm happy.	Don't matter none.
Don't Believe in God	Bad. God not so happy, so I'm damned.	Don't matter none.

The long and short of it being that it was way smarter to believe in God. Worst-case scenario leaves you with a neutral outcome. Whereas neutral is the best-case scenario for not believing.

In my case with the Deer Woman:

	She Exists	**She Don't Exist**
Believe in Her	Good. Prepared for her to be out there, so try to make nice.	Don't matter none, 'cause ain't no one around to see me make an ass out of myself.
Don't Believe in Her	Bad, 'cause then she's got the jump on you, and you've done nothing to make nice.	Don't matter none.

So that's why, by the other fire, my bow sits arrowless next to one of my remaining prized snack packs of Oreos and a piece of ramen as my peace offering.

Next to me is all my other salvaged stuff. Including the quiver of arrows.

A pot of lake water roils to a boil over the fire. I take it off and pour it into a half-full Igloo cooler. One pot of sterilized water at a time.

Not sure how I'm going to haul a water-weighted cooler anywhere with my busted bike still sitting at the bottom of the barrow. But for now, it's just the kind of vessel I need. I look over at the gimpy trailer. It still rolls well enough. I guess. Maybe I'll just pull it myself. Jackass.

Down at the lake's edge, I check my fishing line dangling off my compactable rod I've staked in the ground.

No bites.

Orange flames reflect and dance across the dark surface. Fire water.

Refill the pot, hobble up to camp, and place it back into the flames to boil. Sit and watch and wait for the water to change states.

Off to the side, on a rock, a hunk of something has shimmered into being out of the night.

It wasn't there before. A clod of flesh. Half a skinned rabbit waits like bait.

My hand's already reaching for my knife. Reflex outruns thought. My eyes dart to the darkness, hunting.

From the gloom, mocking notes of poetry: "Tiger, tiger, burning bright in the forests of the night…"

She steps out of the blackness and into the light of the second fire, carrying the other half of the rabbit. My pistol tucked into her waist. My shotgun oddly absent.

She puts the rabbit down next to the bow I left by the fire.

No pack. No supplies. Which don't mean nothing. Whatever she's got is most likely keeping my shotgun company wherever they're hiding and with whomever they're hiding with out in the darkness.

As it is, the only other stuff she has with her hangs off her slight, angular frame: a smudged tank top, somewhat covered by a dirty, geometric-patterned zip-up fleece, black jeans. Or dark blue. Can't really tell in the dim light. Could just be real filthy. And sneakers that look like they've been ridden hard and put up wet. Her dark hair's pulled back into a thick ponytail. There are bits of dead leaves, twig bits, and what looks like burrs scattered throughout. Like she's been crawling through underbrush.

That one looks like she woke up on the wrong side of the tracks this morning. Momma tended to mix and match her sayings without realizing. Somehow they still seem to make sense of the world.

She's around twenty-three. Give or take. Hard to tell. Months wear on you like dog years these days.

A large, nasty-looking Bowie knife dangles from her belt. Massive and menacing. Its hilt glints near the blaze.

She holds her hand up to the fire, less for warmth, more like she's taking its temperature. Grabs a nearby twig, stirs the coals, and blows some more life into the small blaze. It flares up and grows. Lit up close like to the fire, it's clear as day she's got some tribe in her. Cherokee or Choctaw, I reckon.

"You're back."

"Not a bad pair of fires." She ignores my comment and proceeds to make two tripods of twigs at opposite ends of the fire and ties a shoelace loop dangling from each.

"The bow ain't for you, by the way. Still mine. Just, you know, didn't want you to feel threatened."

She stakes a stick through the rabbit's flesh and hangs it from the shoelace loops across the fire. A spit for cooking. Clever rig. She hasn't even bothered to look at me.

So be it. Two can cook at that rabbit game. I grab the hunk she left for me. Not too fast though. Not too eager. Not like I need it.

My stomach don't play it as cool as me though. A groan echoes around its emptiness. Shut up, you goddamn traitor. I place the meat on the sloped side of one of the tall rocks my pot of water straddles in the fire. It hisses against the hot stone.

"Got my bullets?" She's had that question locked and loaded. Just been waiting to fire it off.

But I've been waiting on that query since I started building both fires. Prepared my remarks, as they say. "A deal's a deal, no arguing that—"

"Who's arguing?"

I try to keep up the momentum. "Although we never did agree on exactly *when* I'd hand over my bullets." I yank the noose tight on that little loophole.

"My bullets."

That wasn't the part of my argument that she was supposed to focus on.

"Whosever."

"You an Indian giver now?"

Is that a joke? Or an accusation? Did she see me noticing her tribe blood? How could she have?

All my momentum's been swatted aside like it was a Sphinx moth. I push ahead anyhow. Like I planned out.

"What? No. I mean, like I said, we never agreed on timing. I'll keep my word. But for right now, it seems best for both parties for you to have, you know, the guns and all, and me to hold onto the bullets. Fair and safe."

There. It's out. Logical and fair. Ain't no arguing it any other way.

The girl blows on the fire.

"What happens when you sleep?" She turns the rabbit on the spit and lifts her gaze across the darkness between us. Flames dance in her eyes.

It's a striking sight.

Perception's more important than fact.

We sat close in the deer blind. It was tight quarters up there, but truth be told, I was happy to be cramped against Uncle Izzy. It was

Colder than a polar bear's ice hole. And heat was radiating off him. *The human furnace*, Momma used to call her brother.

In nature, when bears come across each other, they get to figuring who's who right quick. Alpha, beta, it's all about hierarchy. Pecking order. The wild needs order. Otherwise it's chaos.

We shouldn't be talking, really, but his whispered wisdom keeps me distracted and quieter than I'd be just sitting there bored and cold.

It ain't about size. No, sir. It's about attitude. Communicate to intimidate. That way they don't hafta fight. Which neither wants to do unless it's positively necessary. Too easy to get mortally wounded, even for the winner. So they communicate. But they can't speak English or Arabic or Russian. All they understand is the language of dominance.

They roar, slap at the ground, stand tall. They'll circle a challenger. And if that don't work, a bear'll run a bluff charge. Loud blowing, clacking teeth, and then explode into motion, take off at full-tilt right at the rival only to pull up short at the last moment. All to see if his opponent's gonna stand his ground or tuck tail.

Izzy sips some coffee from the thermos. Sucks it through his teeth while taking in the forest.

Size don't mean shit. Claws, teeth, speed. None of it. Facts is just figures. Nothing more. In the end, it's all about who's got the most luster in his bluster.

I reach into the fire and flip my rabbit on the rock. Then I shrug and force a yawn. "You wanna slit my throat in my sleep, go right ahead. But you and I both know it ain't been three days. So for all intents and purposes, I could have the Stripes."

One of the last and only bits of useful information the news broadcast was that the Stripes can incubate for at most three days before instigating symptoms and the telltale patterns on the skin.

Chasing the flutter out of my throat, I add, "Also, then you'd never find out where I buried the bullets."

Her glare burns through the dark.

Then suddenly she smiles.

"Tend to your rabbit, Shere Kahn."

Rendered fat's greased up the side of the rock, and while I've been posturing, it's gone and slid off into the coals.

"Shee't. Shee't." I try to peck through the heat with my hand, flinching back from the flames, reaching this way and that.

Her laughs seem to fan the flames.

"Dangit, dangit, dangit, HA!" I manage to snatch the rabbit meat up and out. Place it on a flatter rock off to the side.

There. I nod and risk a quick glance at the other fire. She ain't looking. Just turning her spit.

"My name's Addison."

It floats on the air like a sour milk-fart.

Somehow, sharing my name is way more embarrassing than the meat falling in the fire.

The girl doesn't respond, just stirs her fire's coals with a stick.

The silence settles in and stays there for the rest of dinner.

Still no bites on the line. Bad bait. No fish. Who knows. I consider trussing up the rabbit bones with the monofilament, try my hand at crawdads. But then I'd have to stay up half the night checking the line.

Plus, I've already done picked the bones to the white. So I toss them in the lake.

Down a ways, the girl squats at the lake's edge and splashes some water on her face. The way she's tucked over, the curve of her belly juts out like she's—

She catches me staring. And gives me a look I don't quite understand. Quicker than a blink, her gaze shifts into a glare. Instinct pulls her hand up to the Bowie knife.

"You mind not eye-banging me."

"What?!" The tone knocks me back, off balance. It finally registers. She thinks I'm… but that weren't… it's like the whole Indian-giver thing all over again.

"No, um, I wasn't, I wouldn't. Not at you with—I mean, it's not that you're not purdy, but, you're—" This wasn't going well. And then it gets worse. "I wasn't, it weren't, no—" Dismay sets me scrambling. "I was, uh, wondering how far along are you?"

My finger points at her belly of its own accord. Somewhere during our silent meal, my brain had gone behind my back and worked out she weren't bloated with malnourishment.

"You look five, maybe six months along." I can't seem to stop myself. Just keep on stepping in it.

Out of the fryin' pan of shame and into the fire of humiliation, Momma would've said.

"What're you some sort of pregger perv?" She's up and the knife's drawn.

Bluff charge or real charge, I stay squatted down by the water. Hold up my hands. Shake my head. "No, it ain't like that?"

"How's it like?" She circles around me away from the lake.

"My momma, she was a midwife. And a doula."

This gives her pause. But only for a moment. "Don't mean you ain't still a perv."

She's got a point there. Ain't no way to assure her I ain't without sounding defensive. And guilty. And creepy. So I don't bother.

"Where's the daddy?"

"Dead." There's no emotion behind this.

Figures.

"I'm sorry."

She scrapes her gaze over me, ticking off some sort of checklist, sheaths the knife, and walks back to her fire. Done with conversation.

I wait. Then fill my pot and limp my way back to my camp.

She watches from behind her fire, clocking my every step.

"It's good you can put some weight on it. The knee should be better in a day or two."

Putting my pot on the fire. "My bike won't be though."

She don't say nothing to that.

So I get my sleeping bag from the trailer.

She nods at my trailer. “You drag that lazy-man’s load all the way from the pit?”

I look at the trailer, all my stuff, then back at her. “No.”

The girl half-laughs at my sarcasm.

“Must not’ve been on the road long if you’re riding into pits.”

“How was I supposed ta know there’d be a pit camouflaged with branches and…”

It was hard to tell in the dancing shadows of the firelight, but it sure as hell look like she was grinning.

Mm. Take a beat. Calm. She’s just poking the bear. Don’t take the bait. “That weren’t no pit. That was a trap.”

“Whole damn meadow open to you and you ride right into it.” She’s definitely grinning.

But that don’t stop me.

“In the gloaming, shit and Shinola were all mixed together. Things’re hard to pick out in twilight.”

She guffaws. “So then why was you out riding at all?”

She has a point. And I don’t have a good response. I wasn’t about to talk about the pretty sunset reflected in the lake or the majesty of buffalo silhouetted on the horizon or that I was still putting however many miles I could between me and the dog I… buried.

If people already got an idea about you, ain’t no use fighting it. So you may as well use it. It’s a cover story that they’ve already agreed to believe.

“Yeah, I only just got on the road. I was hunkered down for a spell. Had a secure bug-out place.”

“Bug-out place? Like it was infested?”

“Oh, um, you don’t—it’s a prepper term. Like a place you ‘bug out’ to when the shit hits the fan.”

I roll out the sleeping bag.

"Bullshit. You mean to tell me you were 'prepping' for this? Before the Stripes started?"

"No. Yeah. Sort of. I mean—" It's weird hearing Uncle Izzy's words roll out of me. "Noah didn't build the ark in the rain. You know."

I always liked that saying. Clever and quick. And it makes sense. But it just bounces off her like green Jell-O off a plastic tarp.

"I was a prepper. But I was thinking more, I dunno, financial collapse, super tornado. I wasn't really prepared for…"

"The end of humanity."

"Yeah."

I'd been planning on chaos. Not emptiness.

The flames pull back into the coals. So I stir the embers up and toss on another hunk of wood.

The exhilaration of company gives way to exhaustion. Without glancing over at the girl—still gun-shy from the misunderstanding down by the lake—I get into the sleeping bag. Lie back. Look up at the stars.

"The whole thing's hard to wrap my head around. And if I'm being honest, the truth is, I dunno if I survived 'cause I was prepared and could hide away, avoid folks, or…"

"If you're just luckier than a hanged man on a frayed rope and happen to be immune. Yeah, me either."

"How'd you make it? Where were you?"

The girl takes a moment and then offers up, "I was visiting my dad on the OTSA when it started breaking out in the coastal cities. So I just stayed there."

"OTSA?"

"Oklahoma Tribal Statistical Area. It's a BS PC term for reservation. What's left of the noble Chickasaw Nation."

Chickasaw. I should have guessed that. They got a big-ass reservation near here, near that fort from the Indian Wars… shoot, what was its name?

Fort Ill…

"Other than our casinos, smoke halls and truck stops."

Fort Kill—

"Don't forget bingo halls," I add.

That gets me another half-laugh from her.

Fort Bill Hickock? Him and Buffalo Bill had both been there.

"So you bugged out there. At the OTSA." I risk a look at her.

The girl nods.

Fort Sill. That's the name. Fort Sill.

I turn back. Nodding myself. "Until the Stripes came."

"Until the neighbors did."

Her words are heavy with portent. I don't look back at her. Don't want to give it any more weight than it already bears. So I keep looking at the stars and offer up, "God damn people."

"God damn people," she echoes. Then shrugs. "Ain't no point beatin' a dead horse."

"Course it can't hurt none either."

That gets me a full belly laugh from her.

Hell if it don't make me grin from ear to ear. It's surprising how natural it all is. Interacting. Conversating. I'd have thought it'd be weird. Rusty. Being so long since… But it was like riding a bike.

Into a pit.

We settle back into the quiet. It feels like as good a time as any.

"Thanks for helping me."

"Thanks for testing my tiger trap."

Son of a bitch. Can't help but shake my head at that. "Apology accepted." If I say it, then it's so.

The quiet don't feel as hollow tonight.

"I missed talking, you know, like back and forth."

The girl don't say nothing.

"What's your name, anyhow?"

Still no response. My question just hanging there like possum balls.

I look over at her fire.

She's gone. As are the Oreos. My bow still rests against a rock where I left it though.

I guess that's something.

I stretch my ears, trying to pick up some hint of her.

Nothing but quiet and crickets.

Guess that's the way of things. Prudence, not predation.

Least the absent Oreos prove she does exist. So there's that. I ain't crazy. Well, I ain't hallucinating her. I still might be crazy.

"Please don't kill me in my sleep," I ask the darkness.

It don't answer back. The girl neither.

If she was gonna kill me in my sleep, she'd've just left me in the pit.

Right?

23

PRIDE

A herd of cattle might feed you. Daddy sits in the corner. He holds the neck of a liquor bottle half full of lava and swirls the amber, molten rock around the inside.

But it drags wolves with it in a wake of want and hunger, Uncle Izzy finishes the saying, from his chair in the other corner.

Between them a hearth ablaze with warmth.

Daddy tosses Izzy the bottle. Izzy raises his hand to catch it, but the bottle disintegrates in mid-flight over the hearth; the lava rains down on the fire.

A lifetime can pass in the seconds between stirring and waking.

I dream of thirst.

I'm a kid again. My body strangled by soaked sheets fastening to my skin. Dripping fire, screaming for Momma. But muted. My voice's gagged with razor blades.

Streptococcal scrapes away the lining of my throat. Flays the vocal cords.

I thrash against its choke hold. The sheets twist and tighten their tentacles around me with every spasm.

And then Momma's there. Cradling, kissing, hushing.

She's peeled the sheets off like dead, sunburnt skin.

Holding me still. *It's ok, baby. Momma's here. Shh, shh, shh. Stay still now. Relax. Still like a statue. And you can stop the hurt.*

Still like a statue.

I calm. I breathe.

Still like a statue.

The razor pushes out against my larynx. But doesn't cut.

Still like a statue.

Doesn't pierce.

Still like a statue.

Just applies a sharp pressure without slicing.

Still like a statue.

The blade of her Bowie knife presses up against my neck, in the crook just below the jaw.

The blank silhouette of her looms above in the bright morning light.

Still like a statue.

The girl clutches a fistful of my hair. She's wild eyed, panicked, and pressing down on the blade on my throat.

Still like a statue.

She yanks my head to the side and hisses in my ear breathlessly, "Not a goddamn peep more than what I ask. Where'd you bury my bullets?"

The terror beats against the inside of my skull. I want to scream, scramble, get away.

All I can do is shake my head. I don't know how to answer her.

She pulls on my hair, up and back. Lifting the jaw, stretching out the neck. Tilting the blade fully perpendicular against my skin, sliding it slightly. The sensation provokes memories of childhood, trying not to cry. That suffocating lump garroting your throat. Only now the lump's pressing in from the outside instead of out from the inside. The skin beneath the sharp edge starts to split apart.

"They're not—"

Another hiss, "Quiet! They're mine 'cause I got the knife to your throat. Now just tell me where ta find 'em. Hush like."

I nod. More with my eyes than my head.

The blade lifts up maybe a millimeter or so. Just enough room for a whisper to get out.

"Ok. They're not buried, that's all. I didn't bury them. I just said that—"

"Where?"

I point at an old athletic bag.

The girl stretches to reach it while keeping the knife connected to my throat. She struggles to unzip it one-handed, but manages to tug it open a couple of inches, sees the boxes of shotgun bullets inside.

She's already up and moving. Accelerating into a full sprint right at the lake. Right into the lake. She wades out almost up to her knees and then starts circumscribing the shoreline as quickly and as quietly as she can.

I lie on my side. Too stunned still to raise myself up. Too confused more than anything.

Watching her wade off with her knife, my shotgun, and the bag of bullets.

The girl keeps on this way, hugging the shore, but staying in the water until she finally runs into some reeds. Lightly, lightly she emerges from the lake, and quick-steps it fifty yards up the bank to a copse of trees around a bend. Next thing I know, I catch a flash of her shimmying right up a tree trunk and disappearing into its foliage.

She's hiding.

But not from me.

Finally, it clicks.

I get it.

Roll quick onto my stomach. Shimmy out of the sleeping bag. Wide-eyed with understanding, I army crawl over to my stuff, grab the monoculars, and scan the horizon in the opposite direction from which the girl ran.

Pressing myself against the earth. Thinking flat thoughts: pancakes, paper, oil slick. Be the ground.

A whistle floats on the wind. Maybe a bird. Probably not.

Keep scanning. Nothing breaks the panoramic line but the distant rise of a knoll.

Always better to flinch than get hit.

I scramble up, still staying low though. Snatch up the hydration pack and quiver of arrows and sprint as fast as my bum knee can go right at the water. But stop short.

Back up the shore, over to the girl's campfire, grab my bow, and haul ass into the water and around the lake.

Heart thumping so hard I can feel my pulse behind my eyes. By the time I make it to the reeds and copse of trees, I'm all fury and frenzy. Still, I ain't about to take shelter up a viper's tree.

A little ways further the reeds give way to an open field of tall grass and wildflowers.

Ghillie, ghillie.

Hunch down, beeline through the reeds, snatch up whatever dead stalks I come across, crouching down further and further with each step. At the field's edge, I crawl my way into the tall grass. Wriggling in, deeper and deeper.

Good enough.

Better to take whatever time I got and get settled than gain a pittance more of distance.

I sink myself into a thick patch of grass and wildflowers, covering up with the dead reeds I gathered up.

Ain't a full-on ghillie suit, but it's what I can manage.

I take out the monocular and watch the knoll.

The air shimmers in the morning heat. Blazing light bleaches the color out of the meadow.

All is quiet. And still. Birds dart across the water, into the trees.

The sun crawls higher, angling down with greater intensity.

A ravenous snarl of mosquitos coheres around me. An ordered swirl of starved chaos. Feasting in a swarm of soft stings. A wave of the hand or quick twist of the torso only buys some temporary relief. But distracts from the uneasiness of it all.

Until they come.

Like a pride of lions, three men quietly summit the hillock ridge, out from the valley beyond. Ambling, loping, angling. They move with menace.

24

HIDE...

Pausing in unison. Lifting their chins as if sniffing the air. Each carries his own gun. Rifles it seems like.

Without a look or a word between them, they spread out, as if on cue, separating thirty yards apart. Stalking their way forward. The middle one nursing a slight limp.

The left one's balding. Not quite heavyset, but large. Grizzly. And purposeful in movement. The right one's younger and sports a close-cropped Mohawk. He's lean. Hollow like. There's a jumpiness to his gait. The limper stands out between the two. Coiffed, calm, older. He feels orderly somehow. Like he might've been a preacher in a past life. The three are all bearded and camo'd.

They stop, spotting last night's camp.

This ain't gonna go well.

Again, without saying nothing, the two on either side flank out as the center one takes a knee, raises a rifle, and focuses on the camp through a high-powered scope.

Mohawk and Grizzly strafe, triangulating. Limp tracks his scope across the empty camp.

It don't take long for them to determine it's been abandoned. The limper stands and the flankers cut in. The triad converges.

Using the barrel of his gun as a probe, Limp rifles through my stuff. Mohawk jitters over to the girl's fire. Feels the air over the coals. Grizzly stands guard atop a nearby boulder, a bear on its hind legs, scanning the meadow and the lake.

Cool shivers through me as his gaze passes over the tall grass covering my body. I can't help but drop my head and press my nose into the earth. Praying for the angel of death to pass over. The horde of flies pulls back from the shift and chill of me.

I peek up, through the monoculars. Grizzly's gaze sweeps on across the refuge.

I can breathe again.

Movement in the copse catches my eye.

Up in the tree, the girl quietly loads the shotgun. She cannot see the camp from where she sits. But glares down at the lake. She knows the interlopers have come. She's known for a while.

Mohawk joins Limp, who's rustling with my sleeping bag.

Mohawk squats in front of my burnt-out fire and holds his hand over it. There's still a little heat.

"This was lit last night, Fish." His voice travels across the water clear and clean.

Limp, aka Fish, barely acknowledges the info.

It's unsettling, being able to hear them so clearly. It makes them feel closer. Like I barely put any distance between us. It's the water is what it is. Carries sound without obstruction. That's what it is. Pools you closer together.

"Zeke, as always, you've got yourself a firm grasp on the obvious. There's also no dust or pollen on top of the sleeping roll." Fish points at it without looking down himself. He stares out at the water instead.

Zeke nods in affirmation, like he's pleased by the validation, not seeming to get the sarcasm. "I don't think this is our—"

"No," says Fish. "Don't look like it. It's somebody though."

Fish squats and picks up the burnt-up remnants of two bottle rockets.

I don't know why I pulled them out of the pit. Useless trash but still I climbed down and pulled them up with me. Spent signals.

Maybe I didn't want to let go of my cry for help. Had to keep holding onto it even if it weren't no good no more. Nor ever.

The difference between a beacon and a warning is who's doing the looking.

All three stand in silence, scrutinizing their surroundings.

"Whaddya see, whaddya say, Esau?" Zeke grins up at Grizzly.

Esau don't say nothing. He just shakes his head and shrugs.

It could be a bluff on all their parts. Pretending not to see me. Set me at ease. An extension of their communicating without saying nothing. Like a cackle of hyenas laughing as a diversion.

"Whaddya wanna do, Fish?"

"We got time. I say we wait and meet our new friend." Fish picks up my Bible. "And they will plunder those who plundered them and loot those who looted them."

Great. Time to settle in and wait.

Shooter... where you going? LG!

Not now, Elmore!

Come on, Shooter. Don't be like that.

I got to focus.

Whatta I say 'bout running, LG? We talked about this. Running only gonna make it worse.

Not if I get away.

The men spend the day going through my stuff. Pocketing this and that: my screwdriver kit, my bandages, my fishing gear.

Zeke taps my broken phone.

Oh, Addie… It's just so damn Christmasy I could cry.

Me too, Momma.

Not sure why I kept that either. Like I'm going to find a repair store somewhere. For a prepper I sure do act like an optimist. It wouldn't matter none, even if I did find someone who could fix it. The phone's bricked. For good.

Still, it pisses me off, him clutching it like Golem with the ring. Tapping its shattered face. Tossing it aside like it's trash.

I need thee, oh I need thee.

Ev'ry hour I need thee…

All the while, me just lying in the field, limp dicked and getting ate up by flies, watching the three of them ply and pilfer my stuff.

I check on the girl from time to time. Mostly invisible in her tree, cradling the shotgun.

Every which way, I've been scavenged. Even the 'squitos're bleeding me dry.

Ain't nothing to do but wait. Stillness is my ally, boredom my comrade, with which I wage a quiet war of hide and go screw yourself.

More times than not, beasts walk away from a fight in the wild, Uncle Izzy instructs. *Risk just ain't worth it to them. Less they backed into a corner with no other way or they convinced they gonna win.*

Or they're horny. Yep. Dicks drive even animals to make poor decisions.

Yes, sir. Gotta continue the line though, I guess. It's what every creature's programmed ta do at whatever cost.

Uncle Izzy rustles my hair. Smiles.

Sometimes the offspring's worth it, I guess.

The heat saps the energy out through my pores, leeching it away into the air and ground. It's so hot now, the bugs have gone and fled to the shadows.

Wait. Watch. Drift. Sleep is a welcome distraction from seeing them sip my purified water out of my cooler.

Passes the time. Conserves energy.

And creates gaps.

Couldn't've been out for more than an hour, judging by the sun. The sound of whooping stirs me awake.

Fish hikes along the lake, casting away with my rod and lures, reeling it in and flicking it back out as he walks. Testing the water.

Back behind him, Zeke's rolled my trailer down the shore and sends it into the lake, whooping and stomping like he's a Pentecostal speaking in tongues.

In one fluid movement, Fish nabs a stone, spins, and beans Zeke with it, cussing at him not to scare away the fish.

Zeke sulks off.

And Esau… he's nowhere to be seen.

Shee't.

I look around every which way. Bring up my monoculars, panning the circumference of the horizon.

Hunting? Tracking? Lying in wait?

Who knows?

Fish keeps coming down the shore. Towards the reeds. Towards the copse. Towards the tall grass.

Whistling quietly.

Fishing away in a pattern of sounds: the sighing *bzzz* of the cast, the satisfying *plop* of the lure into the water, the tired *rrrRRR-rrrRRR* of the reel spinning and spooling the line back in.

Bzzz.

Plop.

rrrRRR.

Bzzz.

Plop.

rrrRRR.

Bzzz.

Plop.

rrrRRR.

Until he comes to a stop at the reeds. He's either gotta pull out the line or risk getting snarled up.

Bzzz.

Plop.

rrrRRR.

He stands there and keeps on casting away. Meditative. Still, constant, like a metronome. Like he's in a state.

Except from my angle, zoomed in on him, I can see he ain't watching the water at all. No, sir. His eyes flicker back and forth, sifting through the surroundings.

Finally coming to rest just up from the reeds. Right where the girl scampered out of the water and up to the trees.

His back still faces the copse. Movement catches my eye. A shift of something in the branches, a glint of the shotgun barrel in the light. Training my lens on her, I can see the girl gripping the gun so hard her knuckles turn white.

Bzzz.

Plop.

rrrRRR.

Fish barely moves his head. The slightest tilt of the chin. His eyes zeroing in on footprints in the silt bank.

He squats down and tucks the rod up into his armpit. Out of his shirt pocket, he pulls out one of them black plastic combs. He sweeps it through the water, real casual. Draws it up and tidies his hair. Parting it real neat and sharp. All the while shooting subtle glances at the footprints. Extrapolating their path.

The angle from where she is, the girl can't see none of this.

Then calm like, as if nothing new has come to light, he pockets the comb, stands up, and finishes reeling in the lure.

Bzzz.

Plop.

rrrRRR.

Fish turns and strolls along, back up the shore away from the reeds. Calm as can be. Not giving away nothing. Away from the trees and tall grass. Away from us.

The girl relaxes, rests the gun across her legs.

She didn't see the look.

Didn't watch the realization.

Didn't notice the plan spring into action, like a wolf trap.

Fish's whistling fills the air as he makes his way back to camp. Where Esau has returned to, a dead prairie dog dangling from his fist, and Zeke dancing around him like a remora on a shark.

"Well, well. Looks like we got us a little sport today." Fish's words sail out across the water, like a Jolly Roger.

I can't get to her. I can't warn her. Not without giving myself away.

25

… & SEEK

The stillness washes up and settles in. Unrelenting. Like the tide.

And I'm drowning it.

As Hell's little horde hunkers down for an afternoon rest, Esau flays and guts his catch. Zeke twitches around the fire he's coaxed back from the dead. Fish's barbarous tongue flutters hushed whispers to both.

And I stay put, staked to the ground, tossed around in a whirlpool of limited options.

Option 1: slowly, but steadily slink my way off. Leave it all behind me. My stuff. The men. The girl.

The more you know, the less you need.

I don't need this. I can just make my way in the world. Like I been doing. It'll take patience and steadiness. But I'm pretty sure I could do it.

Except I can't seem to bring myself to do it.

And at that point I may as well go with—

Option 2: beat the bushes and flush her out somehow. Although I'm pretty sure Fish's already got a bead on her. But if I can set her off right when I'm ready and she were to take flight… that'd sure stir up a ruckus and get their attention. Basically, be one hell of a distraction.

Not to mention that she's all locked and loaded up with my ammo. Which option 1 already has me kissing goodbye. Least this way there'd be plenty of sound and fury to give me some decent cover and a chance to accelerate my own escape and not have to worry about disturbing the stillness.

If I'm real lucky, she'll take one of them out, maybe wound another, before getting felled herself.

D'ju know that in Nam the Viet Cong trained to shoot to wound, not kill? Yes, sir. Built their mines ta do the same. Detonate a whole lotta shrapnel and shih'yat, but only so it'd go yay high. Uncle Izzy circled his hand in the air, palm down, indicating waist height.

And do you know why? I'll tell you why, 'cause if you kill a man, then his buddies simply yank his tags, leave 'im for dead, and keep going. But you wound a man and they're gonna stop and help him. Carry or drag his ass to safety.

One good, nonlethal shot, and you take two or three enemy combatants outta the equation instead of just one.

Shrewd sumsabitches, Addie. Shrewd sumsabitches indeed. You remember that, when the shih'yat hits the fan, best ta have your umbrella tilted sideways.

And if no one ends up shooting anyone, well, then either they're all off chasing after her. Or they catch her.

And distract themselves with that.

Addie...

I know, Momma. But you got to choose smart. I told you that. And numbers can be bad.

That is not how I raised you. That is not the Christian thing to do.

You mean like the Thirty Years War, like burning witches, like the KKK. Like them Christian things?

You know what I mean, Addie.

Her hypothetical reprimand hammers home the shame.

No, I will not leave my momma.

Option 3: flex my bow and try to take them out myself. To make that work though, I'd have to shimmy my way a hell of a lot closer. Undetected. Either move in on them or draw them to me somehow.

Even if I manage either of those, there's another problem.

Arrow always points in two directions. Towards its target and towards its archer.

Uncle Izzy had a point. Say my aim is true, for once, and I get one clean through the heart. Kill him outright. Pretty quick the other two pick out my hiding spot right away.

I might be fast enough to loose another arrow. And with a shit ton of luck holding my shakes steady, maybe, MAYBE take out a second or wound him. Again, my aim would have to be true.

But by that time, the third one'd get me for sure.

For sure.

Maybe the girl'd take the cue though, jump on in, and put my shotgun to good use.

Maybe she wouldn't.

Maybe she'd use the opportunity as her own version of option 2.

Option 4: stand up and make myself known. That's it. Simple. Straightforward. Could be this is all a misunderstanding. Could be these fellas saw my signal and, unlike the girl, came to see and help.

Could be that my whole impression of them was tainted from the start by her Bowie knife at my throat and her fear in her eyes.

And I went and took the wrong cue from a thief.

...A thief who got me out of a tiger trap.

A trap that she set.

...A thief who shared her rabbit with me.

A thief who's well on into her second trimester.

Truth be told, these men don't strike me as the helping type.

These men deal in misery.

The day lengthens between them and us.

I lie there well into the afternoon. Amongst the yellow wildflowers, blasted by the sun. Trying to make the water from my hydration pack last me through until nightfall.

With no good options.

Watching.

They cook. They feed. They rest.

They rise. Suddenly. In quiet coordination. And separate. Spread out and make their way around the lake.

In the western sky, storm clouds billow and rise in the afternoon heat. Dense, towering omens heaped upon each other.

A reckoning is coming.

Esau slips out of sight around the bend while the other two stroll their way along the shore.

Towards the reed patch.

Towards us.

Harbingers.

Come on, come on, come on. Think. Think.

It's hard to tell, even with the monoculars, but it sure as shit looks like the safeties on their rifles are off. The wildflowers and grasses keep swaying back and forth in bright yellow and green-brown blurs across the foreground of my focus.

Where's Esau? Where'd that Grizzly get to?

It don't make sense. A man that big being so quiet. Able to disappear into the land with such ease.

Think, think, think, think—

A notion bubbles up out of the hot haze. Pops into being. From delusional depths. Deranged, desperate, shapeless. It's still forming as I wriggle my way through the field. Trying my best not to disturb the surface of the sea of grass blowing in the breeze over me. Don't want no furrow to Bugs Bunny my whereabouts.

Molting off a trail of my belongings behind me. Shuffling and leaving off everything I'm able, so it can stay hidden. Bow. Quiver. Shirt. Shoes. Pants.

Just in case—

Just in case this actually works.

And exposed skin is crucial. That and the hydration pack I drag with me.

Like a snake rubbing against a rough boulder, wriggling along the ground, towards her, shedding away the last of me. Snatching up every wildflower and dandelion I come across.

See the way he's all lit up, all gaudy with them sharp, vibrant color patterns. Black, yellow, red, yellow, black. Again and again. Uncle Izzy poked at the brightly colored Texas coral snake pretzeled up in the sun. *Really makes it pop and stand out.*

The pretzel started to unravel.

Now what's that called?

Aposematism. He'd taught it to me a while back, and I'd studied up: snakes, poison dart frogs, crown-of-thorns starfish. All of them flashy and neon'd up.

Aposematism. That's right. That's good, Addie. Real good. And what's it all about? Hm?

I wasn't sure what he was after. *Advertising?*

He took it in with a thoughtful nod.

Well, sure. In a way, I guess so. It's an adaptation. Right? Nature don't like waste. Ain't no use in being toxic as shi'yat or choc' full of venom if the world don't know it. So all these bright colors is like a biological warning signal. A big, bright antipredator sign flashing out to the world, saying Don't Mess with Texas coral snakes. Or you're going to get yourself a double fangful of poison.

Like I told you before, Addie, it's all about intimidation. Nature's arms race. And in an arms race, it don't matter how big your arsenal is if the other guy don't know it. The whole point is for your enemies to see how thorny, dangerous, and powerful you are. That way, they don't wanna start something 'cause they know it's gonna cost 'em dearly. Too unprofitable.

When other animals see that brightly colored black, yellow, red, yellow, black, they steer well and clear. No fuss, no muss. No waste. Snake don't nee'ta strike, and other animals don't nee'ta die.

And then in a flash, Uncle Izzy flicked the stick, snapping the snake up into the air, and caught it.

I screamed as he slid one hand up to the head and another down to the tail. At some point I'd jumped back at least a dozen yards.

Uncle Izzy keeled over and stomped the ground, violent grunts hiccupping out of him.

Me convinced he done got himself bit. Another Pentecostal bites the dust.

Until he finally straightened up, and I could see those weren't grunts at all. They were guffaws. He was laughing. At me. At my fear.

Him holding out the Texas coral snake end to end like a magician would display a handkerchief after pulling it out of thin air.

The trick is, Addie, sometimes nature bluffs. This ain't a Texas coral, no, sir. This here's a scarlet king snake. Completely harmless.

Uncle Izzy stepped towards me, and I retreated on instinct.

Come on now. Come here and see what I'm saying. It's a solid impression, but with a keen eye you can pick up on the difference. The black bits are thinner, with a little curve to 'em. See?

I saw.

Now that little trick there's known as Batesian mimicry. A perfectly harmless animal evolves to effectively mimic the aposematic one. Deception. Doubly efficient with half the effort. This here snake didn't have to bother evolving venom glands. It just had to put on the same outfit as the Texas coral. Piggyback right on that demon's badass reputation and the world don't know no different. Predators steer clear just the same as if it were poisonous.

Clever as the devil and twice as pretty.

Adapt or die.

Zeke and Fish've made their way back along the lake's edge and come to stand by the reeds. Zeke out in front, oscillating with the furor of a wasp. Fish slow and steady, behind, nursing his limp.

Coiling to a standstill. A few feet from the footprints.

Glimpses of them flicker through the grass stalks rippling in the turbulent air currents. Wind gusts with the approaching storm.

Fish gives a nod. Zeke sees the prints. They turn away together and glare up the bank.

They don't see me draw up just short of the edge of the tall grass. Don't notice me fall to digging with a stick I found. Soft, silent red dirt gives way. A hole grows out of the scrapes. Stretching open until it's a small but adequate crater. I take a draw of water from the hydration pack, spit it into the earthen cavity.

Staying this side of calm. Working to not worry about Esau. Still out there somewhere, invisible in the ether.

Steady and smooth. Not fretting over Fish and Zeke—weapons in hand—fanning out again, hunting their way up the bank.

Neck hair lightens, lets go of gravity, grabbing up at the charge in the air.

From where I lie, it's hard to see the girl. Pick her out of the foliage. I think I can make her out, still treed in her hiding spot as she catches sight of Fish and Zeke.

Or it's just a mirage coalescing out of the frenzied, electric swelter. An illusion of her tensing. Shaking in anticipation. She leans forward and props up the shotgun on a branch for aiming. Adjusts the pistol in her waistband for easy access.

Frantic to head it off at the pass and throw my body across the road, I drive handfuls of dandelions and wildflowers into the mud-red bowl of earth, using the stick as a pestle.

Ears dilate with intent, doing my best to track the noises of the two men making their way up the bank.

Still no sign of Esau. No sound of the Grizzly sniffing around.

Slow and steady.

Adapt or die.

The color isn't quite right. It's the ruddiness of the soil. Spit in another mouthful of water and toss in more flowers. The soup thickens and puddings up. Yellowing. Color's close enough. Especially in the graying light.

Paint and dapple. Paint and dapple. Here. There. Below the jaw, across the gland—

A hush's moved in, like a fog. It distracts with its quiet.

The men are missing.

I risk a slight wriggle. A little lift.

Got them. Crouched down low. Creeping up on the west side of the copse of trees. Progressing slower now. With caution. But progressing nonetheless. And almost there.

The air feels as if it's about to spark. The moment they break her eyeline, ignition, all Hell's going to rain down.

And me lying there, playing with flowers and makeup. Scraping handfuls of dandelions across my ribs, up into my armpits—

I catch ahold of another notion and lose the boxers—in the final throes of the blight, almost all the victims end up voiding the entirety of their lower intestines—dapple the jaundiced hole-pudding up along and above my groin as an added touch.

Angle my way along the edge, for the best line of sight.

Check their progress, gauge the distance to the western side of the copse.

Through the underbrush, I make out Fish motioning with his hand for Zeke to halt. Which, from the sound of it, Zeke does.

They found something. I'm too late.

Fish squats down. Scans the trees.

I can't see her, but swear that I can feel the air tighten as her hands tense around the shotgun. As if she's spooling in the strain of it all, taut. Constricting. The air tightens, tangled in the tension of her grip.

Fish moves into the trees. A flash of Zeke follows.

Shee't. It's fifty-fifty they catch sight of me. Worse odds that my play works.

Dropping down, staring up at the iron sky, wishing for it to seep in, steel my will, harden the desperation.

Bracing. Considering all the options in a millisecond. All bad.

Eff it.

Turn facedown and push my lower half out of the tall grass, into the open, all the while issuing reek out of me. My final touch of Batesian mimicry. Authentic as shit. Literally. And hopefully three times as repellent. Poop, the final touch on my sickened self-portrait, picture-perfect pestilence.

And wait.

Motionless.

Play plague possum. Arm stretched out, lengthening, yellow-striped ribs. Dapples of ruddy, infectious carbuncles.

Shallow breaths, try to tame my torso into a dead calm, keep it hidden and still, facedown in the grass.

Wait and wonder.

Exposed.

Vulnerable as bait.

Can they even see?

Green and yellow grass sways around me. Too much cover.

That or they've already picked up the scent of her sweat. Breathing it in. Heard her shakes rustle through the branches. Tunnel vision, fixated, Fish taking note of a broken branch on a bush, as she lines up her sights on Zeke fluttering his way into her path of fire.

I need to be out more. Exposed.

I was too chicken shit. To keep the men from closing in. On her.

I can still scoot out a smidge. Maybe. Without moving. Without drawing attention to the motion at least. But needing to still draw their attention to the spectacle of death. My corpse needs to draw their focus away from their cornered prey. Keep her finger from hooking around the trigger. Tightening.

I got to scoot. I got to push myself further out of the cover of—

The whistle pierces the air. Freezes the world in a moment.

My blood chills and thickens into a glacial flow.

The whistle. It came from further west.

From behind.

Where they weren't.

Esau!

Somehow he'd circled the entire copse. In no time. Without a whisper.

A breathy owl hoot echoes back, out of the trees. Fish? The call and response between the pack. Whistle and hoot?

The men come.

26

A DEAD TIGER CAN'T CHANGE HIS STRIPES

Calm. Shallow breath. No breath. Shallow breath. No breath.

Think empty. Cold. Inert. Vacant thoughts.

Eyes smoothed shut.

Not even going to risk a glance through half-closed lids. Don't trust what I'll see. Don't trust how I'll react to what I'll see.

Shallow breath. No breath. Hold.

Listen. Drink in sound.

Pat—drag—pat. Pat—drag—pat. Pat—drag—pat. Fish clears the trees. Hauling his limp through the underbrush. Zeke zips in a scattered orbit around him. Tap—patter, patter. Tap—patter, patter.

Two short, sharp whistles from Esau, still behind, but less so. More north of me now.

How does he move so dang quiet?

The other two soft-step their way around to him. Circumscribe my body. Giving it a wide berth. Esau must've pointed out my general whereabouts. Waved them back.

No breath, no breath, no breath.

Quick breath. Hold.

Pant legs hiss, stretching cloth on cloth as the men squat. Defensive position. Wary.

They should be wary.

They should steer clear.

If they're smart.

They sure as hell should keep their distance.

If they know their Stripes.

And they should not, for any reason, puncture or open up an infected corpse. Not with a knife. Not with an arrow. Not even with a bullet fired from a ways off.

Stripe victims are like swollen, tender bagpipes pumped up to the seams with mustard gas. Bloated and ready to burst at the slightest provocation, blistering spores longing to pop and spew virulence into the air.

So the last thing they should do is stab or shoot a corpse just to be sure it's good and dead. No, sir. They should steer clear.

If they want to survive.

... if...

I hate ifs. But ifs are all I have to go on. Even if it is way too many.

Darker ifs follow close behind. They're quicker. More dangerous. And I can't think about how a good burn would cleanse the whole field. How if it were me, I'd burn it out. Cauterize the vitiation.

If.

Lactic acid singes my lungs as asphyxia tries to tears its way through the soft tissue. I permit myself to draw in just a sip of air—

"There. In the grass." A voice out of the vastness. Esau. Not hushed. Cold. Like granite. It pushes through the wind. Its stone tone sinking in a gust.

Bright spots in search of oxygen firefly against the inside of my eyelids. The light beyond has darkened. Filtered through the storm clouds into a blue gray. Or that just might be the hypoxia tinting everything darker.

Moisture condenses along the strips of sticky flower pigment running from my armpits to my ribs. Sweat beads up just beneath the skin.

Clumps of feces stick and stretch between my thighs. Irritating. Itching.

Don't move. Don't twitch.

Air. I need air. I need air. I need—

A shallow breath drags in a waft of the feculence floating around me. May it leak their way. Wafts of reek and decay.

Think bloated thoughts.

Distended belly.

Swelled groin glands.

Fattened fingers curled by rigor mortis.

Boiling blisters.

Puffed cheeks.

A flawless counterfeit "corpse." My best Batesian mimicry.

A perfectly harmless animal evolves to effectively mimic the aposematic one.

The three don't move. It's unclear whether it's out of a skittishness or in murderous contemplation.

Stares in the dark.

Fireflies swarm and flare inside my eye sockets. A part of me wants to pass out. Wants to give in. Give out. Give up.

Their silence slashes against my eardrums.

Until finally—

"Maybe fever drove him to the water."

"And chills drove him out?"

They're reasoning it through. I allow a slight exchange of relief. Exhale, inhale. A shoal of air.

"Nah. That's not it." Fish. "No sense in it."

He sees through the death mask. He knows I'm not dead.

I'm dead.

"No sense in any of it. No rationalizing inside the Stripes. Pain and terror twist a soul this way and that without any thought other than escape."

Stripes. I ain't never been so happy to hear that word uttered. Fish took the Batesian bait.

Are the other two going to bite? Or are they weighing it out?

Quiet stretches thin through the in-between.

"So he's the one who made camp." Zeke. It's muffled. Like he's speaking through the crook of his elbow, covering his mouth and nose.

"It ain't a he no more. It was a he. Now it's an it." Esau's voice sounds like steel on granite.

"The clothes at the campsite seemta be about his size. You know what they say, now, if the shoe fits…"

Zeke loses it at Fish's pun. Snickering and snorting like an asthmatic hog.

"Why the two fires?" A question carved in granite. The mass of it ripples through the ground.

More quiet. More weighing. No movement though. No approach. A Mexican standoff with a would-be cadaver.

"Z'easy, Esau." Zeke. "Dee-coy."

"Decoy fire? Decoy fr'whut?"

"N'case somebody were ta come up on him in the middle of the night. Duh."

"Then why not just one fire that he don't use? *Duh, duh.*"

"'Cause it'd be cold, d—"

"It's not a decoy."

Fish is definitely the smart one. Goddamnit.

"It was a beacon. A signal."

The only difference between a beacon and a warning is—

"An invitation. By the same lonely soul who set off a final gasp of fireworks."

And that's why you don't launch off fireworks.

"A last plea in the desolation, to not be alone in the final hours of this life sentence we call existence."

Definitely preacher-like.

"I will execute judgment on him with plague and bloodshed." Zeke speaks by rote, without depth. Like a kindergartener reciting the Pledge of Allegiance.

"And so I will show my greatness and my holiness." Fish finishes the thought. Like a prayer.

I'm guessing Bible quote.

Stretched leather boots sigh as someone stands.

"You wanna burn him, it?" Zeke asks. With way more excitement than one would expect.

Silence stretches out for a good decade between the ask and the answer.

"Storm's close. Losing light. Best we get to cover and see if we can't resuscitate that campfire before it opens up on us."

Fish walks off. Away from me. Away from the trees. Dragging his leg with him. From the sounds of it, at a pretty clipped pace.

Sweet retreat.

The other two swiftly follow in kind. Picking up speed. Hastening.

I stay where I lie, facedown. Motionless. Sucking shallow breaths. Striped. Carbuncled. Shit soaked. Happy.

I'm ok. I'm ok. I'm ok.

27

EVE

Will you let me know when? Riley Anne stood at the end of the chem lab counter. She picked at a chip in the Formica.

I hadn't heard her come in. But kept going about my business cleaning and setting up the Bunsen burners for the upcoming class. Mr. Brinson, the principal, made it so I could do a bit of work-study. It wasn't charity or nothing. I did a lot of the technical grunt work around the school. Less like a TA and more of an assistant custodian, if I'm being honest. With budget cuts, I guess it was cheaper to pay me than a teacher.

So Riley Anne could've known where I was and sought me out. Or just been passing by.

When what?

I'm not going to try to stop you. She kept picking at the chip, head hanging down so her hair covered her eyes.

Stop what? What are you talking about?

You know. I mean it. It ain't like I tipped off any of the teachers or cops yet, have I?

I finished fitting another burner and lit it to test the connection.

Cops?! Seriously, Riley Anne, I have no idea what you're talking about.

She sat herself up on a stool. Stared down at the blue flame floating a centimeter above the Bunsen burner.

If I... She stopped. *I know we ain't hung out for a while. But I always liked you. I always been nice to you.*

I didn't know where she was going with this.

I get it. I do. The people here ain't... They're all worthless clumps of she-yit for the most part.

Her hands're hooked over her shoulders, arms crossed, in a protective V across her torso. The vertex of her elbow propped on the table. The bottom half of her face buried in the crook of her arms. Kind of like she's tired. Or calm. Seemingly.

Or scared and hiding.

Could I, like, I mean would you consider—her voice flickers. Like the blue flame.

I turn off the burner. Connect another. Spark that up to test. Something about her tone makes me want to focus on the work instead of her.

Addie, I mean, what else are you stockpiling for? I know you been buying ammo. Arrows. All that.

It clicked in. I got it. "Come on, Shooter. There goes LG." Nicknames have a way of defining a person, fixing an identity in a way that truth or character can't ever compete. A good story'll trump a fact every time.

Maybe it's not that exactly. It's not the fact so much as how that fact's interpreted. She weren't wrong. I was stockpiling.

How do you know I been buying—

My cousin works at the Walmart.

That'd be Harper.

Then does she see that I'm also buying every discounted, dented can of beans they got?

Riley Anne didn't say nothing. She just hooked her thumbs in her pockets. Stared at the Bunsen burner.

There was no defending yourself. Not in a way that didn't sound defensive. Which makes it seem like you're proving the accuser's point.

I moved a laminated periodic table out of the way to set up another burner. There was a comfort in holding it. A description of every known element, ordered, and described as exactly what it is. No variance. No wiggle room. Each distinguished from the others by a specific count of protons, neutrons, electrons. Atomic mass. All of an element's traits and behaviors tied to those specific numbers. Unwavering. Unless you cracked it apart, split an atom right through. And unleashed holy Hell on the earth.

Still. Facts is facts.

I'm not a shooter. I'm a prepper. I'm not trying to hurt anyone. Just saving my, getting ready for the shit hitting the fan, is all. Just in case. That's it. You know that.

Mm. She nodded. She knew.

She stood up. Dug her hands into her pockets. And finally looked at me. She half smiled, kind of embarrassed like, kind of apologetic. Then real quick, she pulled her right hand out and handed me a folded-up piece of spiral notebook paper. Ripped and jagged along the frayed edges of the torn, perforated binding.

Just in case, she said. And ran out.

There it was. Maybe she didn't know. Nobody understood me. I guess that's how the shooters felt too. Crud. But I wasn't one of them. I wasn't. Ever.

I unfolded the paper.

On it, she'd written five names: three students and two teachers.

Shee't.

The dented can of beans glistens in the rain between them.

Zeke holds the machete, like you would if you were stabbing something. But not quite like that. He holds it light like. A loose grip. Pointed down. He pumps his arm once, twice, three times and lets go.

It sails in the air towards Esau, twisting in the wind, but staying straight up and down.

Esau snatches it out of the air without turning his head or moving his shoulders at all, like he knew where it was headed and was just waiting there for it.

It reminds me of an orangutan I once saw at the zoo. At feeding time, a zookeeper hucked chunks of oranges at him from a good twenty yards away, and the orangutan could just tell where it was going. Like it weren't no thing at all to anticipate. Just catch the flying piece of fruit without even looking. It wasn't worth his attention. He'd keep going about doing his thing while his arm seemed to move of its own accord to where it needed to be to pluck the orange missile out of the air.

Esau adjusts his grip on the knife and looks Zeke over, measuring him. They both take a single step back. Esau reaches way down, then springs up quick, like a catapult, and launches the machete into the air back towards Zeke.

Zeke flashes this way and that, an outfielder for the Damocles Diamondbacks, finally dodging to the side just as the blade passes, and then dropping down with the knife to match its descent and nab it right before it hits the ground.

It almost slides through his grasp, all slick with precipitation.

"Hoo-wee! Yeah! Yes! That's right. Slick as a whistle." Zeke struts around in a tight circle, like a beheaded chicken in combat boots. He taunts Esau, bobbling his head about. "I'd snatch you bald-headed, but you already got a good head start. You know how it goes—pigs get fat; hogs get slaughtered."

Esau's a statue in the rain.

That man can strut sitting down is how Momma would've described that one.

Finally, Zeke finds his way back to the spot where he last caught the knife. They each take another step back.

It's like the egg-toss competition on Field Day after church. Only with a machete.

Even in the rain, their voices carry across the lake. Even though they've gone and moved further on down the shore, to an outcropping of boulders. It gives them a little cover from the rain, sure, but mostly it puts some distance between my tainted stuff and their new camp. Nobody wants a sleeping bag rolled in smallpox.

Apparently their quarantine doesn't apply to my canned goods.

Damnit.

The distance is good though. Means they probably won't double back to check on me. They won't see the Stripes and carbuncles drip and streak off my skin in the rain.

I don't risk moving though. Don't want nothing to trigger their peripheral vision. It took me a good half hour just to rotate my way around so I could keep an eye on them. I timed each degree's rotation with a storm surge. It took me another twenty minutes at least to snail my way back to my monoculars.

Now, flat as mud, I just lie there and wait, through the rain. For darkness. The sun's already set, disappeared past earth's end, but the last light's hanging on. Oddly brighter now than earlier. Down past the horizon, the sun's snuck its way below the sky, and light's now bouncing up off the bottom of the clouds. Like a giant ball of phosphorus's burning up out past the edge. Glittering through the raindrops. It'd be pretty if it weren't glimmering down on anything other than this particular field of play.

The two of them go back and forth. The blade arcing between them. Zeke hooting and hollering. Esau silent, staring through caged eyes. Each round putting more distance between them and upping the risk of getting cut with every step in retreat.

Until Zeke hesitates, switching this way and that, like a sprayed roach, as the knife slices a parabolic path down towards him. He flinches to back off, then adjusts, hesitates, reaches in, mistiming by a millisecond, and the blade slices open the webbing of skin between his thumb and forefinger.

The machete splatters into the mud. Sated by a taste of blood.

Zeke dances off, in much the same way as when he gloats, only a little less energetic. Hooting and hollering and cussing while sucking at the red dripping off his hand.

Esau don't pay him no mind though. Paces his way back to the center. Back to the beans. Leans over and stares into Zeke as he grabs the dented can.

Zeke stops dancing, but not sucking.

Esau picks up the can, tosses it up, and catches it, again and again while lumbering like an ursine ballerina back to camp.

Zeke watches him walk off, snatches up the machete, and follows him back to the fire.

As night closes in, the men hunker around their blaze. It hisses and spits at every raindrop that slants beneath their rock bivouac.

Fish reads a book under the cover of an overhang.

Esau scrapes his spoon against the bottom of the can of beans. Grinding away, metal on metal, making sure to get out every last bit of beans. He sucks the spoon and clucks his tongue against the roof of his mouth, savoring every bite. Cleaning every last remnant from his spoon.

Saliva floods my mouth. I'm no better than a dog. I'd rather not watch, but need to keep an eye on them.

Zeke fumes across from Esau, vibrating at the irritation of every scrape. Until he can't sit on it no more. "I hope you fart yourself awake all night." With that, Zeke stomps off into the dark for a piss.

He ain't good lookin', but he sure is dumb. Amen to that, Momma.

My body shivers in the night rain. It'd been warm at first. Hours ago. But it was weathering me down, eroding away any semblance of resistance or will. Lying bare, just a sodden bundle of reflexes. With barely a say in what goes on as I try to keep still. I got to wait them out if we're going to have any shot in hell in getting clear of them.

. . .

It ain't until much later that I finally make my move. When their fire's almost died out. Both Esau and Fish deep in sleep. And Zeke leans back against a rock. Glaring into the darkness, nodding off. When he's supposed to be looking out.

The rain picks up again. The patter crescendos into an applause. Enough cover. Enough waiting.

Time to go.

The girl starts awake. Flinches and almost knocks herself off the branch. She'd drifted off, wedged against the tree trunk.

She looks around, hunting for what woke her. Grasping the shotgun tight, like it's a tuning fork that'll help her divine the source of her stirring. She listens.

So I "click" again up at her. Sounding sort of like an insect. Least that's the idea. They probably can't hear any of it, but ain't no need to tip over the outhouse and make a stink. With the chatter of the rain on the leaves all around her, must be hard to tell which direction my clicks're coming from.

I watch her look around, frantic, divining with the shotgun.

"*clickCLICK*," I chirp to her from the undergrowth. Finally, she looks straight down and sees me standing behind a bush, sucking my teeth at her. In nothing but wet boxer shorts.

The double-barrel divining rod homes true on me.

I hold up my hands in the universal sign for *Don't Shoot, I've Come to Help Get You the Hell Outta Here* gesture.

It takes her a second, but she finally turns the gun away. And stares.

At me. Covered in remnants of my own shit. Decorated in smeared stripes and dotted with "scabs."

"It's dandelion pollen and mud." I risk a hushed explanation.

She nods. More to herself than me. Like she's putting two and two together, solving the riddle of the men's mysterious retreat earlier.

We don't got time for this. No telling how long the rain'll keep up at this level and drown out any sound of our own retreat.

I jerk my head easterly. Another universal gesture indicating it's time to move out.

The girl hesitates and hunts around more.

I get it. And point off across the lake, past our old camp. She can't see it from where she sits, but seems to get I've got a bead on our buddies.

To reassure her, I take a peek through my monoculars and give her the thumbs-up. Zeke has fallen into a deep slumber.

If he had a brain, it'd die of loneliness.

I laugh at that one of Momma's, picking my way back through the grass. It ain't easy in the dark, but I manage to retrieve all of my belongings that I'd molted off earlier.

The girl follows. Ten paces or so behind me.

Down at the water's edge, I put my clothes on, wet. Better than carrying them. And I'm already soaked through to the bone between the rain and a quick dip to wash off.

She seemed relieved, waiting and watching me clean the stripes and such off. I guess riding in on a white horse don't quite have the same impression when you're dripping shit all over it. Fair.

She mostly watches the wavering fire out across the lake.

I finish. We grab our weapons and go.

The night's wrapped itself in a thousand shapes. We keep our heads down and muddle on through. The magnitude of it all spread out across the black landscape.

We move slowly. Partly out of caution, partly 'cause of my dinged-up knee, mostly out of exhaustion. Walk shin deep through the water following the shore, up a creek, scramble up a stony bank, climbing to a bridge and onto the paved road. Sticking to whatever path'll best mask our trail. Counting on the rain to wash away any missed trace.

We push through the night, through the bigness of it all. Its breadth made all the larger by our blindness to it. Visionless, yet exposed all the more so.

An abandoned antebellum fort rises from the inky landscape. Watches us go by and continue on.

The amaurotic void swallows us up.

Somewhere along the way, the girl loses her grip on things. Particularly the pistol ammo.

The void swallows that up too.

28

MORNING, GOODNIGHT

As sunlight peeks over the horizon in front of us, we leave the refuge behind. The storm has blown past. Steel-blue sky. An hour or two later, we stop, north of Lawton, at an old industrial park.

She moves towards the office trailer, but in a moment of clarity, I stop her. Nodding at the old shed I spot around back. Not as appealing as the warehouses and nowhere near as nice as the trailer. A wooden relic from an earlier iteration of industry.

Not much to look at all.

Hopefully.

She doesn't fuss. Just nods and makes her way there.

Inside, sunlight cuts through between the clapboard siding.

We don't care.

Before the door can even clap shut behind us, the dirt floor rushes up to catch our falling bodies.

Through closed eyelids, in the red darkness of morning light, a voice reaches out.

"My name's Ava."

. . .

Never overlook the pleasantries of life, Addie.

But, Momma...

No. No buts, Addison. It's manners that've built civilization. It's manners that bind this whole world together. Manners keep the peace. Now please remove your elbows from offa the table.

"Get some sleep, Ava."

Oblivion overtakes me before I can smile.

29

IN THE LIGHT OF DAY

We sleep, dead to the world. Although, I guess in this day and age, it's the world that is dead to us.

The air is hot. And filled with the sound of a drill boring through steel without lubricant. Cicada songs. An irritating mating call if ever there was one. Males thrumming the tymbals, contracting ribbed membranes together against the base of their abdomen.

They prefer the heat of day. After thirteen years underground, who can blame them? A lifetime in the dark, feeding off roots and sap, inside a burrow. Hiding away all that time just to avoid predators. Smart strategy. Just outlast the hunters. Patience is all it takes. And resignation to an existence of excavating, coated in mud, sap, and their own anal fluids in a drive to survive. Only to one day, after more than a decade in the dirt, tunnel up to the surface and break free out of their cave of a universe, into the light. The revelation of it all is so powerful, they molt en masse metempsychosis. Leaving abandoned exoskeletons behind, frozen in the moment of rebirth, still clinging to some old piece of bark.

I remember plucking the exuviae off trees as a little boy. Collecting them in one of Pop's old cigar boxes. Much to Momma's horror.

. . .

They're pests, she'd protest to my laughing Pop.

They're a collection.

Of vermin.

Of his.

That slowed her down.

It's just... so disgustin'. And I won't abide them in my house.

Come on—

No. It's unhygienic. And I'm a nurse. I can't be going in to work with my uniform covered in dried bits of dead insects.

They ain't dead. They're discarded exo—

I don't care what the details are. Just get rid of 'em. We can't afford for both of us to be outta work.

That shut down the conversation right there.

Later that night, while she was working a double, a smell like burnt hair and mushrooms infested the house. I caught wind of it getting up to go to the bathroom. Followed it down the hall until I came across my pop sitting at the kitchen table. A glass of bourbon in one hand, a lit cigar in the other, my cigar box of exuviae emptied onto the table.

He drew deep on the cigar and then spilled the smoke out of his mouth into the glass. The cloud sank down and settled over the pool of brown liquor. The devil's cocktail, burning with brimstone. He ashed into the box, then blew on the tip of the cigar, flaring it into an angry orange red, until finally he turned it around and bore down with the glowing end onto one of the larger cicada carcasses. Like a curling iron through plastic, it melted a hole right through the exoskeleton.

The stench intensified.

Pop buried his nose in the glass, exhaling the smoke out of the way as he drew down another belt.

It's unsettling to think on how different the world was the last time the cicadas were here, thirteen years ago.

Pop was here.

Momma was here.

The world was here.

Now it's all turned around. Instead of the cicadas, it's humankind leaving its abandoned exoskeletons behind, frozen in a moment clinging to some old bit of wood on the rising tide of death.

It'd be nice to think what's been happening here is like with the cicadas. Some cyclical die-off. Much longer than thirteen years, but some sort of pattern. Of death and rebirth. Only with the Stripes, there's no gestation. No procreation. No birth. Just desiccation.

The cicadas only have four to six weeks in the world above. Just over a month to take it in, find a mate, procreate, and secure their eggs away. Come the end of July, they're all going to die.

The girl, Ava, lies still. She don't stir none as I reach over her. I can feel the wet heat coming off her body, mixing with the dry hot air of the shed.

I stretch my arm out across her, just beyond her hand, and wrap my fingers around the pistol lying in the dirt.

Freeze a moment.

Still no stirring.

I'm up and gone without a sound.

Into the bright, white swelter of the afternoon.

PART IV

30

CYCLE

Maybe it ain't a cycle at all though. Maybe the Stripes is some sort of experiment and all of Oklahoma's the lab. Shee't, all the United States. And we're the guinea pigs. Some corporate genetically modified organism gone sideways. Or some bioweapon that broke loose. Or were let loose.

First came the chaos, then the panic. Both destructive. The chaos started with stuff like some planes that fell out of the sky when pilots or crew or passengers had some sort of breakout in the air. The panic was when other planes, suspected of being infected, were just quarantined off on the runways. Sealed flying coffins, in which folks either were taken by the Stripes or starvation. And God forbid if they opened up those emergency doors and set off the inflated slides. They were met by a fireball of frenzy. Literally. Flamethrowers and incendiary grenades wielded by National Reservists. At least until the Stripes started slicing through their own ranks. Versions of this took ahold everywhere. Hospitals, roads, cities. Borders.

Chaos and panic. The fleet-footed hunting dogs that sprinted on up ahead of the Four Horsemen, beating the bush, flushing out the prey.

The idea that it was intended or at least caused by us feels more comforting. Like we had some say in it. The wrong say, sure, but it was still our say. If it were just random, just "nature," shee't, that's just… too much.

Ava starts awake. The metal noise of my return must've woken her. She doesn't see me through the slats of clapboard, standing outside.

Disoriented. Alone. She looks over and stares at the empty ground beside her. Gone. Abandoned.

Is that disappointment on her face? She shrugs as if she was expecting this. She reaches for the space where the pistol was and pulls back. The expression on her face speaks volumes.

Goddamn little thieving bastard.

Not wanting to see where this could end up, I break up the quiet of the afternoon with a clatter, rolling into motion.

In a stuttered view through the wood slats, like on a zoetrope, I catch a glimpse of her scrambling to the back wall.

It's all so quick, I can see it happening, watch what I've instigated unfurl, but too fast, with no time to pull back and jam on the brakes.

Me kicking the door open with a clatter.

Her spinning, long ponytail tracing out a trail of her movement through the air, the *clackCLACK* of the pump-action.

And once again me getting a full-on frontal view down the barrel of my own shotgun. The startle of it all catches up with me as my hands, knowing the drill by this point, shoot up into the air, palms out, in the universal sign, once again, for *Don't Shoot.*

The two bikes I was holding, one on either side of me, tilt away, almost in slow motion, and clatter against the ground.

She takes in the bikes I found us, and then looks back up at me.

I keep taking in the barrel and paying particular attention to her finger that's curled around the trigger.

"You always wake up this way?"

"Just when my alarm clock's an asshole."

She lowers the gun.

I about shit myself. For the second time in twenty-four hours. Nothing impresses the ladies like fecal incontinence.

31

MONTANI SEMPER LIBRI

The partially open Leatherman makes an upside-down V as it spins from its knife point to its screwdriver tip and back again, "walking" its way across Oklahoma from Lawton to Ouachita, measured out in inch-and-a-half rotations. I open'd it just so it'd cover the width of the map's scale. Each inch and a half translated to fifty miles. Revolving it point to point, like it's a geometry compass and I'm the navigator in one of them submarine movies, calculating the best route through the underwater canyons to evade the Russians.

The scowl on her face dissuades me from sharing that fun fact. It's hot in the trailer office, but the desk is handy, and miraculously, they had survey maps.

So I trace out a slightly adjusted route from my original plan.

Ava studies each rotation, her lips moving silently as she counts along with me.

Sweat drips from my chin. The parched cartography paper sucks up each drop into a splotch. I wipe my forehead and face with some paper towels that I found. Not that it does much good. More perspiration and humidity flood back to where I just wiped them away from.

It's not just the heat though.

I'm weak. And shaky. And chilled. All at once. But I keep a lid on it. Just tired. And hungry.

That's all.

Tired and hungry.

And dehydrated.

Sweating like a pig in a bacon factory.

"So it's roughly three hundred fifty miles to Ouachita. If we can do fifty miles a day, seven days. Less time, obviously, if we can cover more. I just don't know how far… you know, in your, um… what your stamina's like."

"Way I've always heard it told, that whole Ouachita area's one big hillbilly hellhole."

"My uncle Izzy's there."

"So are a bunch of welfare, Walmart mentals and meth heads."

"I'm betting there's not too many of them left."

She guffaws and rolls her eyes. "But your uncle's somehow made it."

I don't say nothing back. I can feel my eyes narrow at her. The insinuation sits there between us.

You'd think she'd be a little, I don't know, apologetic or something. But the look on her face ain't sorry. She just sort of doubles down and gives me this *well, it's a reasonable point these days* look.

It is a reasonable point. These days. But so's leaving a pregnant girl behind so I can make better time.

I don't point that out though. Just wipe the sweat from my chin, catching it before it soaks the map.

She's sweating too. Just not nearly as much as me. Then again, she didn't wake up early and, with a sore knee, hump her ass to the edge of town to scrounge up a couple of bikes and then haul them back here. Now did she?

Addie…

I know, Momma, I heard it too as soon as I thought it. Ok? Ok? I know she don't mean nothing by it.

Almost as if to put a point on Momma's disapproval, Ava scratches at and then rubs her belly.

Still, I got to say something. "He's a prepper too. He's the one who taught me. Used to be a marine. Was in Afghanistan. Been a forest ranger there, in Ouachita, a couple of years now, working, prepping, surviving."

She seems to soften. Maybe thinking she went a little too far. Maybe not. She's hard to read.

"Izzy?"

I guess it is a little outside the norm, if you ain't used to hearing it.

"It's short for Isaiah."

"So what? He got so used to being out on his own doing tours, he couldn't reacclimate into society? So he took on prepping."

"I guess. I mean, not that he couldn't reacclimate. He could. We saw him most holidays for visits. Before Gran passed. Uncle Izzy… just didn't see the point. Didn't really like what society, societies had been doing to each other. What they keep doing to each other. And he didn't want no part of it."

That doesn't reassure her much.

"He was always happy to lend a helping hand. Like he didn't hate people. Or nothing. I mean, well, he did hate people. Not like that though. Like, he useta always say, 'Addie, individuals are great. I love each and every one of 'em. It's people who're awful.'"

"It's too hot in here." She goes out.

I find her standing in the shade of the warehouse. We opened the door earlier to hunt for some water. In the end, it was the hose spigot around back that somehow still had enough pressure inside to still push out a steady flow. There must be a water tank on top of one of the warehouse roofs or something. After all that rain, it feels silly to be this thirsty. But the blaze of the sun just drew all the moisture out of the ground and into the air.

"Best to travel mornings and evenings, so as to beat the heat. Plus, I really like my siesta time." Didn't even get a smile out of her with that one.

We stand there, both leaning against the wall, in the shade, staring out at the overgrowth that's amassed itself on the border of the parking lot and invaded the various cracks in the asphalt that present themselves. Crickets strum their way through the grass and weeds.

In another time, we might be enjoying ourselves a cigarette break. Maybe not with her being pregnant and all. But, that sort of thing. I go and pull us each a long stalk of seeding grass. It squeaks as I draw the flowering stems out of their swaddled sheaths of tight grass blades.

I pop the bottom end of one in my mouth and hand her another. She stares down at it with a foreign look, like what do I expect her to do with it, but I don't react none. Just chomp on the end of mine with a satisfying squish.

She takes a moment, but finally shrugs and does the same with her piece. Like a natural. Like she done it a thousand times. Can't really grow up here in these parts and not have done it all the time as a kid at least.

It still feels like she doesn't quite get the plan.

"He took the ranger job there 'cause it's a prepper's paradise."

"The bug-out promised land?"

"*Montani Semper Libri.*"

She crooks her head sideways at me.

"Mountaineers are always free," I translate.

"What's that. The Ozark anthem?"

She has a point. She also has freckles. I hadn't really noticed them before. It's surprising, her being Chickasaw and all. But there they are.

Stop staring.

I turn away and rub my knee. It throbs. My other joints ache pretty bad too. Mostly in my hips. That can't be good. I slide my way down to sitting and lean back against the wall. Wipe more sweat from my brow.

Tired and hungry. Tired and hungry. Tired and hungry.

That's all.

Maybe some water. I wonder if there's some sort of canteen or something in the warehouse I can nab for her for the trip. Otherwise we'll have to share my hydration pack.

"Look, I ain't trying to sell you on it. And I can't make no promises neither. But it's where I'm headed. You got somewhere you need to go, I understand. Take the bike. And the shotgun."

I let that sit there. It's a real nice gesture. Especially considering she's the one who lost all the pistol ammo.

"I'll make do with my bow and the pistol. And what's lefta its ammo in the cylinder." Just to put a point on it.

She still gives me nothing. Seriously, this one should have been on the World Series of Poker tour.

"Me though, I gotta go there." I nod at her belly. "Uncle Izzy's got some medical training too, come time…"

I try to get a read on her. Nothing. Her eyes stare out, untouched behind a thousand invisible wounds. And freckles.

I turn away. Feel like I'm going to heave up a piece of my shrunken stomach. I catch it in my throat before it can get out. Luckily it's nothing. But I swallow just for good measure.

I don't think she noticed.

"What is it you want?" she asks.

"Whatcha mean?"

"From me."

I don't quite know what she's asking. I mean, I get it. But I don't know how to answer it. Not sure I know the answer myself. The longer I wait though, the more charged the air gets.

"I'm not, I don't. I don't want nothing."

"No? You're just helping me out from the kindness of your heart. That it? And, what, I'm supposed ta rely on the kindness of strangers?"

Her tone's gone sharp. Cutting.

"You ain't, you're not supposed to do anything. As far as I'm concerned. Jeez. I'm just offering—"

"I know what you're offering."

She says it in a way that shrivels up my insides and makes me feel guilty. But for what, I couldn't tell you.

Then she steps off a bit, checks the shotgun magazine, and turns towards me. Not quite pointing the weapon in my direction, but definitely angling it between us. The message is clear. I'd have to outrace thunder if I were to try to get at her.

"Ava…"

"I appreciate what you did for me back there."

"Ok."

"But I didn't ask you for nothing."

"No. You just took my gun and my bullets."

She just glares at me with that one. We already had this discussion. Those're her bullets and gun now. That was the agreement for getting me out of the pit. So I'd best watch myself.

Considering the angle of the 12 gauge, I couldn't agree more. I can feel the pistol digging hard into my hip. Ain't no way I could draw it out without snagging it. Even if I could, no way I'd get a bead on her before she blew a hole right through my middle.

Not to mention I got no interest in either getting shot to hell or taking a shot at her.

As Momma would've said, *Damned if you shoot, damned if you get offed with buckshot.*

"Other than my appreciation though, ain't no other obligation from me to you."

Is that what she's worried about? Owing me something?

"No, ma'am, there ain't."

She shakes her head, clearly annoyed at the ma'am bit. Shee't. I can't help but glance at her hands, measure the tension in them. How flexed or relaxed they are makes all the difference right now.

"You're right is all I'm saying. I did what I thought was right in the moment. I wasn't planning on getting nothing from it. Shee't, I already offered for you to keep the shotgun and shells. I was just thinking I'd keep the pistol and six shots of ammo in case of emergency."

I shouldn't've mentioned the pistol. Her hands flex and twist closer into position around her cannon.

"If it's that important to ya though, shee't, take the damn pistol too."

I really need to stop talking about the pistol. Her eyes keep going to my hip the revolver's tucked against. Jesus, what's wrong with me? Just shut up, Addie.

She wrinkles her nose, gazing out at the bright blaze of sunlight bleaching the world that lies just beyond the edge of the shadow. A soul in want.

"It ain't like you could use or even take two bikes with you," she says.

A soul in want of a bicycle…

"No. Not t'all. I wasn't planning on it. I got one fer me and one fer you."

"Why?"

"Because… bikes are faster? An' easier?" Duh…

"You playing dumb or just born that way?"

"…uh…" Well said, Addie. Articulate as goddamn ever.

"Maybe I'll head down to Lawton." She floats the thought out into the light.

Not sure if I'm supposed to respond. So I don't. The less I say, the less likely I am to bring up the dang pistol again. Which is seriously drilling hard into my pelvis at this point, but I sure as shit ain't about to adjust it.

"Or Wichita Falls."

"Down in Texas?" It just comes out. I wish it hadn't. She turns and considers me, like someone who already caught the spider in their living room and is deciding whether to release it outside or…

"Sure, ok. Wichita Falls might be good. There's an air force base down that way. If that's what you were thinking."

She half smiles at me. Sort of sympathetic. Sort of as if she's wondering to herself, does a spider really need all eight of its legs?

"Or maybe I'll just see where the road takes me."

I look down at the dirt. And keep my mouth shut.

"After I slash your tires of course."

That gets my attention. Her half smile's turned into a full-on grin. But not a welcoming one. A satisfied grin that's just for her, not for sharing.

"I'd rather you didn't. But if it'll make you…" Nope, just stop there. Don't presume; don't assume. You stated your preference. That's enough.

"So we're clear though, taking the second bike you brought back don't make me beholden."

She waits for a response.

"No. You wouldn't be beholden."

She keeps waiting.

My mouth can't help but add, "If you don't take it, I'm just gonna leave it here. Either way, it ain't coming with me."

Her hands haven't moved their position from at the ready on her gun.

"Ok then. I'm taking it."

"Ok then."

She don't move.

Me neither.

She sort of squints at me. Then relaxes.

"It's funny," she says. "All this time I thought I was a survivor. Turns out I'm just a refugee."

Once again, I don't know what to say to that. So, once again, I don't say anything.

"Screw it," she says and spits out the grass. "*Montani semper libri.*"

32

THINGS AIN'T LIKE THEY WERE

"Hold up," I interrupt before frustration gets the best of her.

Ava stands back from her bike, holding it at a distance. Like she didn't want it to take offense as she decides where to kick it. In her other hand she grips the shotgun barrel, the butt of it resting on her hip.

She'd been struggling to "mount up." I hesitated to jump in. If there's one thing I learned from Momma about her work with pregnant ladies, it's always be ready to help, but always wait until you're asked.

Ava didn't ask though. Between her belly, the bike, and the gun, nothing was cooperating, especially her.

Her annoyance shifts from the bike to me.

"What." It's an accusation not a question. The air glows orange around her with the setting sun. "You can go on ahead. I'll catch up once I'm situated."

"If at first you don't succeed—" I smile and hold up the roll I found on a shelf in the warehouse "—use duct tape."

She shakes her head, but that don't stop her from stepping aside and gesturing with the gun as if to say, *Well, have at it, prepper boy.*

. . .

You know, it shouldn't be about what you do for the ladies. It's about who you are.

Uncle Izzy rifled around the back seat of his 1982 Jeep Cherokee SJ.

I shifted from foot to foot anxiously behind him.

It's just a favor for a friend, I said.

Mm-hm, Izzy grunted while still digging around. *I know. You told me already that it's not for you.*

It ain't.

I know. He nodded at the back seat. *And you should say 'it isn't' not 'it ain't.' You're a smart boy, so why are you talking like a redneck?*

A hayseed by any other name would smell as wheat.

Izzy turned to give me a look over his shoulder on that one.

What? That's Shakespeare. Paraphrased. From Romeo and Juliet. *We read it in school.*

Mm-hm. Not sure you're smart enough to improve on the Bard's poetry just yet.

What did he know? That there was a clever goddang twist of phrase.

It was clever though. He laughed. *Smell as wheat*.

His laugh put a big shit-eating grin on my face. *What are you reading nowadays?*

Catcher in the Rye.

That's quite a swing. From Shakespeare to Salinger.

Yeah, my teacher's focusing on "teen" lit. It kinda works, I guess.

Any Jack London? Got it! Izzy backed out of the Cherokee, turned around and leaned back against the seat. He held a small old coffee can wrapped in Saran Wrap. As he peeled away the tight plastic sheets, Izzy picked up where he'd left off with his previous point.

So who's this friend?

Just a friend.

A girl.

I nodded.

Addie, if your uncle's doing you a solid, maybe you pay him the courtesy of answering his questions?

She's a friend. From school.

A friend or a friend *friend?*

A friend.

Finished tearing off the Saran Wrap, he tosses the shreds back on the seat with all the other clutter.

But you'd like her to be a friend *friend.*

I dunno.

You don't? Izzy pulled the coffee can up, like he was going to toss it back. Like he was having second thoughts. *You call up your favorite goddamn uncle, tell him you need a favor, that he needs to get you some of that primo government grow from his buddy in Arkansas, and then drive it all the way across the state, all for some shrug of a girl?*

I knew he was just digging at me, but I felt lower than snail shit in a ditch.

He must've seen it.

Wasn't nothing. Not for my favorite nephew, at least. I was headed this way for a visit anyhow. Come here and look at this.

He peeled off the top of the coffee can. It was full of an orangey dust.

Curry powder. He started digging in with two fingers. *See, the trick with subterfuge is sacrifice.*

Izzy hooked out a Ziploc baggie. Inside, beneath a smear of color, I could just make out two old, withered joints.

My heart sank.

Riley Anne would not be impressed at all with this.

Izzy watched me closely. I knew he saw my disappointment.

And he just busted laughing.

Love looks not with the eyes, but with the mind.

He then started to unscrew the bottom of the can. About an inch of it spun off the bottom. A secret compartment.

A false bottom. An oldie, but a goodie. See, you can wrap this stuff in plastic, toss it in curry, seal it in a can, but you still won't fool a drug dog. That's what the joints are for.

They're the sacrifice.

For the subterfuge. And with that he opened the false bottom. *Let them have the joints, a minor infraction that explains the dog's reaction. So you hand it over 'cause you still got this.*

Izzy tossed me a solid ounce of weed, vacuum sealed in plastic, that was hidden in the false bottom.

Who's the best?

Uncle Izzy.

Uncle Izzy, that's right.

Thank you—

Now tell your friend *to go easy on this. That's some medical-grade ganja. Whatever she's used to, divide by three. And don't tell your momma nothing about this. She'll give me hell for getting you messed up with drugs and double hell for getting you messed up with girls. So definitely don't tell her I gave you this neither.*

It looked like an oversized red plastic stamp that'd been branded with ring worm.

You know what this is?

A condom.

Yep. I ain't saying you gotta use it now. Or that you should expect to. Just, if things end up going that way, down the road, I want you to be safe. I'm good being the best uncle, I don't need to be a great-*uncle, you catch my meaning?*

I nodded.

Ok then. You know how to use it?

Another nod. The health teacher had stayed late one day and unofficially showed all us who was interested after our mandatory abstinence-education seminar. She'd used a zucchini.

Ok then. No telling on me.

I won't tell. I was already moving towards my bike.

Addie.

I stopped.

If it's just about what you can do for her, instead of who you are, then she's just using you.

What if who I am is someone who does nice things for a friend?

Izzy smiled at this. *Well, we already know that. The question is, does she? Just keep your eyes open. See what's there, not what you hope is there.*

I nodded. And grabbed my bike.

Addie.

Yeah.

If she ends up not seeing you for you, don't learn the wrong lesson from it. Don't let her lack of character stop you from being who you are. You got a generous spirit. Especially for a prepper.

The moon lights up the entire stretch of road in a diffuse, pretty silver light. The shotgun rocks back and forth, snug in its duct-tape "holster" dangling from the top tube of her bike. Not a bad job.

I liked it so much, I done the same for my bow.

"Like one of those leather wine-bottle carriers hipsters use when they want to pretend they're going on a picnic in Brooklyn," she noted.

I'd cocked my head at that one.

"Our tribe actually makes a bunch of leather works for a distributer in Williamsburg. And even some hemp woven ones for the vegans."

My head must've cocked more so towards my shoulder.

"Williamsburg is an overly trendy part of Brooklyn."

"Ok. And they got a lot of vegans there?"

"Vegans and orthodox Jews. We sell a bunch of leather stuff to them too. Tefillin mostly."

I tried real hard not to look like I didn't know what those were. Not hard enough apparently.

"Tefillin are those leather straps they tie around their arms. At the end it's got a small leather box that they put parchment prayers inside."

"Why?"

She shrugged. "Not sure. Guess it's like wearing your heart on your sleeve. 'You shall put these words of mine on your heart and on your soul.' Deuteronomy."

"You know your Bible pretty good."

"It's a popular inscription. For the tefillin."

I hesitated. She saw it. So I went ahead and asked. "But Chickasaw ain't Jewish folk… are they?"

She laughed good at that one.

"Nah. We're Chickasaw. But we don't need to be Jewish to make Jewish stuff. A rabbi in Brooklyn just blesses our work and then sells them himself."

I nodded.

The shotgun pendulums from one side to the other with each push of the pedals. Her legs piston back and forth. She's long limbed.

Her muscles're pretty taut. She's definitely put a lot of miles on them. No fat. No softness. Lean. And she can maintain an impressive rhythm, the up, down, up, down, up, down of her knees, the flexing, unflexing of thighs. Butt muscles alternating bulging and relaxing back and forth from cheek to—

"Getting a good look?"

"What? No. I wasn't—just highway hypnosis, you know?"

"Mm. Probably healthiest for you not to talk about my hypnotic ass."

"I wasn't saying, I didn't. I was just drafting offa you."

"Seriously, you ARE a pregger perv."

"What? No. I mean…" This girl's getting me all wrong. I think. I mean I was looking, but I wasn't looking like that. Entirely. Shee't. "I can take the lead if you want. So you can draft offa me. It's a good energy-saving tactic—"

"So you can crop dust me?"

"With what? I couldn't even. It's been so long since I ate something, I ain't got no gas in the tank..."

She laughs. Hard.

"I need a drink." She accelerates away. Up ahead is a small bridge over a creek. She veers off to the side and dismounts.

Ava splashes water on her face.

I rub some on my arms. Rinsing off the heat.

Between our exertion and the humidity, hot still clings to us. In spite of the night air.

The cool runs through me. Too quick. It doesn't feel right. But passes. Exertion, exhaustion. Either way, ignore it.

I submerge the hydration pack and refill it.

Ava cups her hands and raises a pool of water to her lips.

"I don't know if I'd do that."

She raises an eyebrow, *Why*?

"*Giardia, E. coli, Cryptosporidium*... take your pick."

"You just filled up your pack with the same water."

"To boil later."

"In what?!"

"In a... I'll find something."

Ava rolls her eyes and takes a good long guzzle.

"Suit yourself."

She does. Several times.

I can feel my tongue swell up, jealous with thirst.

"It tastes good."

I shrug. Taste ain't the best measure for that sort of thing.

"You know, it's not like... things ain't like they were. There's no more cattle farms. No industry. No shitty people. And this water's flowing fast. The bottom's sand and rocks. No mud."

"That don't mean nothing."

"Roll the dice, man. We should be so lucky that bad water's what does either of us in."

She has a point.

I cup a little up to my lips.

The cool is delicious. I lean down, purse my mouth, and kiss the creek, sucking in as much as my belly'll hold.

"Attaboy, Addie. Embrace the suck."

That makes me snarf the water right up my nose. She literally slaps her knee at my choked coughs.

"Woo, it's a wonder how you made it this long. I never seen someone drown just from drinking."

I gag laugh too. And lie back on the bank, catching my breath.

We go back and forth, making each other laugh harder and harder until it finally peters out.

Ava cups water up to her neck and rubs it up into the base of her hairline. Some of it drips down the back of her sweaty tee shirt. Holding her hair up like that shows off the line of her neck. Like one of them models in a shampoo commercial, she looks—

Right at me.

Shee't.

"You know what I been thinking about?"

Her eyes narrow at me where I lie still splayed out on the dirt.

I ignore the suspicious gaze. "Williamsburg vegans."

"Ok. I'll bite. What about Williamsburg vegans?"

"Well, not about them per se. About a vegan cannibal."

"A vegan cannibal?"

"Yeah, like a cannibal who'll only eat vegans. 'Cause they just taste so fresh. And pure. And they're so much healthier for you. In the long run. And all his cannibal friends always get annoyed at him because he's so high and mighty about it. And such a pain to eat with. Especially at dinner parties. And he's always asking if the folks they're eating were hormone-free grass fed."

I grin at her. "It's kinda funny. No?"

The corners of her mouth turn up a little, but mostly she just shakes her head.

"I guess I'm super hungry."

"Are all preppers as weird as you? Or are you a particularly weird one?"

"I… don't know. Preppers don't really socialize so much."

"Huh. Go figure."

Staring up at the sky, I spot the Big Dipper, sight Polaris, and do a quick calculation. "It's getting on past eleven."

Ava pulls her chin back into her neck with a look of disbelief. "Oh, is it? How'd you figure that?"

"There," I say, pointing at the Big Dipper. "See the Big Dipper."

"Sure."

"Ok, now see the two outer stars on the far side of the ladle?"

"Ok."

"Those are Dubhe and Merak. They point—" I drag my finger across the sky "—to Polaris. The North Star."

"Yeah. So that's north. Direction and time are two different things—"

"Now imagine a clock with Polaris at the center and an imaginary line from it to the second pointer star in the dipper. That there's your hour hand."

"Got it."

"Ok, now two things about this celestial clock."

"Celestial. Someone's been studying for the SAT. What're you, a junior?"

I let that go.

"Two things, one: it's a twenty-four-hour clock, not a twelve-hour one like we're used to. So each hour sweeps out 15 degrees, not 30."

"And two?"

"It moves counterclockwise."

"You're just messing with me."

"No, it's, the earth rotates to the east, so…" I spin my finger in a small circle around Polaris. Then I draw an imaginary line for her. "See how the 'hour hand' points about here. So about here would be about 90 degrees, plus another 45 degrees or so to the left, which is where it's pointing. Roughly 135 degrees."

"Which makes it about 9 a.m. according to your little equation. Wow, it sure is dark for 9 a.m."

"Except it's August. Ish."

"That AND you're full of more bullshit than a slaughterhouse."

"You gotta subtract two times the number of months since March 6. It's roughly early August. Five months. Times two. Ten. Nine a.m. minus ten gets you…"

"Son of a bitch."

"Give or take a half hour or so."

"Well, then we'd best get moving if we're going to make that movie."

Ava struggles a little to standing. Rolls towards her side and pushes herself up. Belly last.

"You all right? To keep going?"

"Shit yeah."

That said, I don't get up much easier. Joints're still aching bad. A shiver ripples through me as I try to sit up. Ava notices.

"Are you all right?"

"Yeah, yeah. I'm ok."

I close up the hydration pack, sling it over my shoulder, and get up.

"Tougher than a two-dollar steak—"

As I get vertical, the stars spin and the ground headbutts the back of my skull with a muffled thud and darkness.

33

LEFT

This is some dope-ass weed, Riley Anne wheezed without exhaling.

I nodded. *That's government grow for you.*

Ironic that the government grows the best weed, she laid herself back onto the floor of the hayloft, her head propped against a bale.

Well, they've had teams of scientists developing and farming it for research purposes. They need the most potent version that's growable.

Yeah, but it's sorta like the cat who ate the canary, dontcha think?

I'm not sure I follow you, Riley.

She laughed. A lot. *I'm not sure I follow me either. Is the barn spinning? Or am I?*

Neither?

She laughed again and took another toke.

I lay back beside her.

You want? She held the joint out to me.

Nah.

She gave me a look.

I gotta study for my A-PUSH test tomorrow.

It wasn't not true. I did have to study for the test. The excuse seemed to satisfy her. Riley Anne already knew I was pretty straight-edged anyhow.

She drew in another deep toke. And in a breathless voice, *I was gonna take AP US History.*

You coulda.

I know. Mr. Moralez said I should. I was gonna.

What happened?

My pop heard the test cost ninety-two dollars. And that's not including any prep materials. So...

It was expensive. But, *They give a discount to those with a real financial need.*

Riley Anne nodded. *You try to get my pops to admit our family's got a real financial need.*

Her pops, like most folks around here, seemed to take pride that they came by their poverty honestly.

Mr. Moralez would've still let you take the class. I think.

Riley Anne shrugged. *What's the point?*

I didn't want to push it.

Why do you take it? She patted my shoulder with the back of her hand.

I turned my head to look at her. We lay side by side, our noses a few inches apart.

Whaddya mean?

I mean, if you're convinced there's gonna be some sorta apocalypse, then why do you take all the hardest classes and study so much? Why bother?

I could feel the heat of her breath. And smell the skunky odor of the marijuana.

My uncle has a saying—

Your uncle, the vet?

Mm. Izzy. Isaiah. The more you know, the less you need.

Is he a prepper too?

I think he's a libertarian.

Riley Anne lost her shit at that one. Slapped my belly with her palm while guffawing.

I grinned as big as a possum eating a sweet potato.

Her ha-has finally died down. We lay there, leaning back against a bale of hay. The backs of our hands touching.

So is that it, then? Riley pointed at me with two fingers, real sophisticated like, holding the joint like it was a cigarette. Then she puffed on it. *You trying to cram in as much knowledge as you can now, so as to lessen the amount you'll need after the end of days? Lessons for lessening, as it were.* She said that last bit in a real posh, sort of intellectual way.

Yeah. In a way. You could say that's what I'm doing.

Riley Anne nodded to herself. *Smart. Crazy. But smart.* She took another hit. *You keep on doing what you do.*

I stared at the dust motes whirling in a sun beam shining down on the old water pump jutting out of the earth. Riley Anne's granddaddy dug that well and set the pump in himself. It's antiquated, but her family takes pride in it. Like it's a monument to a long history of them not needing nothing from nobody.

It's an anchor more than anything else.

Beyond it, Riley Anne's garden was really starting to sprout up. Especially the peas. She's got two green thumbs and a green leg to boot.

A V of geese honk past overhead.

What're you thinking about? The curvature of the earth? She exhaled a plume of smoke.

What? I was praying she didn't actually remember that.

How when you lie down in a field, you feel the curvature of the earth? Can you still do that?

I don't know what you're talking about.

Addie...

Must be some other dude.

Oh, yeah. My mistake. Totally was my other kray-kray prepper friend.

She was lying super close to me now.

When'd I tell you that?

I dunno. Riley Anne shrugged. *Eighth grade?*

That weed must be SUPER strong.

Shut up. She elbowed me in the side. Our torsos were basically pressed against each other. Ribs to ribs.

No. I wasn't thinking about that.

She turned on her side so she was facing me. I was still flat on my back, staring straight out at the pump and her garden. I didn't want to risk a side glance or nothing.

I was wondering about Holden and why he's so obsessed with where the ducks go?

What?

From English class. Catcher in the Rye.

She gave me an *are you serious* look? Which I only sort of caught in my periphery.

No, seriously. I mean, I know there's, like, a bunch of symbolism and crap, but I mean, come on. Holden Caufield's no dummy. I mean, yeah, he gets kicked out of schools and shit, but not because he's stupid. So, I mean, it, like, just doesn't make any fucking sense. When winter comes and the pond freezes over, either the ducks fly south in the winter, like every other bird, or they get picked up by some truck. Who cares? And on top of that, it's not like it's really a big mystery. I mean, growing up in New York City, did he ever see the ducks fly? If he did, then they weren't domesticated ducks that the Park Service was stocking the ponds with. They were wild ducks who knew a good thing when they saw it, i.e., plenty of tourists to feed them. So, like, duh, of course they flew south in the winter. But, I mean, if he never saw them fly or saw some Park Service people dealing with the ducks in some way, well then, there yeah go. It just doesn't make any sense—

That was when she kissed me. It was quick. No tongue or nothing. But sweet. I could taste the watermelon gum she'd been chewing. And smell the sweet perfume of Pantene and hay mixed together in her hair. Her lips opened ever so slightly, gently tugged on my bottom lip. But I was flexing them. I think. My lips were too hard for sure. I needed to soften them or something. I needed to—but she'd already pulled away and lain back flat again.

She took a final drag on the joint.

She'd kissed me.

I thought about asking her for a hit.

But didn't.

We'd just kissed.

You know, sometimes, I feel like the apocalypse has already happened, she said. *We just ain't realized it yet.*

I got what she was saying. But it was too… sad to really address.

Shee't, Riley Anne, you sound like a budding prepper. If you want, I can bring you to one of our meetings.

Shut up. She laughed. *I ain't nowheres near weird enough.*

I wanted to kiss her again. Every body hair on my side closest to her was raised, like antennae. Like little receivers searching for any opening.

I dunno. Plus, with your mad gardening skills, you'd be real popular. A prepper princess. I poked her in the ribs and leaned in, my forehead nudging up against her temple.

She didn't move away. Every part of me focused on the point of contact between us. Forehead and temple. The silence of the moment filled the barn.

And then, for some reason, I said, *You know, my bug-out place's not too far from here. I could show it to you if you want?*

It looked like she was thinking about it. But things're rarely how they look.

I leaned in to kiss her.

That was when she bit me. On the chin. Hard.

OW! It was not a love bite. It was a *bite* bite. I couldn't help but recoil. A little.

Which gave her just enough room to put the palm of her hand over my face and then play push me away.

I rolled back towards her, but she was already getting up.

Nah. When the end comes, I don't want to be left behind. I'd rather embrace the annihilation than face the aftermath on my own.

Super bleak. She felt it too.

The moment for kissing was dead and gone.

All right, Addie, time for you to go study. I gotta go meet up with Elmore and the gang at the Lost Lake.

And that was that.

We'd kissed. Then she left.

To see Elmore.

Uncle Izzy was right. It's people who're awful.

When I wake up, Ava's gone and left.

I'm on my own. Again.

What's left of a fire flickers in the center of a circle of embers. Her parting gift, I guess. Smoke curls up, a dark column leaning up into the morning light.

The creek gurgles a few feet away.

I am alone.

Again.

I rest a few more moments, not yet willing to face what'll happen when I sit up.

Turn my head this way and that. The weight of my skull rocks around, pushing down on the soft brain tissue inside.

I could just lie here.

I could.

I don't.

My entire body moves with a dull soreness. But it moves.

My Sooners sweatshirt ripples away and puddles onto the ground next to me. Ava must've draped it over me. For warmth.

Before leaving me to die.

"Bitch."

"So you're up. Can you stand?"

She comes out of the woods behind me. I don't turn.

She circles around at a respectable radius, squats down, and looks at me.

"Well?"

The anger's still there in me, even if her abandonment was only imagined.

"Gimme a second."

She does.

I turn over onto all fours first. Wait. And push up to standing. It ain't enjoyable, but it's manageable.

"Ok then," she says. She heads up to the road where the bikes wait. "You ride behind me. Try not to lag. 'Less you wanna get left behind."

34

DAZE AND DAZE

We ride through shortgrass prairies and shrublands—open, exposed stretches that emphasize the emptiness of it all, passing through cross-hatches of remote woodlands of junipers, pinyons, and ponderosa pines hugging the banks of creek beds. We cross a wide plain split open by masses of sporadic granite boulders. Along their gray stone sides run streaks of chartreuse, wild and prolific rashes of *Pleopsidium flavum*, lobe-edged lichen. Bedrock stands stained with the occasional outbreak of graffiti. We siesta beneath one such crimson lament scrawled just inside a massive cavity in the towering slabs.

God broke his promise.

God is dead, tagged someone else in different spray paint.

I didn't even know he was sick, added a third color.

Despite the heat, chills tremor through me. Neither of us says nothing of it though. Still, she keeps her distance.

In the late afternoon, we ride on, the sun pushing at our backs, driving us through the throat of red slate hills into what was Comanche country once upon a time. Into a treeless and barren land littered with the invisible remains of warriors, murderers, and innocents. A white-tailed deer watches us pass with barely a twitch. Seemingly all too aware of our demotion down the food chain.

We are still riding when the sky turns orange behind us, following our shadows until we reach a brown river thick with silt. A patch of rare bigtooth maples clusters at its edges. We stop there for the night. Gather what sticks we can, make a fire, and watch the brown water churn into black ink with the fading of the last light.

Night is a welcome break. In spite of our efforts, our progress is wanting. Mostly due to me.

It would bother me more if the fatigue allowed for it.

Ava slips off into the night. I don't know where. Can't work up the energy to ask. I don't care.

Exhaustion overtakes me, and I slip away into a fitful sleep of chills and sweats, curled at the fire's edge.

Somewhere in the night, I become of aware of a second fire bending downwind in the dark. Ava's sleeping form curls along the far edge of it. The sterilized buffer of two small blazes burning between us.

The reality of it barely registers before the aches chase me away from the surface of consciousness down into the dulled depths of black numbness.

Hallucinations and memories periodically skip along the shoal of sleep. Twisted bodies disgorge pledges of wasps from their maws; mounds of mass graves blister across farm fields, swollen clusters of burial barrows; wet towels drag smooth across my eight-year-old brow in streaks of cool as her distant hymns echo in canyons. Her voice almost. Whose? I can't quite grasp it. The only two clarities are the rolling pain and the longing. The burning desire to go back, sink down, and hide away in the hole I left behind. My earthen womb, stocked with canned goods and a calendar of death. The security of the CC.

And the anguish of wanting that. Of being unable to reach back any further for comfort. Memories of Momma have ebbed out of reach, into the deep currents of beyond. All her time and effort and love and she has ebbed beyond the reach of recall. No more tangible than my disappeared dad. The new normal, my default fetal, is—was my cinder-block cellar. The grief of her is gone. Our last connection. Which leaves behind its own type of torment. A needling gap. Like an abscess.

I wake up hungry.

Ava squats by the river. In her sports bra and shorts. She's using her shirt to try to filter out silt while refilling the hydration pack. Her belly rounds out just below where her sports bra ends.

She stretches the soaked tee over her head and shoulders as she walks up the bank towards me.

"I'll carry the pack. I know how you feel about unsterilized water."

It's a joke. I think. She smiles. Sort of. I try. Not sure if I succeed.

Again, she takes the lead. Because I can't. And so she's upwind of me.

We continue to steer clear of civilization's relics and the threat of others, sticking instead to the wilds. Foothills give way to Permian red beds and distant fitful buttes. The occasional body of water glides by: ponds, lakes, rivers. We ride through fracking fields, where herds of pumpjacks stand motionless, arms at the ready, patiently waiting to swing back into rotating drudgery.

Fatigue pushes into us like a headwind. Hunger pulls back at progress, like we're dragging parachutes. The only saving grace is that Oklahoma, as a whole, slopes downward from west to east. Not that it feels that way from mile to mile.

A burnt bus waits stranded on its wheel rims, angled across the center of a two-lane bridge spanning a rocky river. Puddled black scars on the pavement mark where the rubber tires melted and boiled into flames. Passing the monoculars back and forth, we make out the remains of about a dozen or two inside. This happened a while ago. Could've been an accident. A warning. A mass suicide. A cleansing pyre.

We won't cross the river here.

We detour south.

By dusk of the third day, we arrive at the Cross Timbers, where the prairie and the woodland collide into the savanna. Wolves howl at the coming night. Maybe grays down from Minnesota or Mexican grays over from New Mexico. Reclaiming lost territory. The new world has turned old again. It's theirs again.

Against my sickly protests, Ava leads us into the town of Hexton. The air's cooled too much as we've passed from one microclimate to the next. If I spend another chilled night outside, I'll concuss myself shivering.

We walk the bikes in, along the short few blocks of Main Street. The wheels circle through random bits of litter, like flotsam and jetsam from some ghost barge that washed ashore in this landlocked village. A thin layer of ash covers everything. The town smacks of traditional Americana. Low redbrick buildings line both sides of Main Street. A sharp, methodical, linear contrast against the billowing gray clouds above. High arched windows, painted storefronts, striped awnings, empty slots for flags, a clock tower rising out of a bank. Old-timey neon and painted signs announce things like Tavern; Hardware; Drugstore; Camo & Lace—an ammo, lingerie, and bait boutique; Post Office; and Aqua Marine—a tropical fish store, of all things.

Charming, right, Addie? Just charming. This town has good bones.

It has real bones too.

In a pile at the center of Main Street. A barbaric white pile seemingly glowing in the gloaming. Mostly human. Maybe some animal ones tossed in for good measure. We don't get close enough to inspect in the approaching murk. Don't care to. What good will classifying do us? What we can see is that they've been picked clean. Edges of the calcified pyramid spill out of their lines where scavengers have tugged off stray bits of carrion. It is a man-made structure for sure. A beast wouldn't bother. Especially not out in the open like this.

As with most symbols in this newly primordial world, the meaning is lost in the emptiness. It could be some sort of trophy monument as easily as it could be an admonition as much as it could simply be an act of boredom.

It doesn't concern us. Nor slow us down. Just pushes our path out to the edges of the pavement.

The last third of Main Street's charred black. Another cleansing fire maybe. But just at this end. Could've been people. Or disrepair, like frayed untended electric wires. Could've been lightning.

We find our way into the local diner. It feels more like a bingo hall that tables and chairs were set up in, rather than any sort of formal eating establishment. But the sign outside says Beacon Diner.

The cupboards are bare, as are the shelves, fridge, freezer, and storeroom.

We weren't expecting different. But we had to check nonetheless. We did find a stash of old matchbooks in a mason jar.

Still, there's room to spread out. The front windows haven't been broken. And there's ventilation above the cooktop for an indoor fire.

It'll do.

Ava leaves me there to see what she can find.

I don't recall seeing any grocery store in town. Not that it'd matter. That would've been the first place to be picked clean.

Rain begins to patter against the windows.

Miraculously, the gas still works.

I light the oven and prop the door open to heat up the place.

I don't know how long she was gone. But it is dark out now. And the clouds've cleared away.

The sound of her dropping packages on the linoleum floor is what wakes me.

Ava squats across from me, rummaging through a new backpack, unloading as she goes: three RC Colas, a box of Caramel Apple Pop-

Tarts, and some hunting grab'n'gos—pork rinds, dried mango with chili spice, and dill-pickle-flavored cashews.

"And…" She pulls out a pot and two collapsible tin cups. "So you can sterilize river water to your heart's content."

I would be overjoyed if I weren't so tired. My mouth barely has the energy to salivate.

"Any sign of people?"

Ava shakes her head.

"Any bodies?"

"Not more than the bone pile. I didn't dig too deep though. Just the stores and storerooms."

I nod. Most Stripers sought out some sort of protected hideaway or barricaded themselves in their homes to convalesce and ultimately expire. A desperate act of escape that only locked them up with the demon contagion. Stores, public places in general were too exposed and saw too much traffic. Especially in the first few months when the mass die-offs were peaking.

Ava juts her chin at the bounty of snacks on the floor, "I'll give you first pick. So long as it ain't the dill-pickle cashews. And we split the pork rinds."

I smile and shake my head at that. Let Ava get thirstier munching on the cashews and pork rinds. And unless she's hiding some ranch dressing to dip in, the Pop-Tarts're basically worthless.

We are all scavengers now, living off of the corpse of what was. Still, ain't no use fighting against the way of things. I tear open the bag of chili dried mangoes. Sweet spice floods my mouth.

"Oh, and I got you these."

Ava tosses me a white plastic bottle that rattles when I catch it. Across the label a big tropical fish with a blue head, green middle, and dark blue tail swims next to a smaller, bright yellow fish.

"Fish Mox Forte. You got me fish food?"

Ava shakes her head. "No. Fish medicine."

I look at the bottle. I look at her.

"Antibacterial fish medication."

"I still…"

"Look at the back."

I turn it around. It's amoxicillin, 500 mg capsules. Holy shit. I bet there isn't a pharmacy in the country that hasn't been ransacked down to the studs. But a goddamn aquarium store…

"You don't have the Stripes. You don't."

She's right. They would've shown by now. Probably.

"And it ain't nothing from the unsterilized water you've been drinking. Otherwise I'd be sick too."

She's right again. Probably.

"You just caught something. Probably when you were lying naked in the field, rolling around in your own shit."

Probably. And I was lying there naked in my own shit, saving your ass, by the way. Somewhere deep inside, some macho part of me didn't like needing her to take care of me.

"So. Take your antibiotics. 'Cause you've been slowing me down for days."

She tosses me the hydration pack.

"We should boil the water first. Now that we can."

Ava rolls her eyes at that one.

The fresh pot of water cools on the range for the third time. Wrappers scatter the floor between us. Their aluminum innards glint a quiet blue, reflecting the oven flames.

Ava sits in a booth by the window, gazing out at the now clear sky. Starlight pricks down through the onyx velvet expanse.

I opt for the floor. As appealing as the plasticky booth cushions are, there's just not enough room to really lie out.

I sit with my legs out, leaning against the back of the booth. No reason she should get all of the cushion enjoyment for herself. I stare out the glass door, into the blackened void of Main Street, just able to make out the vague outlines of the cast-iron lampposts lining the sidewalk.

Dark streets disturb me more than charcoal woods or black prairie. It's the intent of it. The context. A physical reminder that this is not the way things are supposed to be here. It's not a power outage. It's an extinction.

Still, it's good to be out of the night winds. Somehow the chill still makes its way under the door crack, seeks me out, and washes across me, like ants finding and swarming around a random crumb on an otherwise empty floor.

"Satellite."

"What?" I ask.

"I see a satellite." She points out the window up into the night. "See it? To the left, like a medium-bright star zipping along."

"I know what a satellite looks like." I can't really see from where I sit. I don't move neither.

"Oh yeah, I forgot you're the prepper king, you know everything."

"I didn't mean it like that."

"Whatever. Big dripping shit, there's a satellite."

She says that and shrugs, but still watches after it.

"I'm just…" I got nothing. She says nothing. Crud. I pull myself up and scooch my way into her booth. I lean towards the window.

She points out the glimmering dot speeding past above, through the inky silence.

"Yeah. I dunno. I just don't like to think about them."

"Satellites?"

"Yeah. I know it's kind of weird."

She don't respond. Just keeps looking out the window.

"Like they're sort of mean," I try to explain.

"Mean. Satellites." Her tone isn't so much judgy as it's indulgent. Like with a little kid crying over the slightest of boo-boos. *Aww, did you hurt yourself?*

"They're just, kinda weird, when you think about it. These vestigial keepsakes of the world that was, memorialized in taunting orbits."

"Vestigial, eh?"

"Yeah, like, oh, something that used to be useful, but—"

"I know what it means. It's like our tailbones. Or your two-dollar SAT words."

"Yeah."

"Yeah."

Shee't. That's good, Addie, alienate the girl. Super smart. I slide an empty porcelain sugar-packet container back and forth across the tabletop.

"For the record," I say in my most self-satisfied of tones, "I'd DESTROY the SAT test with the bell curve being what it is these days."

That gets a laugh out of her.

Small victories.

"Anyway, alls I meant was we're all gone, but all the satellites, *our* satellites are still up there circling, keeping watch, listening, talking to each other even. Not caring at all that… Houston's dead and gone."

Ava sort of nods. Or is nodding off.

I fidget with an empty napkin dispenser and watch the blue will-o'-wisps of gaslight dance across one of the crumpled RC Cola cans scattered on the floor.

"Not from the stars do I my judgment pluck, and yet methinks I have astronomy; but not to tell of good or evil luck, of plagues, of dearths, or seasons' quality?"

In the dimness, Ava can still make out the expression on my face.

"What? You think you're the only one with some learning?" There's an edge to the question. And a barb in the look she whips at me.

Before I can defend myself, Ava softens.

"I was an English major. My mom used to read me poetry when I was little. Guess I got hooked. Yep."

It's nice to hear her share anything. The thought flashes past that she might just be lying. Still, that she'd even bother to lie is nice.

I prefer, myself, the fake ones, my pop said.

It was a rare memory of him and Uncle Izzy together. Sitting on the front steps, passing the bottle back and forth between them.

Momma was working a night shift.

Jed, I mean this with all due respect, but you're more fulla shit than Taco Bell's septic system.

I listened through the screen, propped up at the edge of my bed, my feet on the edge of the nightstand. From there, I could catch the occasional glimpse of one of them reaching for the bottle or bending forward with laughter.

Hear me out, hear me out.

A reading from the Gospel of Laziness—

Lazy, hell. Just think about it, when a woman cums for real, well, her eyes roll back, moans echo outta some deep cavern, and she disappears off into some other world of pleasure.

Them French call it le petit mort. *The little death.*

Firstly, fuck the French right in their perfumed, chicken-shit asses. Pop gestures with the bottle.

So that's how you get 'em to some 'other world of pleasure'?

Anyway, that's my point exactly, a little death. Gone off to another plane. Get it?

Ok.

Ok. So they're gone. In their own little world. Not thinking about you. Not thinking about anything.

Pop waited for Izzy to interject something. Izzy just drank and shook his head.

On the other hand, if she's faking it, then that means she's thinking about me, concerned about my feelings. She's putting in effort to make sure I feel good. About myself.

Instead of you putting in effort.

Yeah. I mean what lazy sumbitch wants to put in effort. Effort takes work.

. . .

Her forehead presses against the window, like a toddler waiting for her parents to come home from work.

I don't want to let the moment pass.

"My momma sang," I say.

Ava turns, looks at me, and smiles. It's nice.

"You ain't gonna sing, are you?" The corners of her lips curl up into a devilish grin. "Just teasin'." She pokes me hard in the ribs. "But don't sing. Please."

I respond with a flat, "You're gonna needta forage me up some aloe for that burn."

I grin at her. I can't not.

She smiles. Again, sort of like you would a little kid. But I'll take it. Besides, there's something else there. Between us.

So I seize the moment. Sort of.

I would've, if when I lean in for the kiss, my elbow didn't slip off the table and launch me at her face, like some sort of pouncing mouth molester.

Ava lurches back, pushing her hands against my chest, half catching me, half shoving me. "Whoa, whoa, whoa. Easy there, tiger. What do you think you're doing?"

It just slips out of me before I can stop it, "Uh, seizing the moment?"

"Really. Kinda felt more like a seizure moment. I've seen epileptic puppies with more grace."

"My elbow slipped."

"Right, *that* was the problem."

She says it in this way that almost seems like she gets it. And kind of sympathizes. And once again the words just slip out of me without any sort of filter in place.

"Uh… so, should we change positions?"

She blinks at me blankly, and then with sympathy.

Shee't.

Ava sort of nudges, sort of shoves me off the edge of the booth.

I take the hint.

"This is not that," she says. "This is bedtime."

Ava goes over closer to the propped-open oven and lies on the far side of it. She points to the near side of it.

"Your side."

She then rolls over, facing away from me.

Which I appreciate. I'd rather not have her see me right now.

I slink my way to the near side and fetal up, facing away from her. Press my palms together under my cheek for a "pillow."

Luckily, the exhaustion still has a good grip on me and I can drift. But not before I can still register her muttering, "Pregger perv."

The moan makes its way into my dream. Eerie. Unsettling. The dream images and stories slip away, but the groaning sound persists.

I feel the shaking well before I really register it. Like the yank of an undertow, only quicker. Shorter, urgent tugs.

"Addie. Addie!"

I surface into night. Into Ava's embrace. Or the delusion of it. Until the world clarifies itself.

She ain't embracing me. Ava's knocking me awake. Wild eyes, a palm over my mouth, but no knife at my throat.

This time.

She must feel my awareness sharpen in the dark, 'cause she stops.

"Listen," Ava hisses in my ear.

I do.

Nothing. Not for a minute or two.

But then it comes.

A distant moaning. From somewhere. Out there.

And then it's gone.

I nod at her. I heard it.

She takes her hand away from my mouth.

The groan reaches out of the dark again.

"Is it…"

"I don't know. Could be. Or could be some animal," Ava says.

"It'd be a big animal."

"Like a wolf."

"Or a bear."

"It ain't a…"

We listen again. Just silence. Until the hollow, pained sound rolls down the street. It's muffled somehow.

"I think it's, like, coming from inside one of the buildings. Like it's not right outside," I whisper.

Ava nods. Still listening. Nothing comes for a bit.

She offers up, "It woke me a few minutes ago. But I don't know how long—"

This time the moan sounds like it's calling for help. Maybe.

"Was that a word?" I whisper.

"I can't tell. Coulda been. Or a cat. Caterwauling sometimes sounds like that."

"A cat that big would be…"

"A mountain lion."

I don't know which to root for, a person or a mountain lion. Both are their own special sort of bad.

Neither of us is particularly eager to go out and face whatever it is. At all. Let alone in the dark. So we wait.

For first light. So at least we can see what's what.

And maybe, in the meantime, whatever it is will just move on. Fade away and retreat to wherever it came from.

It doesn't. The misshapen moans continue for another hour or so. Until a gray dawn breaks.

It hasn't passed us by. Maybe it's waiting for us to pass it by.

Shee't.

"Do you want to wait it out or make a break for it?"

Ava considers my question. It's been at least five minutes since the last pained wail. We're positioned behind the counter, as far away from the door as we can be and still keep an eye on it.

She looks around the diner and considers the wall of plate glass facing onto Main Street. "This ain't exactly the Alamo in terms of defending."

"And I ain't exactly too keen on that kind of ending neither."

It isn't sarcastic or nothing. I'm way too scared for sarcasm.

"Right." Ava nods.

She's on edge, quiet. Calm. But on edge.

"We got the bikes in here with us. We could just slip out the back."

Ava shakes her head no for a while before giving an explanation.

"We haven't seen the alley behind. Maybe it's blocked. Maybe whatever it is, is back there. Or something else. Waiting for us to show ourselves."

She's thinking like prey.

She's thought like this before.

"Best we stick to Main Street if we wanna go that route. We've already seen it. Know the lay of the land better than any other option. There wasn't much that'd keep us from going hard in either direction," Ava thinks out loud. "Least there wasn't anything yesterday when we made our way into town."

Another inhuman wail calls out.

It stops us cold. Every time.

Whether it's a person or an animal, a trap or cry for help, it don't really matter. Whatever the case may be, it's all dangerous.

Ava digs through the backpack she packed an hour ago. She tosses me the Fish Mox Forte.

"Take your medicine," she whispers. "And one of these."

A Pop-Tart lands on the counter next to the hydration pack.

"You don't want to take antibiotics on an empty stomach."

As I open the bottle, Ava checks the shotgun magazine. I swallow the capsule and open the Pop-Tart, doing my best not to crinkle the tinfoil wrapper too loudly. I hold out one of the two tarts to her.

Ava's lost in some reverie though. She nods, having made a decision after a long conversation with herself, and heads towards the door.

I don't say nothing at first. I don't believe it.

She crawls into the booth, shimmies to the wall, and peeks her head up just enough that she can see out the window.

Her head twists this way and that, taking in both directions as best she's able from her vantage point. It reminds me of one of them National Geographic shows, where a startled antelope freezes on the savanna, save for its ears, which flick every which way, trying to get a read on whatever it is that tripped its instinctual fight-or-flight system into high gear.

Ava slides her way back away from the window to standing.

She scans the room, then turns back to consider the door and which way it opens. I can see her calculating the angle it opens at, to where it clears the back of another booth bordering the entrance. Ava follows the line with her eye to a couple of tables.

She waves me over and is already turning the first one on its side by the time I make it to her, nodding at me to turn the other. I follow her lead and push my overturned table on its side towards hers. Ava stops hers short so there's a two-inch or so gap where the now vertical tabletops make a corner.

She walks around and squats down behind them, peeking through the gap towards the door.

Ava re-angles my table slightly. Checks the gap again.

It finally clicks.

We just made an arrow slit.

Before I can consider the implications, Ava's already moving towards the door, pointing back behind her, to the arrow-slit cubby.

"Hunker down in there. Have the pistol at the ready."

"You're not going out there. Alone."

"Anything follows me in when I come back, shoot it."

"Ava—"

"Do NOT shoot me."

"Ava!" I hiss through my teeth as loud as I'm willing.

Ava stops, hand on the door handle.

"We don't know enough to make a good decision. I don't want to jump out of the frying pan and into the fire, but I also don't want to wait here for whatever it is to find us."

She gives me a second to take it in.

It makes sense. A calculated risk to balance out a bigger, unknown risk.

"Why don't you stay here and I go out?"

She almost laughs at that.

"Because last time I checked, knights in shining armor aren't wielding a bottle of amoxicillin. And also you seem to have misplaced your white horse. Now get over there. Please."

I draw my pistol and lie down on floor and rest the barrel across my forearm, sighting the door.

Another convulsion of squalls echoes down the street.

Ava waits it out, her grip tightening around the door handle.

"If something does end up giving me chase…"

"I won't miss."

She nods.

I nod back.

"Please don't leave me—" she's out before I get to "—here."

She keeps her hand on the door, closing it behind her, soft, silent. She waits.

Ava steps out across the sidewalk, towards the street. The top edge of the booths cut off the bottom two-thirds of her.

She waits again.

And the sound comes to greet her.

Ava drops out of view, into a squat.

I try to decipher any footsteps beneath the agony.

Nothing. Only the pain.

It finally subsides after what feels like hours.

Ava's head pokes into view as she rises.

Breath seeps out of me. I haven't been breathing.

Outside, it's clear Ava has homed in on the sound. It's towards the singed end of Main Street.

The shotgun barrel points the way for her, a sharp compass needle orienting on an unseeable pole of misery.

Ava follows the gun and disappears past the corner of the diner.

It's hard to put words to the waiting. The silence of the diner grows, closes in, and blankets everything.

That still gets me. The true quiet of everything nowadays. It's more pronounced in town. Context is king.

Before, in places such as here, there was always something, a din of white noise, electrical couplings, a bleed of music leaking out of headphones. A ticking clock.

Now there is just nothing.

But the aperiodic moans. Which you could not set a watch by.

The broiler burns orange still in the partially open oven. If I'm going to meet my end, at least I'll be warm.

It'd be better if there were a mist. Some sort of omen of a fog washing through the street. Like in the movies. A visual cue that could then at least validate the apprehension and disquiet of it all.

As it is, it's just another gray morning.

Birdsongs start to chirp through the air.

As if everything were like it always was.

All of which makes it worse. Wrenches up the unease of it all.

Come on, gimme something.

Otherwise… otherwise doubt questions whether any of it is real. I can't help but wonder if Ava just walked past the edge into some hallucinatory void.

Or if she'd ever even existed in the first place.

Of course she existed.

The cans of RC Cola and Pop-Tart wrappers litter the floor, monuments that bear witness to her existence.

The bellow sounds more mournful this time. Like a baby's bawling. Sharp. Momentary. Then gone.

Leaving behind a quiet distrust once again. Doubting it happened even though it only passed moments ago.

The pistol grows slippery with sweat.

I wipe my palm on my Sooners sleeve and reorient my sights on the door, which hasn't opened.

She could've left me.

It wouldn't be out of the realm of possibility. Would've been kind of smart, actually. Leave me sitting there as an offering. To buy time. To make her own getaway. Like that old joke, *I don't have to outrun the bear... I just have to outrun you.*

She had to leave the bike though. So as not to tip her hand. Set me into motion after her.

That'd slow down her flight.

But if whatever it was would be satisfied with the morsel of me, then worth it.

Unless she'd found herself another bike. Somewhere in town. Last night while she was foraging, and I was just lying here. Like a goddamn—

Ava brushes past the windows, quick with purpose. A trail of phantom essence, like dust motes, miraging behind her and coalescing into hardened reality.

The door clanks open.

And she's inside, already moving to the back. Not harried, but determined. I keep watch on the door, waiting for whatever might be following.

"It's in the bank," is all she offers.

I keep an eye on the door between casting quick glances her way as she disappears into the back room.

To check the alley?

Sounds of a methodical search fill the diner.

The urge to go back, to retreat from the arrow slit, to ask what's what... tugs at my spine. But the fear of what follows nails me to the floor, behind my barricade.

She's a blur of motion, stopping at the door only a moment with a—

"Wait and keep watch—" and then gone, down the sidewalk past the window, past the edge of existence once again.

Leaving me to try to piece together the bits of observation her brief visit provided.

The yellow rubber kitchen gloves.

The apron.

The serrated knife.

The dish towel hanging from where it was tucked in her waist.

The coffee filter held over her mouth with bits of duct tape.

The gun! She didn't have the shotgun with her.

It sits, useless, on the counter.

Apprehension gives way to a panic that drives me towards the door.

It's the howl that stops me.

Different from the others.

Like a release. That then cuts out. Mid-moan.

Then nothing.

When Ava comes into view again, her pace's slower.

The articles she left with have been shed away. Discarded. Out there. No gloves, no apron, no knife, no dish towel, no coffee filter.

She lets the door bang shut behind her. Makes her way to the counter. Retrieves the shotgun. Sort of leans back against the stool. She scratches at her face and finds a piece of duct tape still stuck to her cheek. Peels it off and rolls it between her fingers until it falls to the ground.

She seems surprised to find my gaze meet hers. Almost nods.

"We're good. We can go."

So we do. And we don't talk about it.

35

TAKING AIM

Through the waves of afternoon heat, I can just make out the movement round the other side of the brush.

A quick shift to the left. I hear her.

I soft step round, to the right. Put the falling sun behind me. All she'll see is blinding brightness curving around the black emptiness of my silhouette.

Her soft high-pitched tones of tiredness poke through the brush. Trying to shake off the disorientation of dawn.

I reorient. Quietly clip the arrow around the bowstring. Not a sound. Move with the wind.

Circle.

Circle.

Stop.

She moves away. Instinctively. It's just a feeling, though. She doesn't know I'm there. The last true sounds I made, I was by the bikes. Groaning and stretching out the kinks from the relentless ride away from Hexton.

Quick peek.

Retreat.

There she is.

I got her now.

Draw smooth.

The bow bends with anticipation. Hungry.

Exhale.

Sidestep.

Spot her.

Let loose.

The arrow *CLIP-FWAPS* away from the bow. A blur of motion. Outrunning the sound of itself. Outrunning the wind.

The arrow finds its mark and erupts into an explosion of feathers.

The grouse soars away out of the billowing plumage. It flies quickly into the cover of trees, well beyond range.

Apparently, all I did was a pretty good job of nicking it in the tail. A handful of feathers fall to the ground into a kind of shame circle.

"Shit."

"So Katniss you ain't."

I jump with a start. She hadn't made a sound tracking me.

I try to shrug off whatever she might've seen. "If everything is coming your way, you're in the wrong lane."

"Mm. You think, therefore you miss."

Turning around, Ava stands there holding a spool of fishing line she pillaged from Camo and Lace. She insisted on going back in before we left, against my protests. Said there were some odds and ends she wanted to pick up. That was how she put it, pick up some odds and ends. Like we was swinging through the Walmart, doing our Saturday errands. Still, I couldn't see myself to do more than shrug in protest.

"What's that supposed to mean?" It comes out way more accusatory than I'd meant it to. So I try to soften it with a, "I don't follow."

Ava doesn't look at me, just picks up a six-inch-long stick with a nub of a branch coming off it, and ties her fishing line around one end. Not sure if she's trying to avoid embarrassing me with the challenge of eye contact or if she just couldn't give less of a shit. This is the most she's said since Hexton.

"You need to try not aiming so much."

Ava pulls out some old earbuds she swiped, knots the wire into a slipknot noose, and ties that to the other end of the stick. All the while meandering over to a break in the bushes that leads down to the murmuring river behind the old factory.

"So *you're* an archer now?" That was supposed to come off aggressive, but sounds more defensive than anything else. "Or just playing offa the stereotype, Sacagawea."

I shouldn't've said it, I know, but she was banging me over the head with the war drum.

Ava picks up another stick, snaps off a small branch coming off it, and stabs the stick into the ground, branch nub pointed down. She steps on it to push it tighter into the earth. It stands there like a wooden abstract of a one-armed man. "Yeah, all of us tribe babies are born with a bow in one hand and a peace pipe in another."

"I knew it!" With a goofy grin and an exaggerated point of a finger, I try to pull us back from the nasty direction I had pushed us in.

Ava doesn't change course. She don't bristle, but she don't soften neither. Just reaches over and bends a nearby sapling downwards, ties the fishing line from her other stick to the sapling, about ten inches from its tip. The earbud wire noose dangles down. "No. But I read *Zen and the Art of Archery*."

She's shitting me. A book. Some froufrou Asian book on philosophy or religion or whatever is going to teach her, teach me about bowhunting grouse?! "Yeah, well, doing and reading's two different things now, ain't it."

She doesn't react like she's supposed to. Doesn't react at all. Doesn't even look at me. Too focused on pulling down on her tied stick, which bends the sapling in a sharp arc down to the ground, where Ava then hooks the noose-stick branch nub under the one-armed man stick she pegged into the ground.

It catches and holds.

Then real light, she pulls the earbud wire noose out into as wide a circumference as possible, lays it around some rabbit droppings that I hadn't even noticed. It loops right up against the two hooked sticks.

The "trigger." She just whipped up a hook-trigger sapling snare like she was tying a shoe.

Then without a word, Ava goes off deeper into the bushes, pulling an uncoiled, thin metal spring out of her pocket with one hand and grasping her spool of fishing line in the other.

And leaves me alone.

The wind blows through the leaves. I can't hear her at all.

"You need me to come with you?" I yell at the bushes downriver.

Her voice calls back to me from upriver, "Nah. You… should get us some firewood."

I want to say something back. Something sharp. But she has a point. We'll want a fire. Later. After we rest. So I can sterilize the water I collected.

I turn my back on where she was. Go over to the circle of feathers, pluck my arrow out of the ground, and half-limp my way back to the abandoned factory.

On the way, I come across an old well. Walls of layered bricks circle around its sides all the way down a good hundred feet or so. Bleached pink towards the top, deepening to coral crimson about halfway down, until all the color's just swallowed up into the black. Like staring down into the maw of a massive creature buried beneath the earth. At the bottom, a pool of blackness, save for at its center where a bright spot of sun reflects back, glaring redly out of the expanse.

There's no rope or nothing. No bucket. Just a deep beckoning.

I spit into it.

The gob disintegrates in the air on the way down, never even breaking the surface of that scarlet pupil.

. . .

The firewood clatters into a heap on the floor just inside the factory. Where we made "camp."

After Hexton, Ava's come around to my preference for places that were already abandoned and decayed before the scourge. The reason being these were sites people had forsaken long ago. They were disowned relics cast off from society when there was society. And as such, none of these shuffled-off shells would be sought out as asylums in the aftermath. What would be the point? Places like these had already been picked over, pulled apart, and left to sink into disrepair.

Worthless ruins would be our sanctuaries.

Our camp is just inside the old foundry. Far enough in that we can bask in the cool of its shade, but not so far we have to worry about the questionable "ceiling" that'd already opened up partly and blistered apart down towards the floor.

As it is, an old ceiling fan nearby droops precariously. All five of its blades sagging down in sharp curves, like a wilted flower, with limp-dicked, particleboard petals. Like it was depressed from disuse. Tired of the banality of it all, but not ready or not able to let go and give in to the fall.

A couple of quiet *pop, pops* call out of the wilderness beyond. Too quiet for gunshots. Ava must be snapping saplings or something.

I sit next to the bikes and get a fire going. Not for heat as much as convenience. Easier to do it in the light of day. Plus there's the added benefit of getting it going before Ava gets back and can make some "observation" about how I could light it up better this way or that. I'll just keep it small for now so as not to add to the surrounding swelter.

The trail of smoke finds its way out through an opening in the ruin of a roof. Past hunks of asbestos that hang out of abscesses in the walls. Rigid fibered puffs of toxic concrete cotton.

In a previous life, I'd be concerned. Truth is that concern would require longevity. So I don't bother. For sure, this entire place is toxic to one degree or another.

Just ask the folks from Picher. That town was the buckle of the mining belt. A lead gold mine. Made most of the US bullets for World

Wars I and II. And then finally took aim at itself. A dry lode chased away the mining companies and left behind nothing but piles and piles of chat for the townsfolk to choke on. What's effed is how they went back for seconds and thirds. Spurned the warnings, rejected the government buyouts to evacuate. A bunch of chat rats thumbing their noses at the world by cutting them off to spite their own faces. If any of them survived the Stripes, I bet they never even noticed the scourge in its wake.

Oklahoma's filled with stories like that. People who take pride in destroying themselves just because the world says that's a bad idea.

There's no worrying about that stuff anymore though. Long-term exposure would be a blessing at this point. It'd mean there'd be a long term.

I guess pride. Pride should still be a concern. Pride can do some damage both in the long and short term. Sure as shit drizzles from bad eggnog.

Ava sits down near the broken window. Leans back against an old, dried-out, upright piano.

Hadn't made a sound coming in. Undetectable as ever.

Useful goddamn skill.

Unsettling as hell, but envy worthy.

The spool of fishing wire peeks out of her pocket.

She rolls her head around, stretching her neck. At least we're both tired and achy. Not just me.

Ava reaches out and touches the brick wall, running her fingertips across one of the many pieces of graffiti that decorate this mausoleum of industry.

We wear the mask
That grins & lies
It hides our cheeks
& shades our eyes

Her hand drops.

She turns sleepily and looks my way. Like she just remembered I might be around.

"You got the fire going."

I nod. Not much to add to that one.

"Good. Won't have to bother with it later. After dark."

"S'what I was thinking."

She nods.

We hadn't stopped since Hexton. Not like we was on a tear or nothing. That would've somehow been admitting something neither of us wanted to acknowledge. But pushing through. At a dogged pace. With no breaks. And even fewer words.

She glances out the window. The scorched day blazes away, uncompromising. Turns back to the graffiti and quietly laughs.

"Yeah, I saw that one too," I say.

"It's a poem."

"No shit."

My sarcasm prods the slightest curve of a smile up from her.

"I mean a real poem."

"Like tiger, tiger burning bright and shit."

"And shit, yeah." She smiles at that. Not sure if she's smiling with me or at me. Take it either way. "The tigers are Blake. This"—she nods at the spray-painted verse—"is a Paul Dunbar poem."

I nod. Not about to ask who Dunbar is. Instead I just poke at the fire, turn the thickest hunk of burning kindling on its side. Flames reorient and find their way up, around, through.

Need to scooch back enough to escape the radius of heat. The tired takes me. I use a random brick as a "pillow" and lie back. Stare up out through the ceiling.

"So what is it that book of yours says is wrong with aiming?"

Ava takes in the question with a nod and leans her back against the piano. Closes her eyes.

"The basic idea of it is that aiming's just a distraction."

"Oh yeah, that makes perfect sense. Why aim when I can Jedi it?"

"Sort of. Like you're putting your attention on the target instead of the things you can control."

"Ok. Like what?"

"Like breathing, form, stuff like that. Results versus process, I guess."

That kind of makes sense. In a way. Like practicing free throws over and over, getting down the movement, the stance, the cadence, so come game time, it's just an action, not a thought.

"Hm," is all that comes out though.

36

HARE'S BREATH

The earsplitting screech snaps the two of us awake.

By the time I get the pistol up and pointed at where I think the noise came from, Ava's already in motion.

Bowie knife in hand, out into the heat through a hole in the wall.

Shee't. I follow after her.

A rabbit thrashes in her snare. A frantic frenzy of furry motion. Disoriented. Panicked. Kicking any which way it can, trying to afford itself some sort of influence on its direction.

I know how it feels.

The sapling bounces with every flinch. Flexible, but unyielding.

Ava pounces on the dangling bunny and in one fluid motion slits its throat. Its legs kick two more times. Then stop.

Blood pours out, abstract patterns in the dirt, which eventually blob together into a small pool of umber.

. . .

On a flat rock, next to the river, she splays out the body, stomach down.

"Maybe if we use my shoelaces next time, we can catch something bigger," I offer from my perch on a small boulder.

She pinches its hide at the base of its neck and cuts perpendicular to the spine. Then shoots me a questioning look.

"They're 550 paracord." I point at my laces.

Ava digs her index and middle fingers from both hands into the opening she cut, hooks them up under the skin. "Which is?"

"The rope they use with parachutes. It has a tensile strength of 550 pounds."

Ava pulls her right hand down towards the bunny's tail and the left up towards its head. The pelt peels away from the flesh beneath in a single piece that looks like a kid's onesie… moist with blood.

"Prepper thing?"

"Yeah."

Every few inches, Ava grabs up a little more hide to get a better grip on the furry onesie. She looks over at me.

"So, were you, like, wishing for all this?

With a sharp tug, she tears the fur off the right leg.

"What you mean?"

Tugs on the left leg. Fur still clings to both its feet. Contrasted against the exposed, naked leg muscles, the feet fur makes it look like the bunny's wearing socks.

"Just, I dunno." Ava wipes some sweat from her brow with her knife hand. "All that time spent prepping, weren't you kinda rooting for the whole new world order and shit?"

She yanks the hide from around the neck up to the base of its skull—

"No, I mean…"

And then cuts off the head, opens the sternum at the top, and pulls out the windpipe.

"I'm not judging," Ava says.

She grabs a socked paw in one hand, the skinned leg in the other, and snaps the foot off at the ankle.

"Just, like, how could you not?"

SNAP. Foot number two.

"You'd be a king of the chaos."

SNAP.

"Only here there's no one left to reign over."

SNAP.

"No, it's not… I just liked the outdoors stuff."

As I talk, she slips the blade inside each sock and cuts through the tendons and muscles.

"Survival," I say. "On your own. I guess I wanted things to be different. Is all. You know?"

"Who didn't?"

Ava tosses all the remains up the riverbank. She turns back to the carcass and delicately makes a small incision at the belly area.

"But not, like…" I gesture to the world in general. Nod up towards the abandoned foundry. "This ain't what I was—I wasn't hoping for this."

She slices open the chest cavity, lifting away the skin with two fingers, gently peeling it away from the intestines.

"I didn't think it'd be this…"

"Hard?"

"Lonely."

Ava digs her middle and index fingers into the chest cavity at the top, presses them all the way in until they hit spine, and in one smooth motion, pulls down, drawing all the innards out.

"I miss my momma."

At the water's edge, Ava cuts through the pelvic bone, clears out the colon, and cuts away the remaining rectal area.

"I miss mine too. And my dad. I always hated this shit," she says, tossing the handful of guts and colon downriver.

She places the mass of meat on a clean rock and plunges her bloodied hands into the water.

"When my dad would teach me—force me to 'learn the land or it'll learn you' traditional shit. It was just not my thing. I mean, I know he meant well, and like, it was how he could connect with me. But Christ, I dreaded those weekends with him."

Ava stands, wiping her hands on her pants. "I just wanted to read my books. Stupid of me." She puffs a stray bang of hair up out of her eyes.

"One of my survival books actually has a psychology chapter. But it's all about planning and small goals, enemy lines and PTSD… It don't say nothing about, you know, how to deal with…"

"Everybody dying everywhere?"

"Yeah."

"I guess how could it? How could someone know how to cope with that, let alone write about it?"

"I guess we could now."

"Yeah. 'Cept who'd read it?"

PART V

37

WHERE THERE'S SMOKE

Whiffs of grilled meat fill the air. Even up here.

I breathe it in. Savoring the scent of it. Relishing the sensation of my mouth watering. It'll be nice to eat something fresh, that wasn't dried, canned, or mummified with preservatives.

It's cooler now with the sun low behind us.

Also, being up above the trees makes it easier to catch the shifting twilight breezes.

Probably weren't the best idea climbing up here, considering the condition of the roof and all. But the clock tower wasn't part of the foundry's structure per se. It abutted it, like a medieval bell tower would a church. It was more of a mask than anything else, a rectangular façade hiding the smokestack within. The brick belfry seems to have done a better job holding its own against the elements over the years. Least the structure itself did. The staircase inside the tower that wraps around the outside of the smokestack has definitely rotted away in places. The steel platform up top, though, was good enough. Just had to steer clear of the rusty ulcer that'd eaten away abscesses in the metallic floor.

Still, I found a stable enough nook, wedged against a concrete ledge, my feet braced against the inside edge of a brick parapet.

The woodlands to the east thicken into heavier forested country. Route 70 cuts a clear swath through it all. That's our way forward. Follow it towards Idabel, grab the 259, and push on through Broken Bow into the western edge of the Ouachita Forest.

A current ripples through leafy treetops. It flows southwest all the way to the horizon, disappearing into the gloam, towards what used to be Paris, Texas. Down that direction, the air turns purple in expectation of the coming evening.

For now, tomorrow looks clear.

Swinging the monoculars west, the air shimmers into a bloodied sky hanging over Love County.

Flat clouds swab the crimson-stained heavens and silhouette a column of smoke billowing black in the foreground, set against the sanguine backdrop.

A column of smoke.

A single column.

Rises. And dissipates.

Smoke.

Several miles back.

The thin, black, solitary pillar leans in the wind. Towards us. In pursuit.

A signal.

Ava's slicing a small hunk from the sweating rabbit meat hanging from a spit over our fire. She blows on it before tasting. Like everything's as normal as cornflakes.

Honey, dinner's ready. Quit reading and put a hustle in that bustle!

All of this registers in a blur, crossing the foundry floor, navigating refuse and debris, accelerating at the fire.

By the time she pops the morsel in her mouth, I've kicked the glowing coals apart and am stomping on the lingering flames.

Ava steadies the teetering spit wedged into the ground, barely saving the rabbit from falling.

She gives me a look, but I ain't caught my breath yet.

"What's up, doc?" A solid Bugs impersonation.

Through heavy heaves of air, I manage a, "They're following us."

Her eyes darken. Her tone flattens with the question, "You saw them?"

Now she gets it. Now she understands me.

I nod. Still catching my breath. But spit out, "Their fire. A couple of miles back."

Ava processes. "You saw a fire."

"Smoke, from a campfire. Yeah."

"You saw *a* fire. How'd you know it's their fire?"

Always better to flinch than get hit.

"Who else could it be? Other than them."

Playing the odds, it'd be hard for it to be anyone else. Maybe. No telling for sure. Probability is a hard thing to predict these days. No real way to calculate the calculus of the apocalypse. Not without the plague of stats that mottled the wall of my hideaway back in the CC. But that was a world away. Comprised of only a local sample space of the destruction within a limited radius of caution. This, now, requires factoring all of Oklahoma. And the borderless beyond. Select the number of chances for it to be the very same three hunters stalking after us, and weigh it against the possibilities of it being any of the meager multitude of survivors who might be trailing our tracks. Or just happening across them. Or just happening. And I just happened to catch sight of them. Well, their fire.

Or maybe it's just a random little fire. The sun having caught just so in a refraction of glass and concentrated its focus on a particularly dry clump of dead grass. And then just continued to burn right there a larger clump of nearby hay, and only that hay so as to create a single column of smoke… instead of walls of it like any wildfire would. Odds were that weren't it.

Always better to flinch than get hit.

Ava turns and looks out a hole in the wall. Almost like she's expecting the three of them to be coming on over.

I can't help but look out too, even though I know better.

High grass bends and bounces with the evening's crickets.

I don't get it.

"There's no reason for them to be headed the same way as us. It ain't chance."

She doesn't acknowledge me. Just scrapes at the dried cuticle of her thumb with her index fingernail.

She's got to know I'm right though.

Ava shakes her head no. To herself? To me?

I don't get it. I don't know what it means. All of it.

"Stumbling upon us is one thing. But tracking us… I don't understand. I mean, they already got all of my shit. Even if they doubled back, found my body missing… Coulda been coyotes. Wolves. Anything, really.

"Even if they figured correctly that I was faking, that I got away. So what? I was naked, covered in feces, and running scared. What the hell else they want—"

"Me."

Ava lays the cooked rabbit on a nearby rock. She won't look at me.

"Whaddya mean, you?"

She finally looks at me.

"They want me."

"They don't even know about you. It was my camp. My stuff. They never saw you."

There's something about the way she's gone back to not looking at me. She cuts up the rabbit. Packs pieces into a couple of big green leaves she harvested. Methodical, plodding. Resigned.

That's when it clicks.

"It wasn't chance that they stumbled on us."

Ava shakes her head.

Shit, please don't let me be right.

"You already had dealings with them?"

Ava uses the back of her knife hand to push her hair out of her eyes.

"It was me that gave Fish that limp of his. Well, one of my traps."

My knee throbs at the mention of her traps.

"Fish…"

"Albert Fish. He's the lead asshole—"

"Yeah. I know who he is—"

She wraps up one of the leaves around a pile of rabbit meat. Catches sight of me. Looking at her belly.

"You were… They, uh—did they…"

Her breath catches, but she forces it out in a sharp exhale. Like she needs to be empty of everything before she can bring herself to say anything about this.

I can't help but glance west. The scarlet sky has scabbed into night.

"They caught me at the OTSA. Took me with them. It was a month before I finally got away. Then they tracked me for a while. Then they stopped. Thought I had finally lost 'em by hiding out in the wildlife reserve. They were better scavengers than survivalists. That wasn't the place for them. But even in the apocalypse, people can't resist a good fireworks show.

I don't say nothing. Don't know what to say.

"Is one of them the daddy?"

Ava finishes wrapping up the other pile of rabbit meat in leaves. She stands, hands me one leaf-wrapped meat bundle, and heads for the bikes.

"Told you, he's dead. We should get going."

Like it was cornflakes.

It works though. I head to my bike.

"Yeah. Keep moving, keep putting miles between us." I nod at the bikes while getting on mine. "We should be able to outdistance them in no time."

We saddle up and head out.

38

PUSH

Running somehow feels better. Feels right. Provides direction. Purpose. In its absence, the pace of things can linger. Doubts have time to catch up and reorient a whole way of thinking. Wonder at the point of it all. Picking a destination, making a plan, setting it into motion. All fueled by the embrace of a delusion that *there must* be better than *here*. If only to be there. But over time, as more theres cross over into heres, their mystique and promise wears thin.

Too much freedom. Too many options. The infinity of it tugs in too many directions. Frays the edges of self. Until any surety of self completely unravels in the expanse of it. The emptiness distorts and dements the truth of things. Exposes that there actually is no truth of things. Just things. Whether we observe them or not. Things and no things.

Do your homework.

Clean your room.

Eat your vegetables.

Be a good boy.

The pillars of a meaningful existence.

What happens when they crumble? Too long laid bare to the abrasive, hollowing void?

Then there is only your thoughts and choices. With nothing to guide you but shadows through a deep black cave.

It makes sense, why we used to see omens in everything: the sight of vultures from the left, the cry of a heron, the pattern of sacrificed entrails pooling beneath an altar, shooting stars, eclipses… anything to help augur our way through the mean meaninglessness of it all.

Desperation yields divination.

The gods know better. The gods know. There's something to know.

Science was supposed to lead us up Mount Olympus. We could carry ourselves to the heights of enlightenment. Knowledge would save us.

Killing god, though, left us adrift. Floating through an existential hell. We thought hell was other people.

We thought.

Hell is this.

Hell is emptiness.

Killing god also pissed him off. His wrath was buried with him. Left and forgotten, but not gone. Locked and latent. Hibernating through the ages. Waiting. For us to break through. And rouse it from its slumber.

Science was supposed to save us.

I don't feel saved.

I feel certain. Running gives me certainty. It feels better running than not running. I don't share any of this. Don't say a word. Just pedal with purpose.

The moonlight streaks silver on the blacktop of road slick with evening dew.

We don't talk.

Just listen to the hum of our tires in rhythm with our labored breathing syncopated by the back and forth of the weapons rocking in their duct-tape bike holsters. All bathed in a whitewash of crickets.

Miles roll past. We drive ourselves hard. Sweat clings to us against the chill, dark air. Ava keeps needing to stop. To pee.

We push on. Not through the whole night. Just until well enough has been left behind.

Finally, after our fourth pee break, we make camp without fire, nor water. Behind a roadside fried-pie joint. Single-story, redbrick, gray-shingled roof. The whole place smells of burnt cherries and caramelized apples. Before, it would've been a heavenly scent. The way things are now, it's a hellish, mocking reminder of our lack.

The restaurant stands as a barrier between us and the road.

The bikes rest against the wall, at the ready. We lie hidden in the moon's shadow, behind a rusted dumpster angled against the wall.

The dark woods behind the pie joint stir with nocturnal sounds. The underbrush has begun to invade the parking lot, where a service road snakes its way up to connect with the blacktop.

It's why we chose this spot. Proximity to an escape route.

Lying there, waiting for sleep, I wonder at my paranoia.

It might've been them.

It might've been someone else.

Who's to know?

Either way, it's to be avoided.

The heat of exertion dissipates. Sweat catches cold in the night breeze. It shivers through me.

Ava shifts on the gravel.

She bumps along the length of me.

Back to back, we kindle what warmth we can between us.

I shudder.

She scoots closer. And the shudder settles.

The next day is more of the same: silent miles punctuated by quiet pit stops. The fish medicine's worked its magic on me. And the kinks've shaken loose from my dinged knee.

As such, her pace has become more and more… apparent.

In spite of the frigid chill at night, the heat still rages throughout the day.

We rest on the outskirts of some forgotten town, tucked into the shade of a bowling alley. Finish what remains of the rabbit. Pass the hydration pack between us.

We share an unspoken strategy, stick to the asphalt. Cement don't leave no tracks.

Come late afternoon, we settle on a farm for the evening's "shelter."

Ava sets snares.

I climb the silo. Scan the sunset with my monoculars for any semblance of pursuit.

There's no smoke. No telltale dust clouds of any posse giving chase. Just a ruddy sky and the flutter of barn swallows and bats picking insects out of the evening air.

The coast is clear. For all I can tell.

Maybe it always was. How would they've tracked us anyhow? Along highways, twists of concrete junctions, miles of monolithic pavement unmarred by footprints of any sort. By smell would be the only way. Scent being the only remnant for them to follow.

Don't make no sense.

Neither do the murmurs neither. Words on the wind. So it seems. So it sounds. My ears play tricks on me. Even if it were so, from this height, miles apart, there's still no way for whispers on breezes to reach.

I ignore the ghostly susurrations.

By the time I make it down, Ava's already dozing in the crib barn. She's found an old horse blanket and wrapped herself up in it. Behind her, another sits rolled up and waiting. For me.

I sit down behind her and use it for a headrest to lean back against the stable wall.

In her sleep, Ava scooches back into me.

. . .

The snares are empty in the morning. All except for one that's a bloody mess. Whatever it was we caught, some other animal made an easy and gory feast of it. And left behind what looks like a small crime scene.

The discovery barely gets a shrug out of us. It's ok. Not like we'd want to light a cooking fire anyway.

The sun blazes overhead. More miles of road roll pass as heat waves undulate up from the asphalt. The wheels hum along in a more muffled tone as they get sticky against the baked blacktop.

Around noontime, Ava cramps. Her bike wobbles beneath her as she cups her belly.

An overpass crossing a creek gives us some respite.

I soak my shirt in the water and walk it up to where she sits, forehead resting on her bent knees, sitting in an upright fetal position.

I rest the wet shirt across the back of her neck.

Relief wheezes out of her.

Ava's hand clasps against it and squeezes streaks of cool out of the soaked shirt.

She sees my look and does her best impression of me, "It's hotter than a goat's ass in a pepper patch."

"Well, look who's turning redneck in the sun."

She smiles and nods. As much as she's able.

For the rest of the afternoon, Ava dozes beneath the overpass.

I pick dandelions and some wild anise stalks.

"You picking me flowers now?"

She made it awkward. Well, awkwarder. I was just trying to hand her the dandelions. But her hesitation has me standing there in a way that makes it like I'm presenting them to her, like a bouquet or something.

Even in the torrid afternoon, I can feel the heat rising to my cheeks.

"What? No. I mean, yeah, but not like that. Not <u>not</u> like that. Just, for the baby. Dandelions are good for you. Prenatal shi—prenatally and all. Vitamins A and C, iron, calcium, potassium. You make a tea out of it, or a salad…"

For a second, she seems to soften. She takes the dandelions from me. Even smells the yellow flowers.

She looks up the open creek bed. It widens, creating a rift in the brush. On either side, former farm fields turn feral and stretch out flat.

"Hm. When I was younger, like your age, I used to imagine a date like this, like sort of the perfect date, a picnic out in the open, totally exposed, yet completely alone and intimate."

I don't know what to say. I don't think she means that this is like a date.

"A salad?"

I nod. I know how to respond to that. "My momma useta make 'em for patients she worked with."

Ava takes a tentative nibble of one leaf and cringes.

"You'd better pick me a bouquet of salad dressing too."

39

COLD SHOULDER

The wall of the old school craters open in concrete cankers. Cinder blocks jut a ragged line around the opening, like a set of bad teeth.

We don't even bother hunting for a door. Just step our way through the lesion, popping the bike wheels up and over rubble. On the far wall, a stenciled motto reads: *It is easier to build children than to repair broken men.*

It'll do.

Silver lining about Oklahoma, ain't no scarcity of abandoned and decayed buildings for us to take refuge in.

Ava don't bother setting snares. Light's fading and we already found ourselves some meat.

A couple of miles back, we'd come across a kill in an old livestock meadow off of the road. A pack of wolves had taken down a heifer sometime earlier that day. The pack of them lounged in a sated semicircle around the felled cow. Bellies engorged, fur stained in dried red clumps and dangling hunks of viscera.

Fattened and feasted, they didn't put forth any true resistance to us waving our arms, clattering our bikes, and making a generally aggressive ruckus. The wolves wavered and loped in larger and larger loops until they finally relented and gave berth to us.

I kept circumscribing the kill astride the bike, hooting and shooing. They squatted low in the distance and watched, occasionally turning a head to the side at my hullabaloo.

In the meantime, Ava took out her Bowie and carved us off some steaks. There was still plenty of meat. Wolves tend to consume organs first and leave muscle for later. The flesh was fresh enough we didn't need to worry.

Still, neither of us was too keen on steak tartar.

Ava chews on a wad of dandelions and watches me make the fire. I get everything set inside and out, traversing back and forth in the waning purple hues of last light.

We wait for the black to settle in. Confident our fervor of flight has rendered us alone once again, still bears out to have caution. Another shared unspoken strategy: only fire up blazes come dark and smother them down before daylight. That way smoke just adds to the night and gives nothing away.

Ava stares as I spark the fire awake, puffing it into a crackling frenzy. Once it's going good, I draw a brand out of the raw fire and carry it outside.

Ava follows.

We circle around back to where the second pile of firewood waits, next to our bikes and gear. I slip the red, coal-tipped branch inside the teepee of sticks and brush it against the fibers of dried seed pods.

The tip glows angrily as I blow on it. It coaxes flames out of the desiccated husks. They lick up through the teepee and take root.

We cook our steaks and eat like cyclops kings.

Feasting on a wolf's dinner, we almost feel human again.

Except for the dandelion tea. Which tastes like green, bitter awful.

. . .

After eating, I trudge back into the school and poke, turn, and feed the decoy fire inside. By the time I get back, Ava's finished snuffing out our cooking fire.

She shivers. The nights are cooling more so now. It's better when we have a fire to huddle against the chill.

"So eastern Oklahoma's a bipolar bastard that gets cold as hell at night, check."

I squat down next to her and settle into my best drawl, "It's like a brass toilet seat on the shady side of an iceberg."

Ava laughs and elbows me in the ribs.

Through a gash in the wall, I can see shadows flicker away from the decoy fire still blazing within.

Ava shakes her head at it. "Who in hell ever heard of a decoy fire?"

"That's why it's genius."

With a stick, I hockey a couple of large stones I'd put in the fire and nudge them into holes we'd dug.

Ava kicks a thin layer of dirt over them. Voila, hot stone beds.

I lie back over my buried hot rock, in our fireless camp, hands beneath my head, self-satisfied for sure.

She grunts and lays herself down over her own hot rock spot.

The ground beneath holds tight to the warmth of the stones, but the air above has lost all heat from the day. It ripples shivers across the top of us. A brief chatter of teeth.

Ava scoots her backside against me.

Could be accidental. Just her shifting around, trying to get comfortable. Could be her trying to trap more of the warmth between us.

The proximity of her's paralytic.

Ava reaches back, grabs my far arm, and pulls it over her, dragging me onto my side.

Big spoon.

Little spoon.

"Now maybe you'll stop shiverin' like a dog tryin' to shit a peach pit. You good?"

I snort. This ain't nothing. No, sir, ain't nothing at all. Be casual.

"Uh, erm, yeah. I'm ok."

Real casual like. Casual and cuddling. For warmth. Yes. Just casual cuddling.

Her body relaxes as she drifts off.

Not mine.

No.

Wired, wide eyed and woke as a deer in headlights.

With my pulse hammering away in my eardrums, like a marching band on meth.

She tucks in. Slightly. Closer. Wraps her arm around mine. And pulls us tighter.

Tripping the trigger…

And I shoot my hips back.

Away.

Put space between us.

"Stop twitching."

Ava scoots back hard in rebuke.

Terror takes ahold as her body tenses with recognition, recoiling her hips and hindquarters away—

From me.

"Jesus Christ on a stick. Are you kidding me?!"

"No, no, I, uh—" Just casual?

She spins and glares me in the eye.

"Biking to kingdom come, running from god knows what, sick as a dog and eating like one, all while it's cold enough to freeze the balls off a pool table, and you're getting a goddamn boner!"

"No, I'm not. I didn't." Real casual like.

Ava looks at my crotch. Then at me.

The dark can't do much to hide my pan handle.

"I didn't mean, I wasn't trying nothing… I just, couldn't help it." At least my voice cracks when I plea. So that's awesome. And casual.

She keeps glaring.

I keep not making eye contact.

We sit there.

A breeze blows through the space between us. Cold and unconcerned.

Ava shakes her head. “Turn over.”

“What?”

“Turn. Over.” She swirls her finger around in the air, like she’s explaining to a simpleton to roll over. “Turn over and point your pecker wood the other way.”

It takes a second to register still. But it’s a relief to oblige, roll over, and lie facing away from her.

Not looking at her looking at me is a welcome arrangement.

I can hear her hesitating.

But she finally lies down.

And spoons me.

Little spoon.

Big spoon.

Boner.

Just go to sleep. Just let it go and go to sleep.

“Stupid teenage hornball,” Ava mutters into my neck. “Harder than a choirboy in a porn shop.”

She sort of sits up and looms at me. I think. I refuse to look.

“You even try to roll over and I’ll knee your balls so hard you’ll be sneezing cum.”

You’d think that’d put a dent in the erection.

It doesn’t.

But I don’t even breathe in her direction.

I don’t move at all.

Ten years pass in a minute. Ava moves closer again. Pressing against my back. Her arm rests on my ribs.

It’s ok to relax again—

“Don’t fart none neither.”

My asshole torques so tense I can feel my scalp move.

“Us freezing in the woods and you decided to go and pitch yourself a little tent.”

She laughs herself to sleep with that one.

I stay up a while longer.

Waiting for the humiliation to subside. Deflated.

I dream Deer Woman dreams again. She's not there. Just the weight of her is. Pinning me down where I lie, outside the school, pressed against the wall. I am asleep but awake to the world. To the crackle of the decoy fire within. To the chill of the dark. To the rustle of the wind in the trees.

Awake to the black pack of shapes flickering soundlessly as smoke in the profound dark beyond the edges of moonlight. Slinking, skittering. Catching scents of shadows in the night.

They scamper between the breezes. Circling downwind. Shuffling, raspy shades salivating with anticipation.

Closing in with the dark.

And I can't move.

The Deer Woman has paralyzed me once again. Staked me to the ground. Like a butterfly. No. Like bait. As they sniff the air. Catch the sweet scent of my panic. Their maws watering with want, hungering for a taste of the fear. They approach.

Hot, feral breath warms my neck against the cold night air. As they slip in—

And I shatter out of my frozen block, into movement. Snap up finally. Tension, wakefulness, cold. Hair on the back of my neck at attention.

It was a dream. It was nothing. Phantasms.

The heat from our hot stones has been swallowed up by the earth.

The decoy fire has retreated to a dim red glow inside the school.

And Ava is missing. Her bike is still here.

A twig snaps. In the woods.

I'm already moving. Pistol out. Ears radaring.

A patter in the dark draws my aim. There's nothing there. Keep moving.

Another soft crack from deeper into the trees.

I stalk the sound, using the pistol barrel to divine the way through the black. Light footfalls through the underbrush so as not to give away my own position. Snaking each step out in front of me, into the ink, to navigate rocks and roots. Light steps. Light steps. Light steps.

To a fallen tree. Against which huddles a fetal form.

Ava!

"Holy—Jesus effing Christ! What are you doing?!" Ava stands. Tugs up at her pants. Buttoning.

She's ok. She's ok. She was—

"Stop watching!"

I turn away. Lower the gun. Humiliated. Panicked. In an altogether different way.

"I wasn't watching. I heard something."

"Yeah, the sound of me peeing. Is that what you heard, freak show?!"

"No, the Deer Woman—"

"Jesus, how many fetishes have you got going on, pervert?"

"I was dreaming. I was, scared. Sorry."

I rush away. Back into the woods. Into the dark. Where I can hide from her accusing glare.

And find myself face-to-face with a different set of eyes. Narrower, glimmering out of the black. Its lupine gaze clocking me.

Soft, panting sounds give rise to a low, threatening growl.

It's a wolf. The snarl moves in, closer.

Pushing me back, retreating, one step. Two steps.

"No." Her voice is sharp. Back a ways. "Don't run. Running is what prey does. We don't want to be prey."

I nod.

The eyes blink. The snarl grows.

"It's testing you. Looking for weakness."

I nod again. And slowly raise the pistol. Towards the eyes.

"Addie…"

As she says it, the shape flickers in my periphery. Surges of gray smoke barreling towards me.

From the left. From the right. From everywhere. The pack.

I turn and fire a shot into the left shadows as a mass of inertia collides and scrapes against my back, knocking me to the ground.

I roll with it. Tossed around in a fury of fear, fang, and fur. Ava rushes in from somewhere. Tall, screaming loud, waving her arms, and swinging a heavy branch, like a club. Connecting with something that yelps. And tagging me on the backswing.

"Get up, get up, get up," she yells at me. "Be tall. Like a bear!"

I veer up to standing, screaming, yelling. Firing off two more shots…

At the dark. At the night. At nothing.

They're gone.

Shadows in the night.

Search the black. Catch a breath.

Back outside the school.

Back against the wall.

Disoriented by the dark. But sore, still, from fighting specters in the penumbra.

Ava sleeps to my left. The Deer Woman sits to my right, smoking a ceremonial pipe.

I'm up the rest of the night. Pistol in hand, still warm from firing. Waiting for another test.

40

BUTTON

Relief rises with the sun. Riding's a welcome exertion to steam the chill out of our muscles. And the silence that accompanies it, a mercy. We cruise at a good clip, but not an urgent one. Momentum has lessened. It's been days without any omens rising behind us. Either our evasion was successful or unnecessary. Regardless, it felt ok to ease up.

The slope of the world seems to dip ahead of us and rise in our wake.

When you lie down in a field, can you still feel the curvature of the earth?

Our path took us into Kiamichi Country, through juniper woods alive with birdsongs, past the roar of dammed reservoirs, across a rusted five-span bridge held together with oxidized pony trusses.

I consider what it would take to light the whole thing up and burn it down. Rusted as it is, the steel would hold out nonetheless. Maybe with enough oil I could get the tarred road to take. But that'd mean finding enough oil. And transporting it. Even then mostly all that would happen is a towering mushroom cloud of black smoke announcing to the nearest six counties, Here we are! And when it finally burnt down, the bulk of its steel skeleton would still remain, as crossable as ever. Maybe not by car. But crossable. Burning a bridge is more work than you'd think. And way more effort than it's worth.

The bike wheels hum against the asphalt, cruising down lonely sandstone hills, along coastal plains, around lakes where leaves and sand pattern natural collages across the road.

We ride through narrow back ways, flanked by bogs and draining tributaries. Two tufted titmice swoon past, carrying a shed snakeskin between them.

For a while even, a Mississippi kite hawk tracks above. Swooping down twice, warning passes to evaluate the degree of threat we posed. Establishing the pecking order in this new world. Testing us for weakness, maybe, like the wolves.

We ride on. Into the dark crescent shadow of the Winding Stair Mountains. Sucking air as the land rises towards the Bok Tuklo range.

Ava's hair trails behind her, floating back on the funneled wind of the valley. She sways and swerves her bike across the pavement, carving out playful swerves of childhood.

Once the sun peaks past its apogee, Ava slows. As we pedal past a small reservoir, she drops pace until she's even with me.

As a general rule, I give her the lead. Let her set the pace as she will, so as to not push her beyond the demands of the little one leaching away at her from the inside.

Little's been said for most of the day. Little need. We have a direction. And a purpose.

And a we.

I nod at the distant shore, where a bear hunkers in hunt at the mouth of the creek feeding the impounded water. Driven by instinct, it approached the creek "downwind" of the sun, so its shadow leans back, uncast over the water it surveys. The bear stands to assess where the rough white water rushes across the entry to the lake before settling into a reflective calm.

It's downright bucolic.

Pleasant almost.

"So how far you ever gotten?" Ava breaks the silence.

I hesitate to tell her, but reckon at this point it don't matter. We've already come this far.

"Never been to Ouachita."

You think this summer I can go work with Uncle Izzy?

I'll talk to him about it. You might still be too young for forest ranging all the way over in Ouachita. I'm worried that maybe you're too worried. You know, 'bout the end of the world and all. I mean, it's ok to just be like everybody else sometimes, Addie.

"No." Ava shakes her head, sort of smiling, sort of rolling her eyes. "I mean with a girl. You a virgin?"

The question knocks me off balance, and I near about veer into a gulley. "What? I… Oh."

I ain't going to lie, it comes out real awkward. I do my best to cover.

"No. I'm, you know a gentleman don't kiss and tell."

She don't miss a beat. "So that's a yes to virgin."

I accelerate out ahead of her a few yards.

"Pshh. Look, I ain't one to brag—"

"'Cause you ain't got nothing to brag about."

"—but I get more ass than a public toilet seat in Times Square."

With her interrupting, I end up talking over her. So when she stops before me, that last bit ends up coming out super loud.

The echo of it bounces back at us for good measure. Leaving behind an awkward silence in its wake.

"So that's gross."

I literally and figuratively start backpedaling.

"No, I mean, I'm not a he-whore or anything—"

"Not you, idiot. Your metaphor."

It takes a second to parse. When I do, I still don't manage much more than, "Oh."

"Jesus, you're green." She doesn't say it judgy, just disbelieving. Which is bullshit as far as I'm—

"I ain't green. I know my way around the infield."

"Oh really, where's a girl's button at?"

"Right beneath her clitoral hood." Boom! Science bomb. I aced my anatomy test.

Ava laughs so hard she has to brake to a stop and stand.

I skid into a slide and stop. I don't get it.

"What?! I'm right. Right at the top of her—"

"Clitoral hood!! Seriously?!"

There's more laughing on her part.

"Where did you learn that?"

Screw this. I know I'm right. I know. I stand up on the high pedal, lean into motion, and keep biking.

Not before leaving her with, "Shut up."

Shut up. Well zinged, Addie. Well, zinged. Indeed. You know what though, sometimes it ain't about what you say as much as how you say it. And I said it like I meant it. Yessir.

Ava takes a few more moments to finish up laughing before she finally bikes on after me.

She calls out, "I'm just teasing."

I don't slow down. But I don't speed up neither. She pulls up alongside me.

"It's… accurate—" she offers.

Shut up.

"—and sweet—"

Please shut up.

"—in a gynecological sort of way."

We bike on.

I know it's accurate. I know I was right. I know. I don't need her approval of my knowledge.

"I read an article." My knowledge is bona fide.

Wouldn't you know it, she breaks out laughing again, even bigger this time. And practically veering off the road into a ditch herself.

"SHUT UP!"

"Sorry, sorry. I'm sorry. For real, Addie."

She sounds it. But I don't—

"It's good you're such an experienced reader."

"You—" I kick it into high gear and pull away. Need space to find a good closer… "—suck!" That was all I got.

Ava gives chase, still running her mouth.

"Dear *Penthouse* forum—"

"Shut up. Oh my god, SHUT UP!!!"

The angrier I get, the more she laughs. Until she can hardly breathe at all.

"Wait, wait, wait. Stop, stop, stop, stop, stop!"

She almost sounds like she's in pain.

"What?!"

I stop.

She stops next to me.

I don't want to look at her, but I check just to see that she's ok. She's looking right at me. Hunting for another weak spot, I'm sure, so she can just jump up and down on it.

"Seriously though. Like, what base?"

Are you kidding me?! I turn and stare off, up the incline of the road ahead, looking for where I can ditch this—

"Addie…?"

Ava places her hands on both sides of my head. Turning my chin 'til I finally relent and look back at her.

I give her a *What?* look.

"Come here."

She pulls lightly at the back of my jaw, leaning towards me.

By the time I figure out what's going on, I'm too stunned to do anything about it.

She kisses me.

Her lips soften with warmth. The heat of her breath blows back across my cheek. She tightens and purses her mouth around my bottom lip, tugging it down, pulling apart an opening just wide enough so the flicker of her tongue can dance past my lips and trip a shiver of sensation down my insides.

I want to melt into her.

My entire self is nothing anymore but the pressure of her lips on mine and the excitement within my tongue as it rises to meet hers and slip into—

Ava pulls back, takes in the realization of me, and stops it cold.

"That's enough."

And then she bikes off. Ahead.

Leaves me reeling like I just got ate by a bear and shit off a cliff.

There ain't nothing I can do. And even less I can say. Other than,

"Fuuuuuck!"

41

CLEAR

From the top of the fire tower, it's a good ten miles or so of visibility. From the Cross Timbers north to the flats, no traces of smoke. Tracking the monoculars across the western horizon, all is clear. No signs of men. No omens of portent. Just distant storm clouds.

On the climb down, I try not to look Ava's way. She's off peeing. Again. Baby must be leaning on her bladder with both elbows, the way she's leaking.

Next town, I need to remember to stalk a store for some ACE bandages or the likes thereof. Try to rig up a belly band for her. Momma used to make those too for her patients. Salads and belly bands.

It's just a weight off a woman's shoulders... but lower. She'd laugh, explaining as she helped her client put it on.

Oh my god, it feels soooooo good. Like I can finally breathe and maybe even sneeze without peeing myself, one of her younger clients would say.

Pregnancy isn't no walk in the cake, but this does help lighten the load, or at least shift it.

I gaze off down the road behind us, averting my eyes as Ava makes her way back to me. Give a cough just to make sure she knows I'm down, and gets everything button upped and battened down. The gratuitous cough catches though and morphs into a small, but real coughing fit.

"Entire world's been killed off by the Stripes, and you're milking a cold."

"With all four teats."

"Big baby."

"Least I ain't peeing like a nervous puppy."

"I'm peeing for two."

I laugh at that.

When she's close, I give a nod up at the water tower. "No sign of 'em. I think we're good. I wouldn't even know how you track a bike on asphalt."

She comes up alongside and gazes back. Wrinkles her nose. Maybe with worry. Maybe with allergies.

She nods.

"Uncle Izzy… he was a marine marine or like a medic or administrator?"

"Marine marine. Killed nine people."

"Ready to keep going?"

"Is a bear Catholic?" Another of Momma's greatest hits.

Ava tilts her head at that. "Only if the pope shits in the woods?"

We push on tirelessly in spite of our tired. Through fields, along the edges of outskirts, stopping at a ruin of a drive-in movie theater. The fallen screen, tiled apart in its collapse; some of the larger bits bulge up in certain places, where speaker poles tent it up from the ground.

Ava and I, shoulder to shoulder, sit on the ground, leaning against the chipped Formica counter in the shade of the concession stand. Between our splayed-out legs, a persistent box of ketchup packets gives us a taste of nostalgia, maybe a few calories, and a whole lot of thirst.

Have a Coke
Refresh Yourself
Ice Cold
Drink
Coca-Cola
Sign of Good Taste

Ava splatters a drained ketchup packet against the rusted, janky soda fountain. She drains another packet, pulling it through her teeth, tosses this one at the dangling menu board.

HA BURGER $1.50
CHEESEBURGER $1.75
BARBECUE $2.00
FISH ANDWICH $2.50
STEAK $2.50
CHIL DOG $2.50
H D G $1.50
O
FR NCH F IEN
ONION I
R
N AC S
ICE R AM 1

"I'd skin a sack full of puppies for a Coca-Cola," I say.

"I'd punch a baby for a milkshake."

My jaw actually drops with that one. "Wow. Just… wow."

Ava laughs.

"What? I've been craving one ever since we got here."

"It's French fries for me."

"Mm. French fries dipped in milkshake."

I laugh.

"I'm ravishing."

"What?" Ava asks.

“It’s something my momma useta say. When she was hungry.”

“Ok. Because she was pretty?”

“Because you were supposed to hear what she meant, not what she said.”

Her knuckles touch the back of my hand resting on the ground near the box of ketchup. I try not to move. But not obvious like. Like subtly stay still. It seems stupid. Our shoulders are already bolstering us both upright. But that’s more of a necessity at this point.

The hand contact’s more, unnecessary. And intense. In an exhausted sort of—

“You wanna shove on?” Ava’s already getting up.

Damnit.

“Yeah. Maybe find some water.”

Cascades of white water spill like salt over a massive rock cliff, raining down into the emerald pool. On the far side, the chill of the green water ripples against our shins.

It’s there, in elm shadows, on a mossy boulder, we wait out the afternoon burn.

Her arms hyperextend behind her, palms pushed into the soft moss, contemplating the waterfall. She’s put her hair up in a bun so as not to trap any hot against her neck.

I squirm and stretch next to her, trying to adjust the sore out of my posture. Intertwining my fingers and reaching up with my palms in one direction and jutting my ribs out in the other, then switching, then back…

Then letting go, stretching my arms slowly out and down. And then with one arm, reaching behind her, maybe cup my hand over her shoulder? Or slip it in the space between her arms and her back? Curl around the small of her back? No, that’s too intentional. It needs to be more happenstantial.

I just let it fall lightly to her far shoulder, not really hanging, more hovering, but my hand definitely resting on her shoulder.

Least for a second. Not even. Before she shifts forwards and sluffs off my hand like a clump of dried mud.

Ok.

So that didn't work.

Ava leans into me.

I don't move, just flex every muscle I need to in order to bear her weight and not give her any reason to shift away.

We stay like that a good minute or ten. Taking in the waterfall, the soothing roar of it, the ripples, the cool shade. If it weren't the apocalypse, it'd be paradise.

"How much further, you figure, to Ouachita?" she asks.

"I dunno, we got maybe six to eight more hours."

"Let's push through." She turns her head up to look at me, still leaning on my shoulder though. "Unless you need to rest more?"

"It's nice here."

"Mm." She nods against me.

I scratch my nose against the top of her head. "But I'm good. If you're good."

Ava pulls her feet out of the water. "I'm ok to keep going."

"Well, ok then." I pull my feet out.

42

CROSSING

The way is slow. A relentless and tiring incline resists approach all the way until the road tees to an end at the river.

Wide, brown, opaque water. Braided through the land like hemp. Or woven wood. The current ripples and vibrates with motion, but there's a permanence to the topography of it. The flow of it bulging and dipping, a frozen, enduring waterscape. With a stillness to its movement. Like a standing wave.

Ava coasts up alongside. Stops. A-framing her legs out from the bike to take in the view of the river at the end of our path.

On the far side, across the water, craggy woods tuft up steep cliffs. Massive rocks rise and jut up out of the earth, a single-sided gorge.

The road that tops our T runs north-south, parallel to the river.

Ava takes in both directions.

"So which way?"

She's still breathing heavily with exertion. And exhaustion.

I pull out the survey maps.

"If we're where I think we are... we'll have to head up a ways to the bridge and then backtrack."

Ava takes in the rising hill of the northern route ahead of us. Sounds like she sighs.

"You… ok?"

Ava steps up onto the higher of her pedals and descends with it as her bike rolls into motion. "I'd be better if you moved faster than a herd of turtles moonwalking through peanut butter."

She veers her way upriver.

Ok then. That's that.

Fold map. Shake head. Follow.

In the hours to come, the way takes us past the rubble of another town. We don't detour, don't hesitate, don't debate. Just barrel past frail, forgotten structures. Locomotion's our salvation. Momentum our sanctuary.

Further up, the river veers away from the road. Nature's never liked straight lines. Around a curve, the water disappears from view. We ride on, laying our faith in the maps of the world that used to be.

Up the highway some miles more, right at the junction, pedal past a Ouachita State Park sign without so much as a nod of acknowledgment. It's not an accomplishment, nor a relief. Just another invisible line signifying some previous attempt at dividing that which is indivisible. These days, the truth of things is more apparent. There might be a here and a there, but there is no mine and yours. Boundaries are myths. There's only land and not land.

Everything else is just the vanity of borders. People's attempt to lay claim, to carve a piece away from the universe and declare it separate. Somehow. Assert a sort of dominion, a godhead. False fringes and delusions of grandeur. You cannot own that which you belong to.

I don't voice any of this.

Don't have the energy. And not altogether sure the logic of it all would hold up when given some oxygen or whether it'd rust away.

Another bridge carries us across the refound river.

From there, it's a quick turnoff from the main thoroughfare, onto a service road that chases the river back down the other side of its bank, to the Winding Stair campground.

Dusk's falling. The sky bleeds and washes down over the entirety of the western-facing cliffs. A steep trail looms down from the heights. A twist of shades and shadows, through jags of white quartz stone ruddied by the blood-tinted air. The dark pathway spills out at the far end of the campsite.

Ain't no way the bikes are getting up that. That much is clear.

Spent, we can't do much more than stare.

Having made it, tomorrow seems all the more intimidating.

Hope has given way to dread.

Still, resignation has a certain inertia to it.

"How ya doin'?" I give a nod to her belly. "The two of you must be doubly tired."

"I'm ok. I guess. You?"

"Phoo, I feel lower than a bow-legged caterpillar."

I give her a big grin with that one. She kind of smiles. Mostly just raises an eyebrow.

"Ok then. What do you wanna do?"

Ava shrugs. "Well, we're not going up that tonight. I guess we just get some rest. Hike in tomorrow. I'll set some snares. Why don't you build a fire."

It's the most she's said at once in days.

I nod.

Almost like we planned it, we both let go of our bikes. They arc away from us and clatter to the ground.

The moon has risen and shrunk down small above the silhouetted jagged peaks by the time we're settled in.

Ava's snares lie quiet out in the black. A mute menace or fool's errand. Only morning will tell.

Another of my false fires burns a thousand yards downriver, out on a small peninsula that pokes out a curve in the waterway, dancing in the dark like a wooden duck on a pond.

Our "genuine" blaze's burning down to the coals, nestled in a large hidden crook I stumbled upon between two boulders. As soon as the night drew in deep, I built it up but good. Coaxed it to radiate its warmth into the rock walls. Should keep things cozy at least half the night.

Ava and I huddle together in the corner, our respective legs making a V around the amber gleam of cinders. We lean against each other and regard the fire. It breathes with the breeze, luminous, blood orange susurrations.

"What are your beliefs on God?" I ask.

She takes such a pause, I wonder if she thinks I was just asking the night itself.

"You mean, do I think God exists?"

"Yeah. Sure, I guess. Not exactly. I mean, if he don't exist—"

"Or she."

"Yeah, or she. Whatever. God. If God don't exist, then the question don't matter. None of this really matters."

"Other than to us."

"Yeah, sure, I guess. But without an us, there is no mattering beyond that."

"I knew I should've taken a left at Albuquerque."

Not a bad Bugs Bunny reference.

"Asking whether God exists is as pointless as a white crayon."

"Ok then, what is it you are asking me?"

"What I'm saying—what I'm wondering is, let's say God does exist—"

"Then God's a sadistic bastard."

"Right. That's my point! Sorta."

"Your point is God can go f-?"

"My point is that either God is all-powerful, but a bastard… or God is all-loving, but weak. Like not all-powerful."

"Hence the Stripes."

"Hence the Stripes. And the die-off. And the desolation. And all'a it."

"'Cause either He was mean or powerless."

"Or she."

"Or she."

The night takes it in.

"That kind of choice, the either this or that of things, you know that's the White Man's game."

"I think racism died when all the races died."

"You know what I mean. It's a way of thinking."

Eye roll.

"You k'in roll your eyes 'til they fall outta your head, don't make me less right. Good, bad; light, dark. If you white folks was right and God made us in his image, then God's a lot more complicated than This or That."

She has a point.

"So what about the Red Man's god?"

"We didn't have god."

"Come on, yes, you—"

"Gods. We had gods. Powerful, petulant, flawed beings that smiled down with favors or menace depending on their whimsy and whatnot. Who wooed and warred with each other constantly. Waukheon, the Thunderbird," she clarified, seeing my confused look, "constantly fought with Untunktahe, the Water God.

"Our bountiful Beaver God was revered for his diligence and forethought packing away stores for a thinner time. Still, when the world was in darkness, when the Moon used to keep the Sun in a box, Beaver snuck up Spider's rope to the sky and stole the Sun Box and all the fire-making tools. The box was too heavy for Beaver though, and it slipped open, and the Sun burst forth. And Beaver fled back down to the world, taking with him the fire-making tools."

A crimson glow undulates in the coals. Fire's nothing more than a stolen relic, a valuable vestige of cunning and covetousness.

"The Coyote too, a constant trickster, a thorn in Raven's craw. Raven was a Creator, but also devious and duplicitous in his own right. Did you know a raven was the first bird out of Noah's ark?"

"Weren't that a dove?" If there's one thing that was drilled into me, it was biblical stories.

"The dove was the first to come back. But the raven was the first released after the Flood. It just didn't come back. Found something that piqued its interest and didn't feel no need to return.

"Our gods were Us, only more so."

We sat with her stories as bats flared about above us, blind sharpshooters, plucking prey out of the air.

"The old gods are gone though. You're hunting for something else now. Meaning."

She makes a point.

"I guess I am. I dunno. Like if the Stripes happened for a reason…"

"Then what? Would it make you feel better if we were the good ones? Or the bad ones? Instead of just the forgotten ones?"

"We're not forgotten."

"No?"

"No. We're the forgetters."

The red coals crack and pop as the flames retreat into them.

Ava shrugs where she lies. "Maybe there's a reason. Maybe there isn't. Neither option will satisfy the chaos of it all."

"So what, there's no rhyme or reason to any of it?"

"There's no rhyme or reason to anything. Never has been. Just the whimsy of chance."

"I guess you have a point. There's no logic to it. To who lives and dies. A random few, some older, some younger, some weaker, some stronger… There's no why to the when or wherefore of it."

"Maybe the Mayans were right. Maybe it's just the wheel turning round and round, and we're back at the beginning of things."

"Forced to reinvent the world. 'Cause the few of us that's left don't remember or never knew nearly enough." The idea of it spins back on itself. The us that's left is scattered and scared. The separation between us precludes any pooling of resources or know-how.

"What?"

Ava's wrinkling her eyes at me. Like she could see the wheels turning in my head.

"My momma useta say that cities were humankind's greatest invention. It's from cities that most invention and advancement came. The great artists, the great scientists, the great thinkers were drawn in and molded by the gravity of population densities. The crowd in them created a critical mass of collisions and ideas."

"Cities is also where the Stripes came from."

"True. True. We are a social species still."

"We're an extinct species. We just ain't admitted it yet."

"I just wonder if the key to surviving is the coming together into a society. Again."

"Some societies you don't want to be a part of." Ava scooches back and lies down.

I nod at nothing in particular and eventually join her.

We watch the last of the smoke curl and snake up into the darkness. The stars have all fallen black behind night clouds.

"You talk about your momma plenty, but I never hear you say nothing about your daddy."

Ava turns her head and looks over at me. But I keep staring up into the murk.

Finally give a shrug. "He left when I was little."

"Yeah. That happens. Did something happen? Or just one day he was gone."

"Momma said he just decided he didn't like who he was when he was with us."

"What about you two?"

"What about us?"

"Did you like who he was with you?"

My memories are just bits and pieces of him. Random moments. Calcified by severity.

"One time, I was little. I musta been eight or so. I was sitting outside on the front steps next to this, uh, rosebush. Big, tall goddamn rosebush. Anyway, I'm sitting there fiddling with the leaves on the rosebush and my, uh, pop, he comes home, and I don't really remember right, but he either ignores me or gives me some shit about something; it doesn't matter. I just keep sitting there, focused on fiddling with the bush instead of him, and I reach out and sorta absentmindedly pluck off a leaf from the bush. My pop sees this and turns around and tells me to stop ruining the goddamn bush. So I turn and look at him, for the first time since he got home, and I pluck off another leaf. My pop tells me again to stop or I'll be sorry. I pull off another leaf, and my pop hauls off and nails me. Wham. And I…"

For a moment, the story trails off away from me, drifting up with the smoke. Then it all comes rushing back down at me—

"I just take it without flinching or crying out. And I turn and pluck off another leaf."

Ava kind of snorts, kind of chortles at this.

"So my pop whacks me again, just as hard. Harder even."

I look over at the coals and blow at them until they're angry and bright with hunger.

"We went through the whole bush."

Ava nods at the night.

Her hand shuffles through the dirt until it finds mine.

"God damn people."

"God damn people," I echo.

At some point later, I stir awake in the dark. The coals've gone black. And Ava's spooning me.

PART VI

43

DAWN

The dawn star streaks through the crags and clefts of the land above. The boulders cornering the long-dead fire have shed the last of their heat.

Birds flit and flicker through the branches above the path to the river. Agitated by hunger and light.

This is a rich place, awash with life. Squirrels and other arboreals shudder through the branches of towering trees. Raptors rise in gyres on the updrafts between the punctuated mountaintops.

Damp clings to my ankles as I make my way past thickets heavy with dew. Bright white solar reflections flash and wink off the quiet brown water beyond, beacons rippling through brush and chaparral.

Follow the blindness.

It's less of a riverbank and more of a bluff, sloping down to a shallow washout. Muddy water flows past slowly, like a twist of moving earth. Static and dynamic at the same time. Alive and inert.

A lot more complicated than This or That.

Looking back, the woods have swallowed up the "path" back to our hidden camp, where I left Ava still asleep.

Wisps of vapor curl and wick over the water, like smoke.

Crouching atop the bluff, it is a sight. Near idyllic except for ripe wafts of sour stink leaching up from my pits.

Too rank for myself.

I unwrap my shoes off my feet and rest the pistol across them, back a safe distance from the crumbly precipice of the riverbank. The rest of my garments I leave on and take with me. Clumps of soil calve off the bluff as I high-step down. Silt cascades after me, following in the avalanche of my sunken footfalls.

The water's warm against the chill morning air. I splash about like a little kid, stumbling over smooth river rocks, until I sort of plunge, sort of fall headlong into it and swim my way out into the wide depths.

Peel off my clothes, rub them rough and hard with handfuls of pebbles snatched up from the bottom. Soak each remnant through, wring it out, and toss it out onto rocks to dry as best they can in the early sun.

Naked as I am in the water, my gaze flicks over back to the bank. No sign of Ava stirring nor following. Thank god. Thank the gods.

I backstroke away from the edge, to a deep eddy carved out by boulders, just short of the heavy middle of the flow, where the current runs fast with relentless gravity.

Diving down deep, rising, expelling a mouthful of water like a whale surfacing, cupping my palms together and pumping them flat to shoot out a jet of water like playful, diligent Beaver. Finally bobbing along, backstroking against the current. Memories wash past, a little boy playing submarine in the local swim hole, descending and surfacing to evade Russian subs, pretending his penis was a periscope.

The sounds of the world dull behind the thick cover of water as my ears dip below the surface. Hearing only the weightiness of water, floating along the border of liquid and air, as hawks circle round above, between the peaks, disappearing into the bright disc of the sun. Beaver couldn't quite make off with his overly ambitious bounty, and he dropped it in the heavens, where it burns a hole in the sky.

"Bucolic, ain't it?"

The gravelly timbre of the voice snaps me out of my reverie. Flipping over and sinking myself into the water, some forgotten instinct left over from before we first crawled out of the sea.

Across the river, Fish walks and casts a line up the opposite bank. Casual as all hell, as if we just come across each other at a popular trout hole.

He holds up his palm to block the sun, looks out across the water at me, and half grins. His eyes're pale and rigid. "Morning."

"Morning."

I didn't mean for it to come out. It's more of a reflex than anything else. But it makes me uneasy. The sound of my own voice responding to his, somehow validating his impossible presence.

"My name's Albert Fish, but everyone just calls me Fish."

This time I manage to keep my mouth shut. Social custom be damned. I will not bonify this apparition dressed in faded Dickies denim pants and a collared khaki shirt.

That man there's a wolf in cheap clothing. Yes, he is, Momma. Yes, he is.

The specter of him nods at me swimming along. "Looks like you're feeling better. A little well-earned R & R after your *Tore dee Fr'ants.*" His tone sounds almost approving. Like he's agreeing about a pitcher icing his elbow after nine hard innings.

Don't look upriver. Don't look at the woods. Don't look towards the path. Towards Ava.

"You ever notice how in all the apocalypse movies and TV shows, no one ever uses bikes? Weird, right. You ever used to watch that stuff? I loved that shit. Didn't, in one of 'em, didn't they use a shopping cart to hump stuff around? Still. It's weird, right? I mean, bikes are fast, versatile, and people powered. But not a single bike in a single story… and none of them talk about gas going bad."

There's teeth in his breath.

"That was a surprise for us. I mean, it makes sense, gas is made of high volatile and low volatile compounds. After three months they separate, and the high volatile components evaporate. No more flammability. Did you figure that out or know ahead of time?"

He sees me. I know he sees me. I mean, he's talking to me. But somewhere in my reptilian brain, I figure I can go crocodile. Motionless, submerged for the most part, hidden, with just my nose above water. Undetected. That or I'm just too goddamn scared to make a break for it back to my side of the river.

"Bikes're just smart. And plentiful in the apocalypse. Just not very scary. Can't very well have a zombie riding a Schwinn."

Fish laughs at that, conjuring up the image in his mind's eye. Then winking at my crocodile impersonation.

"Also, biking is just better for the environment." He sucks his teeth and twitches his chin to the right. "Least we don't have to worry about global warming no more. Nature has taken her planet back. Didn't take long, did it? Less than a year. Shit, less than six months since the *fish-kill* finished up. And the big panic took out pretty much all the infrastructure a little before that. Been fascinating watching the ecology rebalance now that we're no longer the apex predator. Resource redistribution. Once-scarce commodities now flourish in abundance while other, almost-taken-for-granted resources spark severe competition."

Fish casts his line upriver again, letting this sink in. It's only now that I recognize that's my fishing gear he's using. Finders keepers.

I risk a quick gander at the bank. Where my pistol rests high and dry up the bluff atop my shoes.

Fish sucks at his teeth, keeps watching the water and me. Can't have him seeing too closely.

"There's plenty of land. Plenty of space." Plenty of fishing gear for you to pilfer. I offer it up in as neutral a tone as I can manage. Not aggressive. Not assertive. Just matter of fact. Pointing out the way of things. Resources abound, so feel free to go on about your business. And I'll go on about mine.

"Mm. True. Real-estate market took a huge blow." He spits into the water. A large gob of mucus. It floats down with the current. "Bullets skyrocketed in value though, didn't they? God ain't making more of those little stingers. You don't want to waste any of those if you don't have to. Am I right?"

Fish reels in his line. He kneels down and looks across the water at me.

I am a log. I am a crocodile. I am invisible.

"Yes, sir. Hell of a thing, this world. These days. Mm. God broke his promise. And now we hafta make do. Forge whatever order we can out from the chaos."

He looks at me like a lion looks at a cub that ain't his.

"You seem like a smart kid. Shit, you have to be, survive this long. That show you put on for us, playing dead, that was some quick thinking. Someone that sharp knows when to stay and fight and when to leave. Knows how to conserve their resources."

Fish takes in the river, the far bank behind me, and the woods beyond. Birds continue to flutter and chirp, paying us no mind.

"I know, I know. You think you got yourself a pretty little partner there. Don't be fooled. She's a competitor just like the rest of us. Killed Esau's brother in his sleep."

He's lying. Maybe. Maybe not. Even if it's true—

"Now us, we don't want to kill nobody. No, sir. 'Specially her. That'd be a waste of resources, now wouldn't it? Even Esau can see that. And that man can hold a grudge, let me tell you." Reel in. Cast out. Reel in. "How's our baby doing? It kicking yet?"

"What baby?"

"Don't equivocate with me, boy. It ain't polite," he snaps, his voice like a metal table getting flipped over. Then just as quick he calms, snuffs out the fire that ignited behind his eyes. He takes out a black comb, dips it in the water, and slicks back the part in his hair. All the while scanning the land. Until finally, he turns his stare back at me. "Now, I didn't insult your intelligence, did I?"

He gives me a moment to think on that. Then he sort of leans in, best he can from where he is to where I am. Takes on a tone, like he's sharing a little secret. Like he's leveling with me.

"Leave the girl and we'll leave you be. To make your own way. Otherwise, we're forced to compete. It ain't personal. It's Darwinism."

He stands up. With purpose. Frowns at the water. "I ain't catching shit here. Think you might've scared all the fish away."

Gives another wink. Then he walks off downriver. Just before disappearing around the bend, he slides out, "Enjoy your swim. See you around, maybe."

44

CABIN

I haven't come this far to be killed. No.

The easy play is to give them what they want. And go my way. They might be excellent trackers, but they ain't got no idea why we're here. Or where I'm headed. And once they have her, they'd have no need to follow me.

If I trust them.

And I ain't got no reason to trust them. Any more than I can trust a pack of wolves. Predators is predators. Ain't no changing the nature of things.

Especially when we got the upper hand. Fish thinks he was being all smart, all reasonable like, springing up on me like that in the river. Give us a chance to talk, man to man. Logic it out.

All he did was overplay his cards. Show off how cautious they're being. His little tete-a-tete there was a bluff charge is what it was. An act of caution. Just like not trying to swim across the river. Too much risk, from the current, from the exposure. Ain't no guarantee that we ain't watching the river, hidden in the woods, just waiting to bear our sites on them and have our fun shooting fish in a barrel, so to speak.

Caution and confidence. Confident that they can catch up to us. Which I guess they've more than proven they can. But confident that his bluff charge will work. That they can take their time. Give me the space to skedaddle. Confident that I'll tuck tail. 'Cause they got the claws and the teeth and the speed. Confident 'cause I already played possum once. So they know I'm scared. And they're letting me know it won't work this time.

Confident they got enough luster in the bluster.

Overconfident. Because of what they don't know. Because they don't know why we're here or where we're headed. Because they don't know we're only a day's hike away. Because they don't know about Izzy—

Camp's empty.

Ava's gone. Just the black scar of our fire remains wedged in the bend between the boulders.

Shit… I worked it out all wrong. Fish was a distraction, a goddamn decoy—

From behind, to the right, a twig *SNAPS*.

The noise yanks me around, pulls my arm up, and orients the pistol.

Ava emerges from the woods, holding the bottom of her shirt up above her belly, cradling a bunch of berries in the hammock of it.

She freezes, seeing my gun trained on her.

"Whoa. It's me. Found some blackberries."

The pistol drops down with relief. Poker face, poker face, poker face…

"What? You ok?"

I nod. I think.

Water drips off my clothes and hair. It patters onto the dirt.

"So what? You just been rode hard and put up wet?"

"Took a swim."

"So I gathered."

"Just anxious. To get moving. Find my uncle."

She nods.

. . .

We leave the bikes behind. Tucked away in the boulders. For safe-keeping.

It's a backbreaking climb. A shit steep path in spite of the numerous switchbacks. Full of crags, rocks, and roots to watch out for as we wedge our way skyward.

Still, I motor along in a semi-meditative state. Occasionally Ava shakes me out of it, struggling behind, needing help here and there navigating a particularly harsh uptick in the path or narrow curve.

We stop at a wooded plateau partway up. Ava sits and slurps at the hydration pack.

From the edge of the cliff face, looking down at the wash of green, the forest has turned thick and imposing below. The river snakes along through it in the distance, a natural border.

A tracking glance back the way we came, over our hidden camp, around the bend in the river. A quick scan with the monoculars. Nothing. No one's following.

They'd have to make their way up to the bridge, across, and back down.

From this height, I can just make out the bridge. Nothing.

It takes most of the day to make our way up, partly because of the elevation, partly because a lot of the trail blazes have faded and we veer off track, and partly because of Ava. Mostly though it's because of the morning weighing me down.

I try not to think about it. About Fish. About the not so veiled threat. About the decision he put to me.

Uncle Izzy'll know what to do. How to best handle them. Ain't no way he ain't armed up to the teeth and outfitted the entire place with a bunch of booby traps and whatnot.

Always be ready to help or hurt, depending on who's knocking.

Done right, there won't be no fight. No need.

In nature, when bears come across each other, they get to figuring who's who right quick. Alpha, beta, it's all about hierarchy. Pecking order. The wild needs order. Otherwise it's chaos.

It ain't personal. It's Darwinism.

That's right, Fish. That's exactly what it is.

It's about attitude. Communicate to intimidate. That way they don't hafta fight. Which neither wants to do unless it's positively necessary. Too easy to get mortally wounded, even for the winner. So they communicate. The language of dominance. In the end, it's all about who's got the most luster in his bluster.

Uncle Izzy's got enough luster to shine those boys up but good.

It looks like a prop in a fairy tale. The way the cabin pops out of the woods and blends in all the same. Like it wouldn't be at all a surprise if Little Red Riding Hood slipped out, or Hansel and Gretel were lunching with Tom Bombadil. Quaint little Swedish cope, handcrafted construction. Debarked timbers woven together in interlocking saddle-notch corners. Purlin, shingled roof, half covered with moss on the northern side. The ceiling extends over the front porch, where four vertical logs hold up a single massive horizontal trunk that spans the entire length from one end of the pitched roof to the other. Atop its center, another perpendicular log stands tall enough to meet and bolster the vertex of the roof. And there's a fieldstone chimney to boot.

No smoke billowing out. No signs of anyone inside, really. Don't mean nothing one way or the other. It could mean a lot of different things.

"How long are we going to wait?" Ava whispers, lying next to me in the dell.

I shrug. "Normally I like to take at least a half hour or so." I scooch down alongside her. "At least."

"But it's your uncle's place."

"Only if my uncle is there."

"Who else'd be there?"

I shake my head at this and raise the monoculars to take another look.

"Watch, wait—"

"Assess. I know, you told me already."

At least she's still whispering.

"How long you think it's been, Addie? Gotta been almost an hour by now."

"God is in the details, and haste is of the Devil."

"We're back onto god again?" Ava rolls her eyes and then rolls onto her back. She rubs the sides of her torso and presses her hips inward.

She's not wrong. It's been well over thirty minutes. Way closer to an hour. And there ain't been nothing to raise an eyebrow at. Nothing at all.

But I can't bring myself to go in. Maybe because of the nothingness of it.

A wave of cold needles washes across my skin. The earth has a chill to it. Ava feels it too. Her arms're crossed over her chest and hands're tucked up into her armpits.

Safety. Precaution. Survival.

Addie, you can lead a dead horse to water but you can't make him sink.

Ava shivers next to me.

Screw it.

Knock, knock, knock.

"Hello? Uncle Izzy?"

No answer comes.

I knock again.

Nothing.

I look back at where Ava's head pokes up out of the hollow. I shake my head. She waves me in.

I try the door. It's unlocked. It creaks its way open.

"Hey, it's me. Addie."

The cabin doesn't respond.

Pistol first, I go.

It's about what you'd expect in a bare-bones survivalist cabin: bed—made with hospital corners just like the marines taught; bed stand with a stack of books—*SAS Survival Handbook*, *First Aid Manual*, *The Complete Works of William Shakespeare*, *The Lost Journals of Eve Tassat*, and *Middlemarch*; and some photos. There's one of Izzy decked out in his uniform and sunglasses, leaning against a Humvee, looking badass next to one of his marine buddies. Another of him and another Ouachita Park ranger with her arm draped around his shoulder, him smiling and looking down with drunken eyes, her holding her curly hair over his head like it's a toupee. And one of him out back behind GamGam's house, standing by the barbeque. A spatula in one hand and nine-year-old me in the other. My arm's wrapped around his neck. He's mid-laugh, leaning back, and Momma's arm is raised, about to hit him on the shoulder. I dangle, tucked into his arm, just beaming in the glow of it.

There's a table with aluminum legs and a Formica top and matching chairs with faux-leather cushions, a kitchen area stacked with shelves of jars of pickled preserves, a woodstove, and half a pile of wood.

An empty rifle rack perches over the door.

The floor groans beneath every step I make.

I pick up a preserve jar. A circle of dust outlines where it sat. I put it back. Everything's dusty. Except the table. Weird.

Everything feels untouched. It's been this way for a while.

Place my hand on the woodstove.

Cold.

Over the table, there's a photo pinned to the wall. A faded Polaroid. It's Uncle Izzy and Momma as kids, holding open their Halloween bags filled with candy. Momma's dressed as Dorothy, blue dress, pigtails, and red bedazzled slippers. Izzy's the Tin Man, axe, oil can on his head, silver paint everywhere, including a large smudge on Momma's dress. They're so happy.

Another's pinned next to it. It's me. An old school picture. Eighth grade.

"Shere Kahn? Addie?"

She whispers from just outside. Must have gotten tired of hiding in the dell.

"Yeah, it's clear. Come on in."

She does. The door creaks open and closed.

"Awwwwwwhhhhhh-" Ava shuffles straight to the bed and plops down face-first into the mattress.

A muffled, "Soft," garbles its way out from the pillow she's burrowed into. "Soooo soft."

Ava twists onto her back and gazes around.

She was expecting more. Shrugging, "It's a roof. I guess. Where you think he is?"

It's a casual enough question. The lack of answers leads to an unsettling silence.

I look out the window back the way we came. Woods and birds. Look back at Ava, casual like, trying my best not to seem unsettled, nod at the empty rifle rack above the door. "Maybe out huntin'. That'd be my guess."

Ava narrows her eyes at me. She's going to say something like I haven't been myself since the morning. I know it.

"Pickles!"

She's up and practically skipping across the small cabin. Snatches up the jar I'd picked up. Ava twists it open and immediately eats one.

Her mouth puckers loudly with savory delight. "Ooooooh. Vinegar-tastic. What are these, turnips?"

"Why don't you get a fire going? I'll go do some recon, track down some water, maybe nab us a squirrel or something." It came out harsher than I'd meant. Tenser. I wasn't trying to cut her off or nothing. Just make it so I could get out.

Fast.

Of course I just make it awkwarder. But it don't matter.

The door groans shut behind me, and Ava's mouth is too full to argue. She barely manages to spit out an "Ok..."

45

BULGE

The woods are full and empty all the same. I hike deeper in, away from where we summited.

Forest. Gullies. Game trails. More mountain.

Water gurgles from somewhere through the trees.

I track it to a creek that's etched its way into a ravine over relentless eons. Refill the hydration pack. Kneeling down at the water's edge, I catch a glimpse of a pit viper across the creek, sliding its way off a stone that's lost the day's heat, slipping beneath the cover of dead leaves, and disappearing down a hole.

It couldn't be less concerned with my presence.

Ambush predator.

We'll be fine as long as we don't corner or threaten it.

I take note of the surroundings. I'll have to show Ava the area, maybe mark off its territory.

. . .

I hitch my way up a tree to get a better view of things. See what I can see, listen for what I can hear. Neither's very edifying. Only that there's a plateau-like shelf a short ways up a nearby peak. Climbing down the tree, I end up tearing a small gash into my leg. It bleeds pretty good. Not much to do but shrug and move on. And try to ignore that somehow it's gone and woken up the ache in my mended knee.

The granite slopes pretty steeply up to the plateau, but it's got good handholds at least. Just need to be careful of the silicate bits that give way and flake off with the smallest bit of pressure.

Well, Addie, sometimes people just grow apart. And sometimes people just don't know what they have. The truth is, your daddy's just taken us for granite.

Ain't nothing taken for granite in this new world of ours, Momma. Other than granite.

I scoot my way to the spacious, brittle edge of the plateau. It just ends. At emptiness. And pebbles off into the abyss.

The sun's dropped and stained the sky amber. From the higher vantage, I drag the monoculars in a wider sweep. Touring the sights: the road, the river, the bend where Fish found me, the bridge.

And the column of smoke curling up from the east riverbank.

Shee't.

They've crossed over and set up camp on our side of the border. Still need to make their way back downriver. Still need to find the Winding Stair trail. Maybe they won't. Without a map or a reason, it'd be easy to miss. Faded blazes and all.

The ashy ribbon twists and distorts its way up. A warped, gray trail smudged across the amber air and deep green woods.

They didn't have to light it. They absolutely didn't have to light it before nightfall.

It's a signal. To me.

A warning. For me.

I can't help but frown and turn away.

The bulge stops me still.

I couldn't see it on my approach. The weeping pine curls over it, shrouding it from view walking towards the edge.

But turning now, it's dead center, nestled in the curve of the branches that form a natural amphitheater focused on the spectacular view beyond.

The ground looks pregnant. The oblong patch of dirt bulges up over the body within. At the foot of it rests a pile of desiccated goat shit. At its head stands a small pyramid of smooth river stones. On the mound itself, white stones form an *I*.

I stare, too stunned to move…

46

FIGHT…

…at Ava's swollen belly.

A fire burns in the iron stove.

Ava loudly sucks the vinegar juice off her fingers, finishing off the last of a jar of pickled turnips.

"Oh my god, I swear I could drink the rest of this."

I poke at the red coals with a stick and try not to look at her.

"Guess these are the cravings they talk about. I hope your uncle won't mind. Wouldn't want him to get back from hunting with a hankering and I've gone and ate up everything. Wonder what's good hunting in these parts. If he ain't back in the morning, I'll go out and set some snares. Saw some promising trails on the hike in. How long you think 'til he gets back?"

"How'd the father die?" It's out of my mouth before I can catch it.

"Huh?" Ava eyes me. Suspicious.

I keep poking the fire. Not wanting to look. Feels like the hairs on the back of my neck're curling under the heat of her gaze.

"I stabbed him… while he was… on me. Right through the lung so he couldn't scream." Her voice has gone cold. Flat. Her hand goes to the Bowie hanging from her belt. "This is his knife."

Her admission gets me to look at her. It made sense, but my mind had been doing its best not to jump to that conclusion. I'd preferred to let that dark possibility float around just beyond the edge of consciousness. So it didn't make it real.

Her saying it made it real.

"He was a bad guy, then?"

Ava won't quit staring at me. "No, he was one of them good rapists. What're you getting at?"

What am I getting at? I don't want to say. I don't want to make it real. But she keeps staring.

"Was he one of 'em?"

Ava's eyes narrow. Zeroing in on what I'm getting at. She nods. More to herself than me.

"The big one's brother."

"Jesus Christ. Just the big one's brother, that all?!" I didn't mean to get loud. It just happens.

"I'm sorry, was he a goddamn friend of yours? My apologies. If I had known, I would've let him go on having his way with me."

"I ain't saying that. I ain't saying that at all."

"Sure sounds like you're upset at me for defending myself—"

"I'm just saying you should've goddamn told me 'stead of lying about it."

"I didn't lie about shit."

"Well, you certainly didn't make it known."

"That ain't the same as lying."

"Fine, equivocating, then. But I guess that's on me. My bad. My mistake for not asking. Ava, is there anything else that might pertain to our well-being that you've been keeping from me? You got any other outstanding vendettas or a case of smallpox instead of the Stripes or some other damn disease that might bite us in the ass and devour us from the inside out?!"

"Where'd you get a word like that?"

The question hangs between us, like a scythe. She's just trying to trip me up. To get the upper hand.

"Like what?"

"Equivocatin'."

"You ain't the only one who took a damn English class, Ms. Emily Sitting Bull Dickinson. And don't twist this around on me. I ain't the one who's been keeping secrets from you."

"Well, how nice for you. How wonderful not getting raped. How delightful you ain't got nothing you're so goddamn ashamed of you'd just want to bury it inside you and let it die."

"Don't you go turning this around. I mean, goddamnit. A thing like that, Jesus, don't you, a thing like that… Ain't much that could stop a man from coming after you after a thing like that?"

"Ain't nothing stopping you from going."

"I ain't the bad guy in this. *I* didn't lie. *I* didn't murder a guy.

"Well, you ain't the good guy. You ain't no hero. You're just a pussy. A sweet little innocent kid who hid from the world and fell in a pit. Who went from crying 'mommy' to crying 'uncle.'"

And she keeps staring at me. The liar just keeps staring.

And takes a sip of the vinegar.

And I… I'm…

God damn her. God damn this.

I storm out.

Into the dark.

47

… OR FLIGHT

By the time I get back, Ava's sleeping soundly in the bed. Red coals pop and crack in the belly of the iron stove. The cabin's warm. Comforting.

The door's quiet creaking doesn't wake her up none. Nor do my tiptoeing footsteps. I retrieve my bag and pistol. Grab my bow and quiver.

The shotgun rests against the wall next to the bed, within reach of Ava. I leave it for her and walk out.

Back down in the dell where we had staked ourselves out earlier this afternoon, I check the pistol. It only has one bullet in the chamber.

Shit.

It is what it is.

The scent of burning wood from the cabin stove permeates the night. Between that and the pine forest, it smells like Christmas.

I don't turn around. Don't look back.

I just make my way down.

. . .

The descent feels more like a forced march. The gravity of it grows stronger with every drop in elevation. The weight drags down on me.

I give in to it. Take on an almost meditative state so I can outpace myself. I'm numb. Or trying to be. Trying to think… about—

Ain't nothing I can do. It's not like I'm proud or nothing. I ain't. But what's the end game? Izzy's dead. There ain't no help to be had here. Ain't no respite. It ain't a sanctuary. It's a siege.

There's three of them. With at least three guns. Probably more. Three of them. And all the time in the world. To triangulate around the cabin, settle in, and wait. Until they get what they want. Pick their moment to pick me off. And pick up Ava.

That's all she wrote.

Running won't do no good either. It hasn't so far. Just delay the inevitable. If they ain't stopped their hunt yet, tracking us clear across the state, they ain't going to.

So, what, then? Fight? Face down three well-armed killers with a single shot in the pistol, a handful of arrows, and some shotgun shells? Maybe we get one. Or even two. Maybe we're killers too, then.

Still. They're going to get some of their own shots off. Sure as shit they are. At the very least wound one of us.

Ain't no way the two of us make it out alive.

Three of us.

Shit.

Three of us.

This way, everyone stays alive. They don't want to kill Ava. Or the baby. They leave me be.

Nobody kills nobody. Nobody gets hurt… or injured. Everyone lives. It's math.

This is about survival.

Ain't no room for sentiment.

There's no morality in nature. No, sir.

Just survival.

. . .

You'd leave your momma?

I stop.

For a drink. I need a drink.

I sit. I sip.

Down below the ridgeline lies woods, somewhere in the darkness. Up above, the black fades into swaths of starlight. A satellite twinkles and cruises past.

Repeat after me. No. No, I would not leave my momma.

The pistol digs into my ribs. I unstrap it and rest it on the ground. Take off the pack too. In spite of the coolness of the night, I've worked up a sweat.

While shifting the bag off and laying it down, I feel that there's something in one of the small pockets.

I unzip and rummage it out.

It's a snack pack of Oreos.

No, I would not leave my momma.

Goddamnit.

I can't do it. Not again. Not anymore.

Too much has been left behind in this world. Too much taken. I'm done with it. I'm done. I can't accept, can't adapt to the way of things no more. There's more to life than survival. I ain't no refugee.

Ok, Momma?! You happy now? You win. I'll go back. I'll wake her, tell her everything, get her moving. We'll disappear into the mountains. *Montani semper libri.*

I snatch the bag and the pistol and head back up, back to her—

SNAP!

A stick breaks underfoot.

Behind me.
In the black.

48

DEAL BREAKER

Fish and Zeke stand, flanking me, each cradling a rifle.

But their fire, it was back by the bridge. Miles upriver from the Winding Stair trail. Their fire… weren't no signal. It was a trick. A decoy.

Fish almost looks disappointed.

"You weren't going back on our deal now, were you?"

My pistol raises my arm. Like it's got a will of its own. Next thing I know I'm pointing it at Fish, then Zeke, then back at Fish. Zeke takes a step away from Fish on instinct. Spreading the distance between them so as to make it harder to focus on both.

Fish don't react at all. Just talks. Calm like. Reasoning. "You don't want to do that now. You fire that thing off, maybe you'll tag one of us, shit maybe even both. But Esau'll hear it for sure."

"Shots just get ol' Esau fired up." Zeke dances excitedly from one foot to the other.

"In the end, it's just a waste of bullets," Fish reasons out.

I back my way up the path. Slowly. Worried about Esau. Searching the dark. "Where is he?"

Fish sucks his teeth. Shrugs. "Out and about, I'd reckon. Where's she?"

"I don't want to kill nobody." The pistol's getting heavy.

"Nor do we, my man. Nor do we."

"But I will if I hafta."

"So'll we." Zeke grins big. Tittering from toe to toe.

"Come now." Fish sounds almost sympathetic. "Killing's a waste of resources. Counterproductive—"

Fish lays down his gun. Gentle like. Slow. Dead calm.

"—for everyone. We should all be aligned together. We're all in the same boat. Are we not? The same pestilence-ridden ark."

Fish takes a step forward.

I train the pistol right at the center of his chest.

Fish raises his hands, palms out, and freezes. But keeps talking.

"This is bigger than us, boy. Can't you see that? We have an obligation. We, the chosen few. To survive. To thrive. We must be fruitful and multiply."

"She ain't yours."

"No. You're right. It's a new world. She belongs to all of us. As does what's inside her. She's our vessel—"

BANG!

I fire the pistol high into the air and take off up the trail.

I hope she heard it.

49

TREED

They flinched. Last I saw. Just enough to give me a second to disappear into the woods at a full sprint.

Zeke crashes through the brush after me. Whooping, hollering.

Like a bat outta water.

The lunatic's revved. A rabid dog finally let off leash.

I heave myself up the slope, fast as I can.

The taste of copper floods my mouth. I can't tell if the thundering in my ears is Zeke or my pulse. Fear shoves me forward, tosses me ahead through the woods. Accelerating around tree trunks, skipping over ditches. Fear and need. A single thought slamming against the inside of my chest. Get to Ava! Get to Ava! Get to Ava!

The cut on my bad leg's opened up. But it don't hurt. Just feels wet with blood.

Change directions. Switch back. Until I burst up onto flat ground. Close now. I can smell the fire.

The proximity prods me faster.

Get to Ava!

Shouts and yips nip at my back.

He's close. Is he close?

I leap a ravine, dash forward, look over my shoulder to see if I can spot him—

THUD.

Black.

50

BLUR

"Sumbitch, my heart's poundin'." The voice catches its breath.

A wall presses against me. It's dusty. My head's stuck to it, right where the pain is. Like there's a nail coming out of the inside of my skull, driving itself into the fictile wall, and pinning me to the spot. Swollen, tender, pounding. Cracked open. Leaking.

If I don't move. If I just stay here. Wedged against it. It's almost ok. It's almost—

"Your heart poundin'?"

The voice. I know that voice.

I pull and pry my skull off the wall, drawing out the stake of pain that holds my skull to that spot. So I can turn towards the voice. The turn is more of a roll though. I'm still stuck to the wall somehow. It's earthen. No, that ain't right. The wall isn't a wall at all. It's the ground. I'm on the ground. Pressed against the earth.

I peel my eyes open. See if I can see the voice. But all there is, is the blur. And the dark.

"Well, hello."

A piece of the blur breaks off from the rest. Steps towards me, winds up, and swings.

A heavy pendulum, maybe granite, swings into my stomach, folds my torso around it, cradles my weight up into its arc, and tosses me back.

It leaves my breath behind. Nailed to the spot where I was.

But the pain scurries after me, frenzied and fierce to catch up before I collide back with the ground.

It dives into my stomach and twists my organs around it, winding them tight, wringing out my insides with such a furious clench that they geyser up into my esophagus and almost vomit their way out.

But then the wall—the ground slams everything back down into place. And my skull explodes in bright, burning starlight, washing everything white with agony.

"How 'bout now? Hear it thudding in your ears?"

The voice. It's Zeke's.

The blur bends over, hands on its knees.

"Man, I hate running. Almost as much as Fish hates waste."

The blur rears back, swings its leg in another arcing pendulum, and kicks me again.

I stay on the ground this time. Absorbing the full force of it.

Everything gushes out of me in a sour burst of bile.

"Hooo-ee."

The blur skips back.

"Yes, sir, sees it as a sin. Killing's only justified to him—"

The blur takes a short run at me and kicks again—driving out another spew of heaving vomit—and dances up, over, and behind me.

Electric spasms convulse through my body.

I can't inhale. Can't catch my breath. Can't unclench.

Just curl in on myself. And choke.

"—if it's a necessity."

The blur of Zeke has sharpened though. Taken form.

His fuzzy silhouette tilts its head at me with wonder. Then flashes into motion, booting my head and jolting it back sharp.

Detonating my skull in a violent flash.

The world fractures.

There is only darkness.

And hurt.

Radiating through the universe.

And a distant, gurgled groan.

I think that's me.

Existence flutters in and out of focus with my eyelids. I want the black. I want the nothingness. Void.

But the will to survive is dogged. It holds on tight and tugs at me. Yanks me out of the black.

No. I'm wrong.

That's Zeke. He's yanking at my boots. Pulling them off.

My gaze drags towards him. Trying to get a fix. Track him.

He leans against a tree, leg bent up, holding my severed foot against his.

No, that ain't right. It's my boot. He's holding up the sole of my boot against his.

Zeke catches sight of me trying to orient on him. He leans his head from one side to the other, like a cat measuring the distance to a mouse. He drops the boots, spits, and draws a knife.

"Fish is right. About waste. To a point. But only to a point. The thing is, Fish ain't here."

Zeke advances.

I try to evade. Back away. But I only sort of roll back. The dark world smears with effort. The best I can manage is just to brace for the assault.

The blur of Zeke moves in for the kill.

But so does something else.

Another blur, behind Zeke, detaches itself and slides towards us. Arms outstretched, cradling a hazy coil of thick, patterned rope. The second blur presents the rope, almost like an offering.

Moves in, silent. Except for the hiss of the coil. The rope rises of its own volition, frays apart at the middle, unhinging.

And strikes.

Zeke squeaks with surprise, arm flinching up to his neck as he starts to turn.

Then his body crumples to the ground. The rope dangles from his throat. Fangs lodged in the flesh, hooked around the carotid artery, secreting pit viper venom in satisfied spasms. The snake unhinges again, detaches from the seizure of him, and slithers off.

Zeke lies facing me. Twitching. Foam bubbles out of his mouth.

A hand reaches down and pulls Zeke's head back by the hair, and another hand lowers a blade and slits his throat.

I try to get my eyes to focus but can't see the forest for the trees.

Just the black.

51

ESCAPE GOAT

I'm not where I was. I'm not prone. I'm propped up against something. Ache throbs behind my eyes.

Hot breath blows across my cheek.

I flinch and raise my arm.

The ache sears and flashes like electricity through every joint and muscle.

I squint and tense against it.

"Easy, Addie. You got quite a knock on the head. Just breathe."

I nod. It hurts. I stop nodding and wait until the pain passes.

I open my eyes.

A bovid face floats in front of me. It's bearded. Wide eyed. It's a goat's face. The animal gnaws at my hair.

The surprise of it drives me scampering back. But the pain stops me after only a few centimeters of retreat.

"That's Billie Goat Holiday. Don't mind her. She's just nosey."

The voice is soft. Different. I don't know it.

I turn towards the sound.

A woman squats amongst Zeke's possessions, along with my boots, my bow and my arrows that lie behind her.

She's older. Maybe late forties. Her hair's wiry. Unkempt curls. Her frame's lean inside a plaid shirt that's way too big on her.

She sifts through his corpse. Taking inventory. There's an efficiency to her movements. A quick but methodical process.

"I'm Bridget. Nice to meet you."

There's something familiar about her…

The goat moves off to munch on a plant. It drags a pink dog leash behind it.

"Here. Eat this. If you can."

She hands me a hunk of speckled white.

"Goat cheese with stinging nettle. Got a bite to it, but'll give you a boost."

Seeing her close up, it clicks.

"You're, uh, I've seen you. You're—you were in the picture. With Uncle Izzy." She's the park ranger who was draping her curls over his head.

"Mm. Right next to yours." She smiles. "I should've made myself known to you sooner. I apologize. But I didn't know you was you. We have a root cellar off in the… I needed to clear out, play it safe. You might have to surrender the house."

But you don't have to lose the farm. I finish Uncle Izzy's saying. Not sure if I say it out loud or in my head.

"I do decoy fires."

Bridget smiles and nods. "He always said that about you. The boy knows how to think through things. Heard so much about you, feel like we're practically kin."

She's staring at me. Not like Zeke. But off-putting, still.

"Sorry. I don't mean to stare. Just… You got his eyes."

Momma used to say that.

"Was it—was it the Stripes?" I ask.

"That what people are calling this plague?"

I nod. And immediately regret it. Almost throw up the cheese I just swallowed.

"Yeah. The plague, the Stripes took him about five months back. Your mama too?"

"Yeah," I admit without a nod.

"Must've gotten your immunity from your dad's side, I guess."

"You think I'm immune? Like, not, it just somehow missed us?"

"Gotta be. I mean, this thing spread so far, so fast. It's airborne for sure. And fast. Gotta be everywhere. I know I was exposed when Izzy… I imagine you were too, with your mama."

I try to swallow down another hunk of cheese so it'll catch and drag with it the shame welling its way up.

"So prepping didn't have nothing to do with it." I lean my head back against the tree trunk.

"Well, not surviving the pla—the Stripes. But it was your prepping that kept you alive through it all. Izzy'd be proud. Always said, 'Anyone can learn some skills, but that boy knows how to think.' That's what got you clear across the state to here. With a pregnant girl no less."

Ava! I have to get to her.

I stand up. And immediately vomit.

But it don't stop me. I veer my way uphill. Towards the cabin. Spewing more chunks along the way. Lurching forward, forward, forward.

"Addie, wait—"

A peculiar whistle echoes through the dark woods.

It stops me cold.

Bridget catches up. She holds a finger to her lips. Hush.

I know. I know. I nod.

She hands me my bow and quiver.

We wait in silence. I can see Bridget weighing her options. There ain't too many. Melt back into the blur. Or stay with me and help.

I move on, quiet, but with intent.

Another whistle. Closer this time.

. . .

The cabin sits, quiet in the dark. No movement within. No point in protocol, the danger's already here.

I crawl my way closer. As a way to stay out of sight lines, but also, being on all fours helps with the nausea.

I stop below the side of the front porch. Sit and lean against it. Listen.

Nothing.

Looking out at the trees, there's no sign of Bridget. She dissolved into the dark.

Like she never existed to begin with.

I slide my way across the deck to the door. It's open. I listen again.

Again nothing.

I nudge it open and peek in.

I can see the bulge of her under the covers in bed.

"Ava."

My whispering is too soft.

"Ava!" I whisper louder.

She still don't move.

I scan the woods beyond and back my way into the cabin.

I crawl my way to the bed and reach up to nudge her awake.

"Ava…"

Only it's not her. It's just pillows under the blanket.

"Would you look at this. Nice place. I see now why you gave us such a run for our money. Whose it belong ta?"

Fish fills the doorway.

52

FISH ON THE LINE

"Come on now. Fess up. Who's place is this?" His hands flex around his rifle.

I can't quite tell if it's leftovers from Zeke's beating or the surprise of Ava's absence, but it's a struggle to focus right on Fish.

"My, my uncle's."

"Mm-hm. And where's your uncle?" He snaps at me with sharp impatience, "Stay with me, now."

"Dead."

Fish steps inside.

"Boy, you ain't got no shoes on. Looks like Zeke shined you up pretty good, huh? Where'd he get off to?"

It comes out as a whisper. "He, uh, he ain't… he didn't—"

The clanging startles the shit out of both of us.

I flinch back against the bed, terrified.

Fish spins right around and drops into a squat. Elbow propped on his bent knee, rifle aimed at the ready.

Another metallic clang wangs at us from outside.

Fish scoots forward, picking his way towards the door to get a better angle. Barrel pointed out at the night while keeping me in his periphery.

Please don't be Ava. Please don't be Ava. Please don't be—

Billie Goat Holiday wanders out in front of the porch. A cowbell dangling and clanging from her pink collar.

Fish laughs. Visibly relieved. He stands up. And laughs again.

"Now look at that. You went off and found me an offering."

Fish takes a step out onto the porch. He clucks at her like she's a horse.

"Come here, girl. Come on."

He steps down onto the porch steps.

Billie Goat Holiday turns to look at him. A strip of Zeke's shirt dangles from her mouth.

As Fish gets a gander of what it is exactly, a loop of black nylon drops down from above, encircling his neck. It's the 550 paracord shoelace from my boot. Confused, Fish grabs at it and glances up.

In the briefest of pauses, there seems to be a moment of recognition between him and an angel of death as he lifts his gun up to the heavens.

The nylon paracord zip-sings around the massive horizontal log beam above the porch as the angel descends in a rush earthward.

Bridget drops down into view as Fish stretches, rising upwards.

A foot above the porch, Bridget jerks to a stop with a sickening crack as Fish's spine snaps.

Bridget lands lightly on the wooden planks.

Everything is still… except for the goat. And Fish teetering this way and that, his toes brushing across the edge of the step.

Both hang, swaying above the earth, severed from its hold. Spectral in contrast. Ornaments of survival and desolation in some arcane prayer to a frozen god.

Bridget hang-squats in place for another few seconds before letting go and clumping down onto the porch.

Fish's body crumples down the stairs in an inert heap. Billie Goat Holiday starts and leaps away.

Bridget half-smiles and stands up. “You ok—”

BANG!

She rotates, spun by an invisible, severe force, and goes down onto the porch.

53

MISSED OPPORTUNITY

Blood courses out of a hole below Bridget's right collarbone.

An invisible menace stalks through the woods. A threat surmised from the blackness by the echo of the hollow, metallic *clack-click* of a bolt-action rifle opening and closing its breech.

Fear and frailty shatter the stillness.

I huddle back against the bed, watching Bridget writhe quietly. She shifts to tilt her head back. Her eyes pierce a fog of pain to find mine. Her lips purse together and split apart to mouth a single word:

Run.

A tremble passes from her to me and shudders my body into action. Grabbing the bow and quiver and dashing back around the bed, deeper into the cabin as another shot thunders out of the dark and wooden shards explode out of the bedpost where I'd been.

The *clack-click* of the rifle re-bolting covers the sound of me opening the back window.

I sort of crawl, more fall my way out and down to the ground and scramble myself into the cover of the trees.

Get away, get away, get away—

But I may as well be running through a tilt-a-whirl filled waist high with mercury.

Somewhere behind me, in the woods, branches snap and saplings groan as the Grizzly with a gun stampedes after me.

It was better when I couldn't hear his relentlessness.

I fall my way forward, pinballing from trunk to trunk. Rasping, croaked breathing, like choked moans. Harsh breaths that cut.

Splash across a creek.

The creek. I remember the creek. By the plateau. I could climb—

The ground skids out from beneath me. Drops away quick. Crumbling down a ravine. Cotton and skin shred against rocks and sticks. Which at least slows down the landslide of me.

Goddamn, that hurts.

Ain't no time to rest. Nor assess the damage. That'd cost momentum. I gather up the speed of the tumble and carry it with me. Mule on through the dark forest.

Sharper breaths slice deeper.

The barrage of Esau has quieted though. Dissipated. He hasn't stopped. He wouldn't've. He slowed down to stealth mode.

Shit.

Movement hooks the corner of my eye and yanks my head around. But not before I can duck behind a tree.

Was it Esau?

He's found me. This is it.

The quivering makes it hard to nock an arrow on my bowstring. Harder still while trying to muzzle heaving lungs. But I don't trust gulps of air not to give away my location.

I try to listen. But can't make out nothing beyond the roar of my pulse hammering through my head. Thudding my rib cage with spasms.

thumpTHUMP.

No shots. If he'd seen, there'd be shots

thumpTHUMP.

No sounds neither. I got to check. Got to get a spot.

thumpTHUMP.

Where are you, you fat fuck?

thumpTHUMP.

The air prickles with electricity. It burns inside my nose as I catch and pull in a slow breath. Controlled, quiet, calm.

thumpTHUMP.

The bowstring moans softly as I draw it back. Calling through the dark.

thumpTHUMP.

Come on, you got him. Breathe in, breathe out.

Shoot between the heartbeats—

thumpTHUMP.

It's a dog-eat-dog world now.

thumpTHUMP.

Breathe in—

Hinge around the tree trunk.

Look past the arrow.

Breathe out.

thumpTHUMP.

The arrowhead disappears into a blur.

Breathe in.

And Ava takes shape. Inside a wide, jagged split in the earth itself. A gully cut into the granite mountain that rises to the plateau graveyard.

It's Ava.

She's stretched long against the incline of a slab of rock. Her feet and hands bound, each set tethered to its own tree. Like she's being drawn and halved by the forest itself. Stretched out as she is, she struggles against the bindings, trying to squirm her way clear.

I cover half the distance before even realizing I'm moving. The second half cleared in even less time.

Her eyes shine with fear then dim with relief as I come into focus. She's gagged. A bandana bound across her mouth.

I don't say nothing, just go to work untying her. Trying to. But the knots are too goddamn tight.

And the crash of Esau has risen out of the woods.

Closer than before. And more frenzied.

Bait. Ava's bait.

Trapping both of us in a dead-end gully.

Esau's charging barrels closer now. Just beyond the ridge.

Slow. Slow. Breathe. Think. Take your time. Haste is of the Devil. Look.

Nearby, Ava's stuff sits nestled in the crook of some tree roots. Including her Bowie knife.

The blade makes short work of sawing through the binds that tether her arms.

But not short enough.

Heavy footfalls splash through the creek with the pace of a rabid grizzly.

The rope frays away from her wrists, releasing her from one of the trees. Another length still binds each wrist to the other.

But I move on to cut away the binds on her feet, when the avalanche of Esau sliding down the ravine billows over us.

Once again, I find myself exchanging a single, anguished look with a wounded woman. For the umpteenth time tonight, I flee. Run away from Esau into the woods. For the last time, I abandon Ava.

And hide.

And wait.

And watch:

Ava freak.

Ava grabs the knife with her still-bound hands and tries to cut the rope tethering her feet.

Watch her slice her way free. Get up, grab the shotgun, and sprint into the night. Into the woods. Past a large trunk. When Esau slams the butt of the rifle into her swollen belly.

Ava goes fetal before even hitting the ground. The wind rushes out of her. She can't scream. Just cradles her torso in anguish.

Esau stares down at her. His eyes narrow, like one might at half of a roadkill. He whistles loud.

And waits for a response.

Whistles again.

Ava writhes on the ground, dry heaving. Her gagged cries are thin. Lost.

Esau regards her holding her stomach in pain, her protruding belly. He picks up her shotgun. Inspects it. And points it right into her belly. He holds the rifle in the other, pointed out into the nothingness. A monument of pandemoniac.

His voice carries through the night. Even his hissed susurration. "One move, one flinch, one twitch and I'll put a hole through the both of you."

Ava manages to still herself.

Esau scans the woods.

I flatten myself against the tree I've taken refuge behind. Shit, shit, shit, shit, shit.

A dozen or so yards off to the right, I see them. My bow and arrows.

"Gimme my brother's knife." His voice drips venom.

Ava drops the knife.

"Good girl."

I slither along the ground. Slow. Quiet.

Esau kicks the knife well out of Ava's reach. He squats down close to her. Reaches for her. And tugs the gag down. Then he stands back up.

"I think he's sweet on you."

That's when Esau kicks her.

Ava moans over the sounds of me grabbing my bow and drawing out an arrow.

Esau turns out to the woods. To me. And yells, "Is that right? You sweet on her?"

He turns back and kicks her again. Loosing another barrage of moans.

The arrow rests between my index and middle fingers. Nocked against the bowstring. I've got one shot at this. He doesn't know where I am right now. Not exactly. One shot. Maybe two. One clean one though. 'Cause he'll sure as shit be firing at me by the time I get off the second.

I stab a second arrow into the ground for easy access.

Breathe.

Draw.

"You sweet on this little whore!?"

Hinge out.

Exhale.

Release.

The bowstring twangs and the arrow whips through the air right at Esau…

And lodges in the tree trunk just to the right, a few feet behind him.

Thwit!

I missed.

Esau's already eyeballing the line of the arrow, arcing his aim back along its invisible trail.

Arrow always points in two directions. Towards its target and towards its archer.

Shit.

I pluck the second arrow from the earth. Fumble it against the bowstring, dropping it.

In my periphery Esau kneels down on one knee, resting the rifle stock on the heel of his hand.

I nock the arrow into place, raise and draw the bow in one smooth motion—

Only to see Esau staring calmly down the length of the barrel, right at me. His finger flexes around the trigger—

Shhhthhik!

Esau's shoulders bend back towards each other in some sort of grotesque prayer. The rifle fires off way wide into the black as he jerks into a turn.

His twisted torso reveals my first arrow… lodged in his back, somehow sticking out from between his ribs.

I lower my bow, still nocked with my second arrow, and watch as he bubbles and spits blood. The arrow must've punctured his lung.

Esau thuds to the ground.

And reveals Ava standing behind where he kneels and gurgles. Her hands are still bound together, but bloodied now from stabbing Esau… with my arrow. She must've pulled it out of the tree while we were distracted trying to shoot each other. And daggered it into his back.

Ava kicks the rifle out of his reach, then backsteps and crumples to the ground. I rush over and skid to a stop at her side. Patting her down, checking for wound or injury.

"You all right? You're all right."

Ava gives the slightest of nods.

"Yeah. I think."

"Yeah," I say.

"You really need to try not aiming so much," she whispers and rolls her eyes.

"Shut up."

We laugh. Only a little though. It hurts too much.

Esau gurgles at us, his arm clawing impotently for the rifle several yards away.

I walk past him, kick the gun another yard away, and retrieve the Bowie knife.

And bring it back. To Ava.

Dawn bloodies the sky and wakes the birds.

"Addie…"

In the morning light, Bridget spots us. And Esau. She's managed to stumble her way to the top of the ravine.

"You all right?" Bridget wraps herself over a boulder to keep from collapsing into a heap. Her right arm dangles down like the hour hand of a busted clock.

I look at Ava leaning against me. She smiles and gives a weak nod.

Whispering, I ask her, "We ok?"

"Yeah."

"We're ok!" I shout up the ravine.

I rest my head against Ava's.

"We're ok…"

She entwines her fingers in mine and squeezes my hand.

And we watch the big body bleed out. A thick rivulet of red snakes its way down towards the creek.

EPILOGUE

The stone knocks against the rock edges of the irrigation channel. Water splits off from the creek and courses along between the edges of the thin aqueduct. I walk along behind it, bouncing like a little kid. It makes me happy every time, to follow the trail of water as it hunts its way successfully through the forest.

The vegetable garden looks good. The beans crawl skyward up the makeshift lattice. Its green pods dangle heavy from the thin offshoots, swollen with growth. Giant, fuzzy-leafed squash plants fan out and invade the neighboring peppers' territory.

Bright red tomatoes balloon and bulge within the funnel of their conical scaffolding. Some of the leaves are yellowing.

They need more water.

Thirsty bastards.

I give a tug on the stone gate that serves as the lock for the tomato channel. More water pours down its drip tributary.

"Why don't you pick three or four for supper?"

Bridget holds a basket half full of vegetables out towards me. I nod and take it from her.

She moves on and keeps yanking up weeds. Her thick, braided ponytail metronomes behind her.

I pick the biggest three and make my way to the cabin.

The porch steps creek as I walk up.

"Hey, can we open another jar of pickled beets, Bridg?" Ava yells out the open door.

She starts, not expecting me. Smiles big. And suddenly freezes. Her eyes close briefly with discomfort. Her hand moves up and pats the side of her massive belly.

"Baby kicking?"

"Like a rabbit playing soccer."

I smile.

She smiles and grabs my hand. "Feel."

Ava flattens my palm against the spot. Sometimes I swear I can feel the baby's pulse. *thumpThump—thumpThump—thumpThump*. Quick and soft.

Some body part pushes back against my touch and retreats beneath the surface.

"Was that a foot?"

"I think. Hard to tell in the tight quarters."

I nod. "Soon."

"Not soon enough. I am so done being preggers."

And as if on cue, Ava surprises herself with a fart. She rolls her eyes at herself. "Damnit."

"S'ok. You're fartin' fer two."

"Shut up."

We laugh. We go into the cabin. We make supper.

THANK YOU FOR READING AFTER THE END

We hope you enjoyed it as much as we enjoyed bringing it to you. We just wanted to take a moment to encourage you to review the book. Follow this link: After the End to be directed to the book's Amazon product page to leave your review.

Every review helps further the author's reach and, ultimately, helps them continue writing fantastic books for us all to enjoy.

You can also join our non-spam mailing list by visiting www.subscribepage.com/AethonReadersGroup and never miss out on future releases. You'll also receive three full books completely Free as our thanks to you.

Facebook

Instagram

Twitter

Website

Want to discuss our books with other readers and even the authors? Join our Discord server today and be a part of the Aethon community.

Nolan Garrett is Cerberus. A government assassin, tasked with fixing the galaxy's darkest, ugliest problems.

GET CERBERUS BOOKS 1 - 3 TODAY!

Forget life, liberty, and the pursuit of happiness... Surviving is a feat in and of itself.

GET REPUBLIC OF RUIN TODAY!

"Aliens, agents, and espionage abound in this Cold War-era alternate history adventure... A wild ride!"*—Dennis E. Taylor, bestselling author of We Are Legion (We Are Bob)*

GET THE LUNA MISSILE CRISIS NOW!

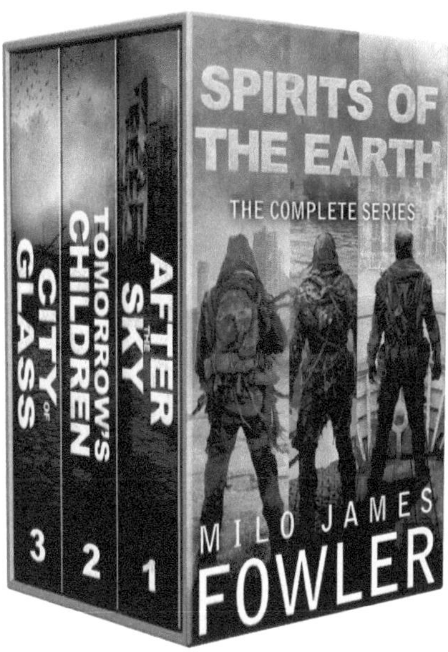
SPIRITS OF THE EARTH
THE COMPLETE SERIES
MILO JAMES
FOWLER
AFTER THE SKY
1
TOMORROW'S CHILDREN
2
CITY OF GLASS
3